UNCHAINED

C.J. Barry

NCP

Be sure to check out our website for the very best in fiction at fantastic prices!

When you visit our webpage, you can:

* Read excerpts of currently available books
* View cover art of upcoming books and current releases
* Find out more about the talented artists who capture the magic of the writer's imagination on the covers
* Order books from our backlist
* Find out the latest NCP and author news--including any upcoming book signings by your favorite NCP author
* Read author bios and reviews of our books
* Get NCP submission guidelines
* And so much more!

We offer a 20% discount on all new ebook releases!
(Sorry, but short stories are not included in this offer.)

We also have contests and sales regularly, so be sure to visit our webpage to find the best deals in ebooks and paperbacks! To find out about our new releases as soon as they are available, please be sure to sign up for our newsletter (http://www.newconceptspublishing.com/newsletter.htm) or join our reader group (http://groups.yahoo.com/group/new_concepts_pub/join) !

The newsletter is available by double opt in only and our customer information is *never* shared!

Visit our webpage at:
www.newconceptspublishing.com

Unchained is an original publication of NCP. This work has never before appeared in book form. This work is a novel. Any similarity to actual persons or events is purely coincidental.

New Concepts Publishing
5202 Humphreys Rd.
Lake Park, GA 31636

ISBN 1-58608-683-9
© copyright 2002, C.J. Barry
Cover art by Eliza Black, © copyright 2002

All rights reserved, which includes the right to reproduce this book or portions thereof in any form whatsoever except as provided by the U.S. Copyright Law.

If you purchased this book without a cover you should be aware this book is stolen property.

NCP books are available at special quantity discounts for bulk purchases for sales promotions, premiums, fund raising, or educational use. For details, write, email, or phone New Concepts Publishing, 5202Humphreys Rd., Lake Park, GA 31636, ncp@newconceptspublishing.com, Ph. 229-257-0367, Fax 229-219-1097.

First NCP Trade Paperback Printing: 2004

Printed in the United States of America

Visit our webpage at:
www.newconceptspublishing.com

UNCHAINED

C.J. Barry

Futuristic Romance

New Concepts　　　　　　　　　　　　　　Georgia

PROLOGUE

It was a scream that woke her. In sleepy confusion, Cidra sat up in bed and blinked into the darkness of her bedroom. All lights were dead on the control panel by the door.

Another scream--her mother's. Never in all her fifteen years had Cidra heard such a terrifying sound. The last remnants of sleep disappeared with the unmistakable crackle of laser gunfire from the far end of the house. Chains of panic squeezed at her throat. Heart pounding, she swung her feet to the floor and crossed the dark room to her closed door. Her hand was on the opener when another barrage of laser blasts and the shouts of strangers rang out, this time much closer.

She hit the alarm on the control panel to warn the rest of her family, initiating a drill her military father insisted they all learn in case of emergency.

As footsteps thundered through her beloved home amid crashing doors and shattering windows, she stared at the lifeless alarm. No power. No alarm.

The smell of smoke finally jerked her out of dazed horror. She dropped to her knees and with trembling hands pried open one of the floor panels that concealed a small opening. Intruders moved down the hall outside her door.

Without looking back, she dropped into the pitch black void of the secret tunnel that ran under her house. Once in the tunnel, she closed the tile door over her head and locked it down. It was then she remembered her light stick. In her bedroom. But the mistake was quickly forgotten with the vibrations of footsteps overhead.

Who were they? These people who were destroying her life?

Silent tears burned a trail down her face as she listened to the pillaging above. There would be nothing left of her room, her home. She knew that. But it could be worse. She only hoped her parents and brothers had already escaped ahead of her through their own hidden floor panels.

In absolute and unrelenting darkness, the tunnel lay empty and quiet but for her own ragged breathing. Stagnant air filled the low, narrow passageway. The dirt floor was cold and alien beneath her bare feet.

Placing a hand against each wall for guidance, she began a blind journey toward the safe house as her father had instructed, fingers groping for what she could not see. The tunnel seemed so much longer than she remembered in their practice runs, endless and terrifying. Something scurried by her foot. Her heartbeat became unbearably loud in her ears. With each small step forward, she fought back the paralyzing grip of utter darkness.

An abrupt incline signaled the end of the tunnel. With wholehearted relief, Cidra felt around for the door latch and stumbled through the doorway into the deserted old house.

Avion's giant moon cast a ghostly glow through silent rooms as Cidra searched for her parents and her younger brothers. Empty. She must be the first one. Exhausted, she slumped down a wall to the floor facing the tunnel's door. They would be here any minute. She wrapped the filthy nightgown around her legs and waited for her family to arrive.

A gentle hand shook her awake. Cidra squinted at a familiar face bathed in brilliant daylight. Slowly, blue eyes and white hair came into focus.

"Syrus," she said, her voice raw.

The old man gave her a weak smile. "Cidra."

She stared at him, wondering why her father's old friend was here with her, why she had slept against a wall, why her eyes burned. Reality invaded in a sickening rush.

She looked frantically around the room. "Where are they?"

The old man worked his mouth for a few seconds before he finally spoke. "They didn't make it. I'm sorry."

Tears rimmed Syrus' eyes as he took her hand in his. "There's serious trouble, love. You had better come with me."

CHAPTER ONE

Ten Years Later

Cidra leaned on her shovel and gazed out over the Lake of Ares.

Riotous colors skimmed across the water, compliments of the exotic birds for which her home planet of Avion was renowned. Late day sunlight kissed the top of each gentle wave, casting brilliance to the kaleidoscope flashes of wings and plumage. Sweeping branches of ancient Bani trees hung low over rocky shores where spindly-legged waders strutted and preened.

A sad, fleeting smile touched her lips.

It was a perfect day.

A good day to bury Syrus Almazan.

Cidra looked down at the open grave and fought back another wave of tears. He had been more than her friend. He had opened his home, guaranteed her safety, and become the family she desperately needed. The tears that stung her eyes burned no less for him than they had for her family, murdered long ago.

Cidra took a deep breath and immersed herself in the songs and whistles resonating through the lush forest until the painful flood of emotion passed.

The moment broken by a nearby groan, she glanced over at her dear friend Barrios, clearly exerting himself far more than he had in recent history. His flushed face dripped with perspiration under a ring of silver hair that circled his head like a crown. Barrios wore his superb culinary skills shamelessly, quite rotund and determined to stay that way sustained by four solid meals a day.

She pushed aside the stark reality that she was completely alone now but for him. Lucky for her, he also happened to be her best friend. As she smiled warmly at him, he grunted hard and looked as if he too, might expire on the spot.

Cidra straightened. *That*, she definitely couldn't handle.

As she was about to return to the grim task at hand, the first tingle of forewarning welled up within her. Laying trust to it, she let it envelop her, turning her senses up to full volume. Slowly, she turned her head toward the single, well-concealed path from Syrus' cottage.

Someone was coming. No one knew of this little clearing except a few, close friends. Very few. Very close.

Cidra gripped her shovel across her body with both hands. She was painfully aware they were trapped. They would not be able to see the uninvited party until he was upon them, and there was no time, no place to hide. Her blood pumped faster, her breathing quickened to match it. A hasty glance at Barrios told her he was totally unaware of her tension or of any potential danger.

She rolled her eyes to the stars.

"Barrios, someone's coming," she whispered as loudly as she dared.

The older man stopped mid-throw and looked up toward the footpath.

Cidra cursed silently for coming down here unarmed. Well, who expected trouble during a burial?

With a slight shudder, she realized this would be the first challenge to her Kin-sha prowess. As only a Kin-sha master could, Syrus had taught her the ancient warrior skill of hand-to-hand combat, weapons use, and the quiet, dignified philosophy that was Kin-sha. His gift to her. Her own personal power.

The flash of excitement faded to dismay with the sheer power the intruder exhibited as he slashed down the narrow path, closing fast. Cidra frowned. Apparently, he wasn't worried about making his presence known.

He was either a clumsy friend or a very confident enemy.

Every fiber of her being stood on high alert. The dense foliage parted and a large man crashed through. He was tall and lean, moving with the confidence of a dangerous predator. Her mind quickly registered broad shoulders, slim hips, and simmering, effortless power. Short, dark hair framed a handsome face and the piercing eyes of a hunter. He wore a white shirt and snug-fitting tan pants tucked into well-worn brown boots.

The laser pistol hanging off one hip and a short plasma blade strapped comfortably to the other thigh made it clear this was a man prepared for anything. Furthermore, he looked neither clumsy nor friendly--a bad sign in a potentially dangerous package.

She could defend herself, but she wasn't sure about protecting Barrios, too. No less a Kin-sha warrior than Syrus, Barrios believed with his heart far more than he practiced with his body. In no way could he be considered in peak form.

If this intruder wasn't a friend, they were in trouble.

The man stopped long enough to survey the scene before him, frowned and walked toward Cidra, moving with long strides. She noticed him glance at the shovel in her hands and wisely come to a halt outside striking distance.

"I guess I'm too late to meet with Syrus." The voice was deep and smooth.

At once, a pair of silver gray eyes locked onto hers with enough intensity to shake her to the bone. A prickly shiver started in her scalp and raced down her back. His eyes narrowed, looking deep into hers. The world around her slid away. The sensation was distinctly uncomfortable and unwelcome.

Cidra took a deep breath. "Who are you?"

"Grey Stone. A friend of Syrus'. He called me two days ago and asked me to come to Avion. I got here as soon as I could, but obviously not soon enough," he muttered, dropping his gaze to the fresh grave.

Cidra looked him over suspiciously. So, he was a friend with very bad timing or a lying enemy disappointed he had been beaten to the punch.

"He died last night in his sleep." She hoped the man would be satisfied with that and leave.

Unfortunately, the man didn't budge and all it did was prompt the vision of Syrus lying peacefully in his bed with the morning light filtering through his window. She shook off the morbid image. It was not the way she wanted to remember her dear friend and mentor.

Besides, at this point she had a bigger problem and he was eyeing her like his next meal.

Barrios finally stepped forward and stretched out a hand to Grey. "I'm Barrios, caretaker of Syrus' home and part-time grave digger," he acknowledged ruefully. "I've heard Syrus mention you a few times. You're an interstellar treasure hunter, right? Sounds adventurous." Barrios flashed a broad grin.

Grey returned the customary handshake. "You could say that, but it's not quite as exciting as you might think. Mostly a lot of tedious research and traveling around in circles."

He turned his sights back on her with unsettling deliberation. "You must be Cidra. Just as Syrus described you. Without the shovel, of course. Is that a new Kin-sha weapon these days? I've been away for a while." A wry smile spread across his face. It was both devastating and distracting. Just what she needed.

Not amused, Cidra answered, "Actually, it is. I could give you a graphic demonstration, if you'd like."

"Plenty of time for that later." He threw out coolly, locking his steely gaze on her. "I'm supposed to take you with me."

"What?" She took a quick step back and shot Barrios an accusing look. He gave a helpless shrug.

Narrowing her eyes at Grey, she demanded, "What are you talking about?"

"I made a promise to Syrus that I would take you on as part of my crew." He watched her intently. "I take it he didn't mention it."

"No, he didn't," Cidra shot back. Panic and anger surged

through her. It was a toss up as to who she was more furious at: Syrus for taking charge of her life and bringing this unnerving stranger all the way out here, or this overconfident man who so casually decreed her future. Her knuckles turned white on the shovel. Lucky for Syrus, he was already dead.

Fine. Enemy it is. Weapon ready.

"I suppose you have some proof besides your word." She thrust her chin up. Even as she spoke, dread welled up within her. *What had that sweet old man done?*

Grey's humor disappeared quite rapidly, replaced by a foreboding coolness. He took a single, intimidating step toward her.

"My word is as good as it gets." He said it as if he lived by it.

She resisted the overwhelming urge to step back. Enemies she knew how to handle.

Barrios cleared his throat, breaking the escalating tension. "I think you can safely assume that Stone is speaking the truth, Cidra. Syrus spoke highly of him. Said he was a man of honor."

Cidra glared at him. "I don't care, Barrios. How dare Syrus do this without asking me first? I won't be forced into something I know nothing about."

Turning back to Grey, she added, "*With* someone I know nothing about."

For a few seconds, nothing happened. Then she watched in wary amazement as he crossed his arms over his chest and relaxed.

"I think Syrus was trying to do what he felt was best for you," Grey said softly. "You clearly meant a great deal to him. Avion isn't a safe place for a trained Kin-sha." Then he paused. "I have a feeling he realized he was going to die very soon. He probably didn't want to worry you."

Cidra glowered at him, unwilling to admit that he was right on all counts. Even as she struggled to come up with a reply, the word 'freedom' whispered in her ear. What started as a flicker rumbled into a flood--an elusive, unattainable dream until this moment.

She looked into his eyes. They didn't waver, didn't give. A hard man with hard eyes. Lucky her.

What could Syrus possibly have on such a man to ask this favor and have it granted so fast? Especially considering who she was. Unless....

Oh no. She almost gasped aloud. Syrus hadn't told him.

If he had, Grey Stone would not be standing here waiting for her response. He'd be running. Fast. In the other direction. She should tell him and watch helplessly as all hope vanished with him. 'Freedom' whispered, louder this time and sweet. She would tell him later.

Her eyes narrowed. *Stone, by the time we are done, I may be your next enemy.*

Barrios shuffled uncomfortably next to her, looking around for an escape route.

"Perhaps we should finish laying Syrus to rest and continue this discussion after dinner. It's getting late," she said calmly.

Out of the corner of her eye, Cidra saw Barrios' head shoot up in surprise. Probably more for the mention of dinner than anything else.

Grey gave her a quick, cool assessment with those hunter's eyes that could drill into her very soul.

"Fine." He moved closer, masculine scent and body heat swept her senses. Then without another word, he turned abruptly away.

Cidra realized she had been holding her breath during the brief exchange. Determined not to give him the satisfaction that he could shake her to the core with one look, she exhaled a slow, silent breath. Only then did she notice that her hands were empty and he was using her shovel to help Barrios. He didn't ask, he didn't offer, he simply took it from her.

Deliberate or not, the point was made. Grey Stone was in charge.

She grimaced. No doubt about it. He would not be pleased when he found out who she was.

CHAPTER TWO

The succulent aroma of delicately roasted game bird and fresh bounty from the gardens filled the cozy dining room. Grey sat across from Barrios and Cidra, enjoying one of the best meals of his life.

Grey conceded that excellent cuisine ranked high as a personal passion of his. With technology came pre-made, instant food but the taste reflected mass processing. Freshly prepared fare was becoming a lost art.

He discreetly eyed Cidra while she stared at her meal. She had been quiet since they returned from the gravesite. He got the impression that he was experiencing a brief reprieve. At least that's what he hoped. He liked the fighter he'd met this afternoon much better. Grey tried hard not to smile. Feisty. Not for every man, but personally he liked feisty.

She had looked rather fierce standing there with that shovel. Syrus mentioned she was a fully trained Kin-sha and she certainly had the body to prove it: lean and graceful, concealed power, hidden strength.

Grey gave her credit for not taking a swing at him earlier when he threw out his bombshell. He had witnessed an honest reaction. She'd held up well, no loss of control. Syrus had not disappointed him.

Grey studied her classic features, enhanced and caressed by soft candlelight. Auburn hair spilled over her shoulders *en masse*. A thin crease etched between her brows, her mind deep in concentration. Full lips lent a sensual pout to her distant expression. Something in those clear blue eyes spoke of an indomitable spirit and maturity beyond her years. Clear, calm, centered.

He shook his head and almost laughed aloud at how Syrus had described her with comments like 'a hard worker' and 'learns quickly.' The old man must have been going blind. Those weren't exactly the phrases Grey would have used. In fact, he was conjuring up a few new ones right now.

Pulling his gaze away from her, he glanced around. The dining room had not changed since he had been a Kin-sha student here fifteen years ago. The large oval table and chairs sat twelve generously. Wood paneled walls and coffered ceiling completed the cozy room.

His eyes finally settled on the vacant chair at the head of the table--Syrus' chair. He felt the loss deeply. The man had been more than a teacher and had made Grey feel like more than a student. It seemed a lifetime ago. The turning point in his life. Everyone had them. Some you chose. Some chose you.

His gaze flickered back to Cidra as she shoved her food around her plate. He wondered if she had such a turning point in her life.

Cidra sighed softly. As usual, Barrios had outdone himself. Too bad she left her appetite down by the lake. Syrus was gone. The fabric of her life was starting to wear thin. This was grief, plain and simple. She had lived through it before. It would pass as it always did and she would move forward as Syrus had taught her, stronger but without Syrus.

She'd never thought about what she would do after he was gone. He had. By all rights, she should be grateful. Instead, she felt trapped. Grey Stone had obviously come a long way for her, just for her. Although he did unnerve and irritate her, she knew that Syrus would have never put her in any danger. If anything, he would have found the best way to keep her safe. She knew without a doubt that she could trust Grey Stone completely.

Stone had one particular point she could not deny. Since the Avion government had banned Kin-sha ten years ago, any use of it would be disastrous or worse. All those years of training would be wasted if she stayed.

She drew in a deep breath. Her choices were depressingly limited. There was nothing left here and nothing to lose. After acceptance gained a foothold, excitement followed. Her future. Could it be possible? Until now, she had no future but the endless isolation of the sanctuary.

The possibilities flooded over her. A treasure hunter. Sounded exotic and exciting despite what he had said. As she gazed up at him, she suspected working for the man would be anything but tedious.

More physically overwhelming than any man she'd ever met, he dominated space. He looked even bigger now than he had outside. More civilized perhaps, but no less intimidating.

Unruly curls of his dark hair glinted in the candlelight. Those penetrating eyes, she was sure, could see in the dark. So sharp and intense, they complimented the hard lines of his face. Even his mouth had a chiseled edge, perfectly shaped and more tempered than the rest of him. She found it strangely bewitching, tantalizing. Suddenly she looked down. How long had she been staring at him?

Beside her, Barrios ate ravenously, talking between bites. "With the main Kin-sha facility dismantled, we've been secretly training a few students in private residences, but it's pretty risky. So far, the locals have left us alone but no one can say how long that will last. I'm afraid if we don't take the chance, the art will be lost forever."

He shook his head. "Avion has changed a lot in the fifteen years since you left, Stone. I doubt it will ever recover from the Dakru incident. That cursed Ximenes Plague. We don't get much news anymore. Is it still out there?"

Grey nodded. "It's taken a few billion lives on hundreds of planets and shows no signs of slowing down. Last I heard, it was spreading through the Sankaran sector."

He grinned at Barrios. "As far as I know, Avion is still the only supplier of an effective vaccine. You can be grateful for that."

Barrios snorted. "You would think so. We thought it was such a blessing, being the first to develop a vaccine for the worst plague of the millennium. Avion, the pride of the galaxy. And the money." He waved his hand in the air. "It made Avion rich, but I'd gladly give it all back. The cost was too great. That missing vaccine shipment to Dakru spelled the end for all of us. Those idiots in the Avion government blamed the whole mess on the Chief of Security and his Kin-sha unit. And you know that Avion will *never* forgive the Kin-sha for tarnishing their pristine image."

Grey asked Barrios, "You must have known Avion's Chief of Security then. Jarid Faulkner, right? He was in charge of vaccine deliveries. Any idea what *really* happened to that first Dakru shipment?"

Barrios stopped mid-bite. "The vaccine shipment vanished along with a full Kin-sha crew."

Before Grey could respond, Barrios looked up and pointed his fork at him. "It left as planned, I can assure you. Jarid Faulkner was the finest Chief of Security Avion ever had. A master strategist. He had a contingency plan for everything. That vaccine shipment headed for Dakru with escort just as he ordered. On schedule." He punctuated each word with a fork jab. "Something went very wrong."

Grey glanced at Cidra and frowned. She listened in rapt attention, her jaw clenched tightly. Her fingers were white around her fork. *Strange.*

Building momentum, Barrios continued. "It disappeared without a trace. No transmissions, no distress signal, nothing. Jarid never found out what happened to it or the crew. The worst part is that it took Dakru too long to notify Avion that the shipment never arrived. By the time they did, the plague had claimed another half a million Dakruians. Another half million died before a second shipment could be dispatched."

He stabbed a piece of meat viciously. "Then that Dakru Commander, Tausek, began condemning Jarid and his Kin-sha team. Some nonsense about the Kin-sha trying to destroy his precious d'Hont fighting force." Barrios snorted. "I'll tell you, the d'Hont are no more than cold-blooded killers. No morals, no honor. They made it sound as if Jarid murdered all those people with his own two hands. Tausek kills that many slaves in those blasted Thoriate mines every year. He had the entire sector riled, including our own people."

Suddenly Barrios threw his fork down. "I still can't believe the Avion government let those filthy d'Hont get their hands on Jarid."

Grey stilled. "What do you mean, they *let* them?"

Propping his elbows up on the table, Barrios put his round face in his hands. "The d'Hont knew everything. How to infiltrate the planetary defenses, where to find Jarid. They even knew when Jarid would be home. They were in and out of here before anyone noticed."

He leaned back, his chair groaning under the strain. "It was an inside job all the way. Personally, I think the Avion government handed Jarid over to pacify Tausek so he wouldn't attack the entire planet."

Grey shook his head. "And in typical Dakruian tradition, they killed the entire family, too. A shame."

Barrios looked at Cidra and folded his arms in front of him. "Well, not quite."

Grey's eyebrows arched up. "What?"

Barrios reached over and took Cidra's hand in his. "He doesn't know, Cidra. You better tell him."

Grey slowly turned to Cidra. For the first time since he had met her, he noted real fear in her eyes. An unpleasant sensation rumbled through his gut that his fantasy image of her was about to be permanently altered.

Cidra looked back across the table at him in defeat. She had hoped to leave her past behind her and start over in a place where no one knew who she was or from where she came. But there was no sense avoiding the inevitable. Eventually Stone would find out. He deserved to know the truth, even if it meant the end of all her hopes and dreams.

"I'm Cidra Faulkner. Jarid Faulkner's daughter."

He stared back at her, his face a strange mix of incredulity and disbelief. A sickening wave of disappointment rolled over her. She wondered how long it would take him to bolt.

"I heard everyone was killed," Grey declared coolly.

"I escaped. I guess they never bothered to count the bodies." She squeezed Barrios' hand so hard, he flinched.

Barrios leaned forward. "Syrus rescued Cidra right afterward."

He made a sweeping gesture with his hands. "He brought her here to the sanctuary where the remaining Kin-sha had gathered. He introduced her as his niece, Cidra Almazan. No one questioned it." Shrugging, he said, "Probably because Jarid was a great man and none of the Kin-sha believed what the Dakruians charged was true." He glanced at Cidra. "Even if it were true, no one deserves to die like that. They couldn't even ID the bodies."

Grey eyed Cidra with wary respect. He couldn't imagine how much strength it took to carry the condemnation of an entire planet on your shoulders, not to mention the fear of discovery day after day. He had guessed right--indomitable spirit. But from the hollow look in her eyes, that spirit was in desperate trouble.

He took a deep breath. Talk about trouble. He didn't even want to think about what would happen if word of this got out. He was a treasure hunter, not a bodyguard. Leave it to Syrus to omit a few minor details. The old man had set him up and now she was his problem. He would keep his promise to Syrus, but he would do it his way.

He picked up his glass of wine, watching her over the rim. "I think it would be best if we continued to introduce you as Cidra Almazan."

Cidra muttered, "Right. I wouldn't want to give you any bad publicity."

With a smirk, Grey replied, "Actually, I'm thinking more of your safety. I doubt even I could protect you from the entire planet of Dakru."

Barrios chimed in. "He's right, Cidra. If Tausek finds out you are alive, there will be no stopping him. His hatred for your father is complete. He rules Dakru now. Vengeance and power are a deadly combination."

Cidra blinked at her old friend as the realization slowly sunk in. Lulled into a sense of safety within the sanctuary, she had nearly forgotten the fact that her mere presence could be dangerous to those around her.

She turned to Grey. "I won't jeopardize your crew. Under the circumstances, you should not feel obligated to keep your promise to Syrus."

Grey's eyebrows went up in surprise. "I always keep my promises. There's no problem as long as your real identity is kept secret. We leave in the morning. I have a business to run."

He downed the rest of the wine and set the glass back on the table hard, effectively closing the subject.

Cidra stared at Grey's grim expression. She'd been right about one thing. He was not pleased when he found out who she was.

Without warning, Barrios abruptly jumped up from the table. "Good Lord, I almost forgot!" And with that, he lumbered out of the room.

Cidra and Grey looked after him, then at each other.

"He's your friend," Grey said.

Cidra smiled weakly. "I never said he was stable."

Grinning from ear to ear, Barrios returned with a small wooden box in his hands. "Syrus gave this to me a few days ago. He told me if anything happened to him, you should have it."

He shoved the dishes aside and placed the box in front of Cidra. She touched it lightly, running her fingers along the exquisite inlay on the lid. In the center was the ancient Kin-sha crest, faded and delicate.

"I don't ever remember seeing this before. Are you sure it belonged to Syrus?" She glanced up at Barrios, who was still smiling away.

He snapped out of his reverie to answer her. "Umm, it looks vaguely familiar, but I'm sure it was Syrus'. He handled it like a newborn babe."

Cidra sat in silence, not entirely sure she wanted to know what the contents were. Syrus had been rather mysterious lately. Lord knows what he might have put in a box in his state. She breathed deeply, leaned forward, and pulled the latch.

So far, so good. At least nothing came flying out at her.

She lifted the lid wide and peered inside. Papers, some odd objects, a holographic recording cartridge. She sighed in relief and smiled. Nothing unusual.

Barrios gasped. Grey's eyebrows shot up. They both leapt forward at the same time.

Cidra ducked out of the way as Barrios went for the papers and Grey grabbed a small vial, neither giving the precious box any regard.

"Am I missing something here?" she demanded in bewilderment.

Examining the label on the vial of black liquid, Grey snapped, "Where did this come from?"

"Government. Classified. Military. How did he get these?" Barrios tore through the documents.

"Thanks for clearing everything up. Never mind, I'll find out for myself." Cidra reached in for a letter marked "Cidra" in Syrus' neat handwriting.

She opened the letter and drew both men's full attention as she read it aloud.

My Dear Cidra,

I want you to know how much you meant to me during the past ten years. You brought sunshine into my dark times. It broke my heart to watch you suffer for your father's guilt when I knew the allegations were not true. Please forgive me. I possessed neither the means nor the strength to pursue the truth.

You, on the other hand, now have both. I have contacted Grey Stone. He is a good man, much like your father, honest and trustworthy. He can provide the means.

You must provide the strength, Cidra--to discover the real fate of the Dakru shipment, clear your father's name, and save the Kin-sha. To free yourself. The time has come. The two of you are ready.

I collected all the evidence I could find. I know your father was innocent. I do not know who framed him and the Kin-sha, but I can get you both started on your quest.

Cidra, I loved you like my own. Travel with care, my child.

                                        My eternal love,
                                        Syrus

Silence filled the room. Grey muttered something under his breath.

Cidra gripped the paper in her fingers. *Your father was innocent.* The words burned in her mind. Words she desperately wanted to hear. Words that healed her soul. In her heart, she had always believed her father was innocent. He was Kin-sha. He was honorable. *Innocent.* And it was up to her to prove it.

She looked at Grey and smiled. "Well Stone, it looks like we're partners."

Grey's gaze slid up from the note in her hands. Her breath caught as she looked into the dangerous eyes of a caged animal. His voice was steely and tight. "I don't do partners."

He tossed the vial back into the box. "So, how long did it take for you and Syrus to dream up this little plan?"

Cidra's mouth dropped open. "What are you talking about?"

Grey snorted and shook his head. "You sure have the innocent act down. Just so you know, it won't work on me."

"Do you think I would have been hiding on this planet for all these years if I had known about this before?" Cidra snapped.

"Without a ship? Yes." Grey leaned toward her. "It just so happens I have one hell of a ship. But you already knew that."

She answered through clenched teeth, "I didn't. Syrus did." She leaned back in her chair, crossed her arms, and regarded him coolly. "He must have picked you for some good reason."

Barrios stifled a snicker.

Grey narrowed his eyes at her, at the speed in which she had turned the entire conversation around. As if by divine intervention, his comm link beeped. He stared at Cidra's defiant expression a few more seconds before rising and striding into the kitchen. He flipped on the communicator.

"What is it, Decker?" Grey snapped.

On the other end, Decker paused. "Captain, you said to contact you when I found, uh, our little problem."

Grey clenched the comm unit. He did not need this tonight. "Who is it?"

"You're not going to like it, sir. It's Mora." His voice was down to a whisper.

Mora, a spy? It couldn't be. "Are you sure?"

"Positive. I found her last message to Sandor Wex, the only encrypted message sent off the ship during the time period you specified. Mora told him to stay close because we were moving in on the Mask of Teran. What do you want me to do now?"

Grey fought back the pure, red rage of personal betrayal that he had come to know so well. He needed to think clearly. "Where was the message's destination?"

"Hold on." There was a pause. Then Decker swore and came back. "Vaasa, Captain. Home. From what I can tell, that's where they've been meeting, too."

Right under his nose. Grey hissed though his teeth. Anger rose in a torrid wave. She had already betrayed two of his lucrative finds to Sandor Wex. There would not be a third. "Notify the crew that we're heading home to Vaasa for a few days."

There was silence.

"That's all?" Decker finally blurted. "Aren't you going to do anything to her? You know how much we lost on those two finds they jumped. And you've done enough preliminary work on the Mask's location to give Wex a good target area."

Grey gave a short laugh. "Not a chance. The man can't find his way through Thendara Market without getting lost. Besides, I haven't told a soul where I really think that Mask is. Go ahead and notify the crew. And Decker, don't restrict Mora's transmissions. I want her and Wex on Vaasa at the same time."

"Yes, sir."

"We'll be coming aboard tomorrow morning. Out."

Grey pocketed the comm unit and leaned back against a cabinet, aware that every muscle in his body was on fire. *Mora.* His ship's cook. The last person he would have suspected. They'd had a brief affair aboard his ship a year ago and had ended it on good terms. Or so he thought. Grey dragged a hand through his hair. He had trusted her. Like a fool.

Standing in the kitchen, he realized something else. He was about to lose his cook. He surveyed the neat kitchen and slowly smiled.

* * * *

Moonlight spilled through the second floor window of the same bedroom Grey had occupied long ago as a Kin-sha student. With restless energy, he folded his hands behind his head and shifted position again on the narrow bed. In the half-light, the bright colors of Syrus' wall paintings faded to subtle shades of gray.

It had not been a good day. He had buried his old friend, been betrayed by a former lover, and somehow been saddled with a strong-willed, potentially dangerous woman and a dead man's mission. And the crush of old memories was undermining his normally logical approach to problem solving.

The moment in time came back in a painful flash: standing beaten and shaking at Syrus' door the night he had run away from his father, Lassiter Stone. The only lesson that lying bastard ever taught Grey was that you couldn't trust anyone, not even your own blood.

That night Syrus took in a bitter young man and did what he did best: bestow the gift of Kin-sha. His gentle ways, so different from Lassiter's heavy, heartless hand, epitomized effortless patience, tolerance, and the real meaning of friendship. Kin-sha emphasized the balance of mind and body, demanding absolute control over both. The standard training gave Grey the tools to defend himself, control his anger, and command his future. But Syrus had also taught him by example, living as a gentleman of honor and a man of his word. The lessons of life and living.

It was a debt Grey now had a chance to repay. Still he felt

trapped, forced into a situation beyond his control or choice. As much as he cared for the old man, he couldn't help but be furious with him. He was en route to the final location of the Lost Mask of Teran when Syrus summoned him. This little detour had blown his schedule all to hell. He wouldn't have put his operation on hold for anyone else. And he wouldn't take on a mission like this for another person except Syrus.

Fortunately, Syrus' mission could wait. He had to deal with Mora and Wex and then he could go after the Mask. After that, he would honor Syrus' final wish.

Satisfied with his new strategy, Grey tried to relax. The uneasy feeling persisted. Giving in to the compulsion, he rolled off the bed and pulled on a pair of shorts. A quick walk around the cottage would ease his mind. He picked up the laser pistol next to the bed and checked the setting. Living in the sanctuary held no guarantee of safety for any Kin-sha. Cidra's hostile greeting of him confirmed that.

Slapping the pistol in his palm, he turned to leave and suddenly stopped at the window. Moonlight filled the night sky, casting the woods in a ghostly glow. And in the middle of the courtyard stood Cidra looking up at the giant moon, her back to him.

He knew without a doubt she was the reason for his uneasiness. He set the pistol down and rested a shoulder against the window frame. Watching her white nightgown flare gently around her legs, his mind drifted to what she would do aboard his ship. Even with her extensive training, he had little use for an accomplished Kin-sha in his operation. Long-dead artifacts rarely gave him much of a struggle. It was going to be a challenge to find a position for her.

But one thing was certain. She was not going to be his partner. Partners meant compromise. He was the captain of his own ship so he wouldn't *have* to compromise.

A faint breeze wrapped the gown snugly around her, cutting a clear silhouette in the moonlight. Those long legs were something. His body raced ahead of his mind as an unexpected wave of awareness blazed through him.

He shook himself, remembering where his libido had gotten him in the past. He'd already made that mistake with Mora. He had ignored his own hard and fast rule: *do not get involved with a crewmember.* He grimaced at the hard and fast part. Not a good choice of words at the moment, but the rule remained. Business as usual, especially with this one. She was trouble all the way, no matter now innocent she claimed to be.

What worried him the most was that he almost believed her tonight when she told him she knew nothing about the box. Almost. He'd already played the fool one too many times today.

It all seemed perfectly clear until he saw her wipe a hand across her eyes, her shoulders shake. Grey backed away from the window and blew out a long breath. She was crying. She didn't seem like the kind of woman who cried easily. In the vastness of the sanctuary, she looked small and alone.

Grey paced his room, feeling guilt and anger and wondering why he felt the need to do something. Then he turned and walked to the door.

* * * *

Night was as quiet as the day was loud in the woods of Avion. Cidra stood alone in the moonlight on a planet she both loved and hated, trying to forget who she was.

The sanctuary swept out around her. A swirl of wind haunted the trees and cooled her sweat-dampened hair, sending a shiver through her. The dinner conversation must have been what triggered that wretched nightmare again. After all this time, she thought she had finally outgrown it. A tangled confusion of screams and fire, smoke and siege, dragging her down into its dark terror. They were the twisted memories etched in her mind of how she had escaped the hand of death long ago.

Cidra drew in a shuddering breath. Like every day for the past ten years, she wondered what happened to them that night, how they died, why she had been spared. She would never know. She wasn't sure which was the crueler fate: dying with them or living without them. Tears streamed down her face in a silent purge of injustice and grief. Cidra hugged herself tight in a vain effort to control the trembling.

There were days when she missed them so much. Too many times she'd wished for a different life, to be someone else, anyone else. Now she had that chance to rectify the past, to build herself a new future. But regardless of Syrus' order, she knew it would be her duty and her mission. Grey Stone had his own agenda.

Anger flashed through her. He thought she set him up. She still couldn't believe it. Why would he think such a thing? Not that it mattered. It was perfectly obvious that he didn't want this mission, and he was even less enthused to harbor her. The only reason he agreed to take her was because of Syrus.

A new flood of tears burned down her face. For once, she didn't fight it, allowing the pain to crash over her in waves as if it would somehow redeem her. She cried for her parents and brothers, her life as she had once known it, for a mission that seemed impossible for her to achieve alone.

Abruptly, another sensation broke the desolation that engulfed her. Her danger sense triggered. Cidra spun around to find Grey standing there, bathed in moonlight like a divine apparition.

Not him. Not now. She lowered her head and struggled to pull herself together.

He stepped closer. "Cidra."

Grey's fingers slipped under her chin, gently lifting her face to his. His eyes were gray pools filled with warmth and strange understanding.

She squeezed her eyes shut. She didn't want his sympathy. The very thought sent a surge of energy and strength through her.

"I'm fine," she said, opening her eyes to meet his. "I can take care of myself."

His expression darkened in the moonlight. Warm fingers dropped from her chin. The air became distinctly cooler.

"I hope so," he stated in a tight voice. "I don't have time to play guardian."

She nearly growled. "Who do you think has been watching over Syrus and Barrios all these years?"

A wry smile crossed his face. "I'm surprised you had time with all the plans you and Syrus were making."

Cidra's eyes narrowed. "I knew nothing about this mission before tonight. If I had, I wouldn't have picked you to help me."

He took a step toward her, charging large and broad into her personal space. She held her position at the clear intrusion.

His voice was low and menacing. "Let's get one thing straight. I'm the best you are going to get because no one, and I mean no one, would take this mission except me. But I don't have to be happy about it."

She clenched her fists at her sides. "And neither do I."

CHAPTER THREE

Tausek, the supreme ruler of Dakru, surveyed his kingdom

from the solitude of his private chambers towering over the land. He stood silent and motionless in the darkness, a black figure casting no shadow, seeing all. The entire floor rotated slowly atop his twenty-story tower building. A bank of windows offered a generous panoramic view of the Capital City.

As usual, the sunset had been glorious. A blood red spectacle only a true native of this scarred, sterile land could appreciate. A violent sunset for an equally violent world.

Far below him, barrel fires dotted the unlit streets of the city like strings of lights. Silhouetted figures moved around the meager flames. It must be cold tonight, he mused. The street cleaners would have a busy morning picking up frozen bodies. The thought warmed him for such was life on Dakru. The weak perished, leaving room for stronger, healthier hands. A most profitable cycle.

Charitably, Tausek contemplated the wretched souls of his world. Criminals, murderers, outcasts, refugees--the collective scourge of every planet in the sector. The hands he needed to harvest the precious black treasure called Thorite from Dakru's underground mines. Thorite ruled supreme as the key component for space travel, an accelerator necessary for the jump to hyperspace. Crystals so rare, so perfect, cold and black as the night. Dakru was infinitely rich with them. The veins ran deep, far, and wide.

Unfortunately, Thorite's crystalline form was brittle, its face layers twisted beneath the ground. Mechanical extraction had proven too damaging to the mineral's delicate hexagonal rods, making manual harvesting a necessity. Hands. Expendable hands.

Tausek never had any trouble finding them. Dakru gladly opened its doors to all, offering nearby worlds an outlet for their social problems, prisoners, and exiles. A surprisingly hardy lot. Finding themselves stranded on this desolate world, they had no choice but to work for food and shelter.

Regardless of their strength or species, eventually they all perished. Thorite was, for all its beauty, quite deadly. Its toxic presence devastated a being's lungs beyond repair. Tausek deemed treatment pointless, merely creating a negative impact on profits. After all, hands were so easily replaced. As long as societies ran on emotions, his steady supply was guaranteed. Anger, rage, jealousy, greed--they were the sins that filled prisons and eventually populated Dakru's mines.

Deme slid her long, furred body along his leg, a fine clicking noise emanating from her throat--uncharacteristic affection for such a notoriously lethal creature.

"Easy Deme, my pet."

An identical set of luminescent eyes peered at him from behind a chair. The pair of corvits were a gift from a grateful customer. Deme and Deik were mates for life, dedicated to each other and their master. Tausek found them immensely intelligent, loyal, and useful. They obeyed his simple commands flawlessly: stay, come, guard, and his personal favorite, *target*. With their razor sharp claws and teeth, they were born killers. Unlike Tausek's human forces, the corvits had never failed him.

A soft bell chimed in the tower room. Deme and Deik leapt to attention and moved stealthily to flank Tausek.

"Enter," Tausek ordered, not turning. His tower was a fortress. There was no need to fear his enemies here. Besides, he knew who it was--his eyes and ears of the universe, Commander Plass.

The door slid open and Commander Plass entered, impeccably dressed in a standard d'Hont uniform, a small insignia the only indication of his superior rank and his d'Hont designation.

He stopped a suitable distance in front of Tausek and saluted.

"Permission to report, sir."

"Proceed."

Plass replied, "I have word from Avion that Syrus Almazan has died, apparently of natural causes."

"So the great teacher of the Kin-sha, fallen at last," Tausek observed calmly. "Is that the last of his family?"

"Only a niece survived him, sir. A young woman. Her name is Cidra, I believe."

Tausek's black eyes narrowed. "Cidra." He tasted the word slowly. "An unusual name. A name not easily forgotten. Tell me Commander, why does that name sound familiar?"

Plass hesitated. "I don't know. Do you wish an inquiry?"

Tausek's mouth twitched. "No need. I know where I've heard that name before. Jarid Faulkner had a young daughter named Cidra."

Plass balked. "It can't possibly be the same person. As you ordered, we killed everyone in that house. There were no survivors."

"Perhaps you missed one." Tausek turned his back to Plass. "You will personally investigate this matter. I'll expect your report shortly."

Before the door had slid shut behind Plass, Tausek knew what the answer would be. Instinct was not an emotion; it was a tool.

He had no doubt that she was alive. While she lived, the daughter of Jarid Faulkner was an unacceptable threat. She was the only person left capable of destroying his power. She must be found and eliminated. With her, the reign of the Kin-sha would end. Using the d'Hont as his own personal weapon, Tausek would control the sector, unconditionally and unimpeded.

Only then would the master plan continue.

* * * *

As Grey's K12 short-range transport jet cleared Avion's atmosphere, Cidra marveled at the breathtaking glory of space. Masses of brilliant stars wove an intricate pattern across an endless darkness, a tapestry crafted for eternity. Opaque veils of light shimmered through a myriad of galaxies, curtains of green, white, and red. Swirls and spirals, rivers of light separated by a black nothingness. Beauty beyond words. Beauty beyond boundaries.

With great reluctance, she pulled herself away from the incredible view.

"So you think this was from the original Dakru shipment?" She held the slim ampoule of Ximenes vaccine from Syrus' box up to the main cabin lights.

Barrios answered from behind her amid a shuffle of papers. "The serial number assigned to that vial falls within the reported range on the printed manifest from Syrus' box. The manifest dates and details match the time of the Dakru shipment."

He mumbled, "I'd sure like to know how he got his hands on these documents. We are talking highly classified information here. They must have been stolen. But the real question is, how did Syrus get a vial from that shipment?"

Cidra pondered the implication. "Maybe it's true. Maybe it never left Avion."

"I don't buy it, Cidra," Barrios stated flatly. "Your father would have done his part."

She hesitated. "You don't think Syrus had anything to do with the disappearance of the shipment, do you?"

Barrios sighed loudly. "No, but he knew that it didn't just vanish, that's for sure. We'll know more when we decode and run this holo recording aboard Stone's ship. Too bad Syrus didn't have a holo deck to play it on."

She glanced back at Barrios twirling the stubby, cylindrical cartridge containing the holo recording from Syrus' box in his fingers. It could hold a massive amount of three-dimensional visual recordings as well as raw data.

"Any idea what's on it?"

Barrios shrugged. "Haven't a clue. Maybe nothing." He grinned at her. "Maybe answers."

An affectionate smile touched her lips. This morning Barrios had accepted an offer as head cook onboard Grey's ship. She suspected Barrios was more interested in Syrus' mission than the position. Regardless, he would never know how much his presence meant to her.

Cidra handed the vial back to him. Filling the back seat of the small K12 jet, he looked relaxed although Cidra had never known him to fly. She wondered if he had logged some time in the SymPod.

The SymPod was the closest she had ever come to actual flying. Not much larger than a one-man escape pod, it simulated the piloting experience of a variety of ships, under any condition and battle setting. The flat console could replicate any ship and every control. Theirs was an older version, gleaned from the Avion government by the remaining Kin-sha, capable of training pilots under actual battle conditions without risk.

She had enjoyed the exercises immensely, logging endless hours, memorizing battle strategies, executing tried and true maneuvers, and making up a few new ones along the way. The SymPod was exhilarating, remarkably realistic, and completely safe. It was also the closest thing to freedom she could find on Avion.

Syrus had isolated her well, protecting her from danger of discovery. Unfortunately, that protection came at a steep price: the absence of friends, companions, peers. As a tremor of excitement whisked through her, she realized that was about to change. She covertly glanced at the man who had made it all possible.

Cidra watched him pilot the small jet, his big hands flowing over the helm controls with gentleness and familiarity, giving the K12 his undivided attention. It was almost sensual.

Suddenly Grey was asking, "Something wrong?"

She snapped out of her contemplation and felt the heat rise in her face. "How long before we rendezvous with your ship?"

"Not long. *Calibre* is waiting outside Avion's sensor range."

"Why outside sensor range?"

Grey gave her a sardonic grin. "Habit."

She nodded and fingered the controls lightly.

Grey leaned back in his chair, evaluating her. "You want to fly?" He saw her eyes light up and abruptly flame out.

"I've only flown in the SymPod," she warned.

His eyebrows arched. "You've never been off-planet before?"

"Never. Is that a problem?"

Grey tried not to frown. *Only if you want a seasoned crewmember.* "No. No problem. Take over for a while. It's a short flight to *Calíbre.*"

They switched pilot and gunner seats and strapped down. Grey asked, "Does everything look familiar?"

She was slow to reply, totally engrossed in the panel of controls before her. "Close enough. Our SymPod was behind a few upgrades."

Grey nodded. "Why don't you try some basic maneuvers?" At least he'd find out what she could do.

She glanced at him sidelong with the most enigmatic smile he had ever seen, and he immediately regretted his suggestion. She pulled the ship off autopilot, weaving and spinning through space with abandon.

While Grey was contemplating the fact that he had just unleashed a holy terror, behind him Barrios roared with laughter. "Did Cidra mention she practically lived in that SymPod?"

"Now you tell me," Grey murmured, watching her flying skills with interest. She was a little wild but not bad. Maybe she could be useful on crew after all. Average would best describe the current level of piloting skills on *Calíbre.* She was definitely better than average.

Grey watched, mesmerized by Cidra's genuine delight as she commanded the ship through a smooth series of loops and dives. Suddenly she turned serious, bringing the ship squarely out of a barrel roll, her eyes wide, focusing straight ahead. Before he could question her, she plowed the ship into a power dive.

"Cidra, what the—" was all Grey could get out before a green laser blast shot across the bow.

"They're shooting at us!" Cidra gritted her teeth while pulling another evasive maneuver. "Who are they? How many?"

Grey scanned the displays. "One, a Victor Class III. Try to bring us around behind them and give me a target I can see."

Cidra didn't want to come around behind them. She wanted to panic. Her heart pounded in her chest. Some things the SymPod couldn't simulate. Impending death was one of them.

Beside her, Grey snapped, "Cidra, we don't have time to swap stations. Move it!"

Immediately, she launched the little ship into a series of evasive maneuvers and then switched to an Avion defensive pattern along with anything else she could think of, pushing Grey's little K12 to the limit. The Victor stuck with her, but its reactions grew sloppier as the maneuvers became more complex.

Concentrating fiercely, she forced a mental review from her armament training while diving and spinning her small jet between laser blasts. Victor Class III. Heavily armored six-man fighter. Good shields, four guns, superb speed. Against their K12 jet, sporting two guns, minimal shields, and excellent agility.

Final analysis: no match for any length of time.

As she was trying to recall the Victor's weak points, a blast rocked their small ship. Warning lights flashed. Grey glanced at her sharply. She knew without asking that they would not survive another hit.

Under Grey's command, the K12's guns swiveled toward the attacker and spit fire. With the enemy little more than a blip on his display screen, Grey knew he was wasting a great deal of ammunition into deep space. He needed them in front of him for any real chance of a kill.

"Hey Captain, need a hand?" Decker's voice boomed over the cabin's comm. Grey caught a glimpse of a familiar silver and red ship racing toward them. *Calíbre*.

"It's about time you showed up," Grey barked. "Fire on that thing. Now!"

"They're too tight on you. I don't think it's safe until we get closer," Decker responded, a worried edge to his voice.

"If you wait any longer, we'll be dead. We need a distraction. Do it."

Instantly, long streaks shot out from *Calíbre*'s cannons, lighting up the Victor's shields. A perfect hit. Grey gave silent thanks. Leena was manning the main guns this shift. She was the best gunner he had. The attacker slowed its pursuit somewhat, but made no move toward *Calíbre*.

"Shields down on the Victor, sir. They should back off now," Decker said. "Head for us, we'll cover you."

"I don't think so," Grey growled. "Cidra, give me one more shot."

With the Victor closing fast on her tail again, she flipped the nimble jet vertical and dove hard left. The Victor followed on an intercept course. Cidra yanked her ship hard around and under the Victor at neck breaking speed. She could hear Barrios' loud gasp behind her.

"Hang on," she ground out. The attacker was now above and behind her trying to swing around. She pulled the K12 straight up and upside down, her guns facing the Victor's unprotected side.

"Now!" she yelled, but Grey was already firing. Orange lines lanced across the Victor, ripping through its vulnerable belly as Cidra pulled them through the inside-out loop. A violent explosion shook the bigger ship, followed by a small series of flashes before it burst into a raging ball of fire.

Cidra brought the transport around to witness the full destruction of their attacker. The tiny cabin was quiet except for her ragged breathing. While she fought to control her thundering heartbeat, it slowly dawned on her that six people had just died at her very sweaty, very shaky hands.

Grey slammed the comm switch. "Did you get an ID on that ship, Decker?"

"Working on it now. We should have it by the time you come aboard." Decker's voice bellowed over various whoops from *Calíbre*'s deck crew.

Grey shut off the comm and scrubbed his hands over his face.

"Well, that was interesting," Barrios said weakly, his face a light shade of green. "Friends of yours, Stone?"

Grey exhaled hard. "Everyone has enemies. We'll find out who it was."

Someone wanted him dead. That much was certain, but they didn't touch *Calíbre*. Either they did not view her as a threat--a very remote possibility--or they wanted *Calíbre* unharmed for another reason. *Piracy*. He would make a list of possible suspects later. He had the feeling the list would be succinctly short. First, he had someone to thank.

He turned to Cidra, who sat staring out into space. "Nice flying, Cidra. We make a good team."

She didn't appear to hear him, her face frozen. He realized she was shaking hard. "Are you all right?"

"Fine." She closed her eyes, her jaw muscles tightening. "Killing is new for me."

He fought the urge to pull her into his arms and hold her. This was her personal battle. He prayed the strong warrior within her would win. He could not afford for her to go soft on him. Out here, a moment of hesitation could be bad. Worse than bad. Downright deadly.

Grey leaned over, commanding her full attention. "Cidra, they were trying to kill us and they would have. We had no choice."

Cidra nodded. He was right of course, but it didn't stop the trembling in her gut that threatened to invade and conquer the rest of her body. They had families, children, homes.

"I'll bring us in." Grey took over the controls.

She didn't argue, didn't have the energy. She pulled the quiet strength of Kin-sha around her.

Numbly, she watched his ship fill the main view screen. *Calíbre*. Cidra concentrated on the sound of it, repeating it until her heartbeat returned to normal and she no longer felt like vomiting. The name rolled through her mind as if it had always held a place there.

A Moorian-built cruiser, it moved gracefully, its red square-tipped nose slicing through space. The silver main body extended back from the nose, short wings flanking each side. A massive space foil looming over the aft part of the ship promised quickness and superior maneuverability.

Sleek, powerful, and dangerous, she mused, much like her Captain.

"She's beautiful," Cidra breathed softly, her voice still shaky from the aftereffects of battle.

Grey glanced at her, his eyes gleaming. "Yes. She is."

He landed the jet in *Calíbre*'s port side landing bay. As they exited the K12, a tall, lanky man strode toward them sporting a shock of red hair and what appeared to be a permanent grin on his face.

The man waved. "Captain, glad to see you in one piece. Nice bit of flying. I didn't know you could handle a K12 like that."

"Barrios, Cidra, this is my first officer, Decker." Grey gestured to Cidra and looked at Decker. "Cidra was at the helm."

Decker's eyebrows shot up. He whistled softly and then beamed at Cidra. "Been a long time since we've had a good looking, crack pilot around here."

She grinned back. "Really, what are your pilots usually like?"

"Average." Decker winked. "And real hairy."

Grey spoke up. "Decker, show Cidra to Cabin Number Two. Barrios is bunking with you temporarily."

Decker hesitated. "Uh, Cabin Number Two, sir?"

"Problem?"

"No, sir. I just thought ... no problem." Decker scratched his red head.

Grey turned to Cidra and Barrios. "Decker can show you around and get you settled. Make yourselves at home." He nodded to Decker and strode out of the landing bay.

Decker waved them in the other direction, ushering them down a hallway of doors. "This corridor runs around the inside of the ship between crew quarters on the outer perimeter and the public areas located in the center. Bridge is at the front, landing bays and cargo in the rear."

They passed under the high, graceful archways that formed the ship's infrastructure. Bright, ambient light flowed from panels above the doorways spaced along the corridor. All surfaces gleamed with low luster metal. Austere, strong, safe.

Cidra paused and pressed her hand against a smooth wall, tuning into the gentle vibration of a ship alive. The engines shifted slightly, gearing up for the jump into hyperspace. She had never actually experienced the vehicle that facilitated intergalactic travel before. It translated into distance, a lot of it in a hurry, between her and Avion.

Decker continued his tour. "Including you two, we now have a crew of eleven. That pretty much fills up the quarters. We all try to get together for evening meal. Keeps the group tight. And for the most part, everyone gets along. We work when there's a job, usually fifteen days max, then get a break for about the same." He shrugged his thin shoulders. "Depends on what we come up with. Our pay is contingent on success."

"So, how *is* the treasure hunting business?" Barrios puffed, struggling to keep up with Decker's long stride.

"It's been better. Our last two finds were claimed just as we arrived." Decker's voice carried frustration.

Cidra spoke up. "That's not an inherent risk in treasure hunting?"

Decker shook his head. "Not for us. Don't get me wrong. Treasure hunting can be a ruthless, dangerous business but our specialty is recovering very old artifacts considered lost forever. Not many hunters bother with those, but Captain has a real talent for it. He's the best I've ever seen. It takes a lot more research and time because the trail is ice cold. But the reward is much higher than a simple search and salvage operation of a more recent wreck." Decker shook his head. "We put a lot of work into those two finds. It was no accident both of them were jumped by the same people." He stopped talking abruptly and looked at them, as if sensing he had said too much.

"The same people?" Cidra repeated. "You're right, that doesn't sound like a coincidence."

"Sounds more like a leak." Barrios snorted, his eyes roving the corridor. "Any place to get a drink around here?"

Decker jumped at the change of subject. "Right this way."

* * * *

Cidra left Barrios and Decker in the crew lounge and headed to her quarters. The cabin numbers were clearly marked on the sleek silver doors of *Calíbre*'s main corridor. As she stepped up to her cabin door, it slid open for the personalized comm unit Decker had given her.

The room was small and, like the rest of *Calíbre*, puritanical but comfortable. Cidra punched up the adjustable lighting. Standard silver metal comprised most surfaces except for the blue mat flooring. One narrow bed occupied the farthest wall. A small desk sat between the bed and a single upholstered chair.

Two doors flanked one wall. To her relief, the first revealed a small private lav and shower. She had expected trips to a public lav on a ship this size.

When she pressed the controls to open the second door, there was a faint click but the door didn't budge. After several failed attempts, she gave up and made a point to ask Decker about the mystery door later.

Instead, she stretched out on the bed. It was small, but surprisingly comfortable. A grin crossed her face as she wondered how well Barrios would be sleeping in these diminutive beds, if only for the duration of her mission.

The mission. Now that she was out from under the dark cloud of Avion, excitement shimmered through her. It was more than she could have ever hoped for. Finally, a chance to find the answers to the questions that had haunted her for ten years. Regardless of the evidence, it had never once occurred to her that her father had deliberately withheld that shipment. Now all she had to do was convince Grey. As much as she hated to admit it, she needed his help, his ship, and his expertise. What would it take to convince him?

A gentle chime interrupted her thoughts. Cidra hopped off the bed and walked to the door. It opened promptly. A young woman stood smiling at her. Her black hair framed her face like a bowl. Even standing still, she seemed to be in motion.

"Hi, I'm Leena. Welcome aboard."

"Thank you," Cidra said. Leena looked back at her expectantly. Cidra hesitated. "Would you like to come in?"

"Sure." Leena bounded past her and surveyed Cidra's cabin with interest. "I've never been in this cabin. It's nice."

"Isn't it like all the others?" Cidra asked as the door slid shut.

"Mmm, pretty much. A little bigger, I think." Leena nodded, agreeing with herself.

Cidra glanced around the tiny room and wondered how it could possibly be any smaller. She sat on the edge of the bed and motioned for Leena to take the chair. "I see. How long have you been on *Calíbre*?"

"Oh, about a year." Leena flopped into the chair. "Captain was looking for a gunner from Vaasa. I was lucky enough to get the job."

Cidra eyed her. "Are you the gunner that hit the Victor?"

Leena flashed a proud smile. "That was me. They were so close on your tail that Decker didn't think I could pull it off. You gave me an edge though. They were too busy trying to keep up with you. Those were some pretty slick moves."

Cidra shrugged and looked away. "I didn't have much choice. It was move or die."

"Whatever the motivation, you sure impressed the deck crew. I know Coon will be happy to give you the helm. Piloting is not his forte."

"No? What is his forte?" Cidra asked.

"If you ask him, he'll say penetration."

Cidra's eyebrows shot up and Leena laughed. "You'll grow to love him. We all do. He's our sweeper."

Cidra's eyes narrowed. "A sweeper. Let me guess. He probes a region for something. Using sensors?"

Leena nodded vigorously, her hair bobbing away. "Yup. It takes talent to pick up a specific object hiding in a bunch of junk floating around in space. He has infinite patience and stamina." She held up her hand. "Don't mention stamina to him either."

Cidra laughed. Dinner promised to be an adventure.

A stray thought hit her. Pointing to the mystery door, she asked, "Do you know where that door goes? It won't open."

Leena looked over at the door in question and turned back, wide-eyed. "Don't you know?"

Cidra frowned and shook her head.

"It connects to the Captain's quarters. It has a release on each side. I think that's why this room has never been used. Captain likes his privacy." Leena stood up and shrugged. "We're filled up, so I guess he decided it was okay. Well, I gotta go. See you at dinner in the crew lounge."

Cidra managed a smile. "Thanks for everything. Especially for hitting that Victor."

"Anytime. I'll introduce you to everyone tonight." Leena waved a hand at her and disappeared into the corridor.

Cidra stared at the adjoining door as if it were alive. She jumped up and locked the release on her side, her pulse racing. Good Lord, calm down. It's not as if he'd barge in uninvited. Or would he?

She leaned back against the door and closed her eyes. The idea was at once nerve-shattering and tantalizing.

* * * *

It was late afternoon and Grey stood on the bridge evaluating provisions over a micropad. Decker approached him and glanced at the deck crew nervously. "Sir, I need to speak to you. Immediately."

Grey lifted an eyebrow. It took a great deal to make Decker nervous. "Trouble?"

Decker cleared his throat. "I think it could be. I just saw Cidra and Mora, uh, talking in the dining hall. Neither one of them looked very happy."

He shoved the micropad at Decker. "Take care of this." He turned and marched off the bridge.

CHAPTER FOUR

Cidra's intention was to join Barrios in the crew lounge. It seemed like a simple enough task. She should have known better.

The lounge was empty except for the woman firmly planted in her path. Not just any woman. The most attractive, voluptuous woman Cidra had ever seen in her life. A red-haired, green-eyed beauty wearing a straining scarlet jumpsuit and a disapproving scowl.

"So you're the package Grey picked up on Avion," the woman

scoffed in a throaty voice, scanning Cidra head to toe with clear contempt. "Hardly worth the effort."

Cidra frowned at her, amazed how an attractive person could turn so ugly from the inside out. *Be nice, Cidra.* Remember you have to work with this woman.

"I'm Cidra Almazan. And you would be?" Cidra started in her most peaceable voice.

"Mora. You're new here, so consider this your orientation." A smile twisted over Mora's face. "I'm going to explain how things work around here."

She stared icily at Cidra. "Rule Number One. I make the rules. This is my ship."

Cidra lifted her eyebrows. If she hadn't been so surprised, she would have burst out laughing. "Really. I was under the impression it was Captain Stone's ship."

Mora ignored that. "Rule Number Two. I don't like Avions. You and your high and mighty people think you own the galaxy, picking and choosing who to save with your precious vaccine. You are not welcome here." Mora's voice lowered to a growl. "Watch your step. We wouldn't want you to have an unfortunate accident aboard ship."

Cidra listened to Mora's threat in disbelief, her sense of humor deserting her. *Good Lord, where had Grey found this one?*

"Rule Number Three. I have Grey's ear. And the rest of him. He's off-limits." Mora breathed deeply, filling her red jumpsuit to capacity. "Besides, you're not his type."

Cidra bristled. "And you would be an expert on the topic?" The first stirrings of anger began to seep into her body. *Control, Cidra.* The conversation had just taken a dangerous turn.

"I know how to make him happy. I know what he wants." Mora lifted her chin to Cidra. "Me."

Blood pounded in Cidra's ears as she narrowed her eyes at the other woman. She was dangerously close to losing her temper. It would not bode well to pummel a fellow crewmember on her first day of employ. The temptation wasn't worth throwing away her future for. Retreat seemed the sensible choice.

"Mora, exhale before you hurt yourself," Cidra muttered with disgust and turned toward the exit.

"Hold it. I'm not finished with you." Mora reached out with her right hand and sunk her fingernails into Cidra's left shoulder. Her attempt to twist Cidra around never had a chance.

Something in Cidra snapped. She would later recognize it as

her self-control. She reached across with her right hand and wrenched Mora's hand off her shoulder, simultaneously stepping back. Using Mora's own forward momentum, Cidra pulled her across the front of her body and flattened the surprised woman against the wall to her right. Cidra pinned Mora to the wall by shoving her forearm under Mora's chin. The whole maneuver took a second, leaving Mora blinking wide-eyed, helpless, and gaping at Cidra.

Grey had rounded the corner of the corridor just in time to see the action unfold. He slowed to a stop. As he feared, the confrontation had escalated. He knew only too well what Mora was capable of, even if he had found out the hard way. Unfortunately for Mora, she'd just picked a fight with a fully trained Kin-sha.

He leaned against the corridor wall and decided to let Cidra finish what she started. Besides, he thoroughly enjoyed the idea of someone getting the best of Mora for a change.

Cidra didn't give Mora a chance to recover. Her self-control had deserted her, replaced by pure fire and brimstone. There was no way she'd allow anyone tell her what to do after ten years of hiding. Quiet fury laced her voice. "Now it's my turn, Mora. Rule Number One. I make my own rules. Is that clear?"

Mora nodded weakly, still stunned. Her breathing came in short gasps and only by the grace of Cidra's grip.

"Good. Rule Number Two. I don't care to hear your opinion of me or Avion or anyone else." Cidra's voice shook with the effort. Mora's eyes widened.

"And Rule Number Three. Stay away from me." It was a low, dangerous whisper.

Mora stared at Cidra before slowly nodding again.

Cidra stepped back and released her hold. Mora sucked air into her lungs, clutching her throat with one hand and bracing herself against the wall with the other. The red jumpsuit looked suddenly deflated. She gave Cidra a murderous look but said nothing.

Cidra spun around and resumed her exit from the dining hall, now more disgusted with herself than Mora. The damage was done. She had barely boarded and already made a mortal enemy. At this rate, she'd go through the whole crew by tomorrow.

Retribution left her shaking and confused. Anger had claimed her and won. Why had she let it? Mora had certainly struck a few nerves, but it was no excuse. Cidra had lost control, plain and simple. Syrus would not have been pleased.

Clearing the doorway, she looked up to see Grey waiting and cringed. From the look on his face, he had witnessed the scuffle. As she approached him, she took a deep breath and braced herself for his reaction. Now she would find out how the Captain ran his ship. This could possibly be the shortest employment contract in history.

"What was that all about?" His brow furrowed, his expression unreadable.

Cidra halted directly in front of him. "Mora and I were just discussing a few things."

"Such as?" His face darkened.

"Rank. Avion. What type of women you prefer," Cidra drawled. "She has strong opinions on all subjects."

Grey swore. Cidra took a deep breath. "I'm sorry if I've caused any problems for you."

He didn't seem to hear her as he took her arm and led her down the corridor. "Don't worry about it. Mora's leaving soon."

Baffled, Cidra frowned and glanced up at Grey. "You wouldn't discharge Mora because of this incident, would you?"

Grey said nothing as they made their way toward crew quarters. He guided her past her cabin. When the door slid shut behind them, Cidra found herself standing in the middle of the Captain's quarters as Grey walked to a low cabinet and opened a bottle.

The room was larger with a similar layout as her own with one notable difference: the standard narrow bunk had been replaced by a spacious, freestanding bed. She stared at it for a second. Of course, it made sense. He was a big man; he needed a big bed but the intimacy of it all left her mouth dry.

She pulled her attention to the rest of the room. Her eyes widened in disbelief. Shelves lining the entire cabin displayed an impressive collection of art and artifacts. Exotic, unusual, some breathtaking, some hideous. Each a striking example in fine craftsmanship from various alien cultures. She eyed Grey in astonishment and admiration.

"Where did you get all these?"

Grey poured two drinks from the bottle. "I'm a treasure hunter, remember? I wouldn't be one if I didn't appreciate art."

He picked up the glasses and turned toward her. She was concentrating on an exquisite Krion statue in genuine fascination, her blue eyes shining. It was enough to stop him dead in his tracks. He suddenly realized that he had never brought a woman into his quarters before. This was his private space, a place he shared with no one.

He tried not to think about what that meant as he handed her a drink. She accepted it, instantly fascinated by the luminescent green and blue swirls undulating gracefully through a clear liquid base. "What is it?"

"Oeno, a Vaasa commodity. It's very good. Try it." He took a big swallow, watching her over the rim of his glass.

Cidra followed his lead, taking a generous sip. It was chilly, alternating sweet and sour on her tongue as she swallowed. Suddenly she gasped, her eyes watered. The coolness transformed to heat, spreading quickly, following the same path down her throat.

Grey grinned guiltily. "It takes some getting used to."

"Thanks for telling me," Cidra sputtered. The burning subsided, replaced by a rush of pleasure. She watched the undulations with new respect. Barrios would love this stuff.

She drew a deep breath. "I lost my temper. Mora said some things that cut too close, and I reacted poorly. I promise it won't happen again."

"Don't promise things you can't deliver."

Cidra blinked at him. That was hardly the reply she had expected. "Why would I do that?"

He shrugged. "From my experience, most people don't honor their promises. They make them casually. They break them casually. Besides, there's something important I want you to promise me." He pinned her with a stern expression. "Really promise me."

Cidra could almost feel the precise moment impending doom descended upon her. "What's that?"

"I don't need to tell you how most people feel about Avion and the Kin-sha. It's not a topic you want to bring up in casual conversation. It also turns off potential customers, contacts, and employees. In other words, it's lousy for business." He spoke purposely, his gaze unwavering. "No one on board knows I'm from Avion or that I'm a trained Kin-sha. I would like to keep it that way. If anyone asks, I'm from Vaasa."

Cidra stared sadly into her drink. So much for loyalty. "I can understand your predicament. I *promise* I won't say a word."

He shifted against the table. "There's something else. That move back there. With Mora. She probably didn't recognize it as pure Kin-sha, but I did. Someone else might pick up on it, too."

Cidra argued, "It was a simple self-defense move. Anyone could have done it."

He nodded. "Granted, but keep the Kin-sha for emergencies. No need to raise any suspicions."

"You never use it?"

Grey lifted his eyes to meet hers. "I had to give it up ten years ago. It wasn't a choice."

Cidra's mouth dropped open as his words hit home. "My father didn't betray the Kin-sha. You saw Syrus' note."

He smiled wryly. "I saw it. So far I have your word and his."

There was a heavy silence. Frustration choked Cidra as she stated flatly, "You won't help."

"I didn't say that."

"You didn't have to."

Grey took a big swallow of Oeno. "I'd like to see what's on the holo recording."

As Cidra stared at him, she realized what he was doing. Stalling. And there wasn't a thing she could do about it. He certainly didn't look in the mood for negotiation.

"Of course, Captain. Well if there's nothing else, I'll return to my quarters." She placed her glass on the table next to him and headed toward the door.

She was across the room when he announced, "Mora's a spy."

Cidra stopped and turned to look at him. Barrios' statement of a leak aboard ship rushed to mind. "Are you sure?"

"Positive. She works for Sandor Wex. Another treasure hunter. At least that's what he calls himself. A scavenger is more like it." He glowered, his fists clenching.

"He jumped your last two finds," she deduced quickly.

He brightened and saluted her with his drink. "Very good."

Much to her chagrin, she blushed. Memories of Syrus' gentle instruction flashed in her mind. She could see his influence on Grey.

"I marked the first incident up to coincidence, but I knew I had a problem after the second one. The odds were astronomical that he'd hit us twice. Not these finds. No one except the crew even knew I was working on them." He shot down the rest of the drink and turned to pour himself another.

She found herself watching him, fascinated by the way he moved. He glided from position to position, purely, powerfully male. It called to her on a level she couldn't explain. Cidra frowned, disturbed that these thoughts were developing with more frequency.

Turning back around, Grey's tone darkened. "Now he's apparently decided jumping my finds aren't enough. He wants *Calíbre*, too."

"How do you know that?"

"Decker confirmed it was his Victor that attacked us over Avion." He shoved a hand through his hair.

Cidra was stunned and appalled. "They tried to kill us!"

"Actually, I believe they were trying to kill me. Easier to take *Calíbre* with me out of the way. Mora must have tipped them off that I would be alone. I don't think they expected any trouble taking me out. They certainly didn't count on your flying skills."

"What are you going to do about it?" Cidra whispered, almost afraid to ask.

"I have a plan." Grey stared at the floor, his mind elsewhere.

She took in his hard eyes, hard face. "Are you going to kill them?"

A corner of his mouth raised. "No. Just teach them a lesson and get them out of our way for a while. A long while." He paused and said pointedly, "If Mora finds out we're on to her, the plan won't work."

Cidra relaxed. "I won't breathe a word." Then she added with a laugh, "And remind me not to cross you."

She never saw him coming. He slammed his glass down, shoved off the cabinet and closed on her swiftly. Slipping a hand under her chin, he held her fast, warning flashing in his eyes.

"I wouldn't recommend it. You don't want me for an enemy," his voice was as hard as his face.

Cidra swallowed, unable to break the connection, his close proximity generating more heat than the Oeno. Alarmed, she placed her free hand on his chest to keep him from coming any closer. He didn't budge and made no move to release her.

Grey had only meant to reinforce his position on the subject, but the lines were quickly blurring. He suddenly found himself enthralled by her clear blue eyes. In an instant, he was drawn into their bottomless depths. There he uncovered her inner strength and courage, her innocence and absolute trust. In the calm mirror lay his own reflection.

Out of nowhere, a thunderous awareness gripped him. He ran his thumb slowly along the edge of her lower lip, enchanted by the fine line. Cidra parted her lips and inhaled sharply. He lowered his mouth to hers, kissing her gently, denying her escape. As he tasted her, each kiss became deeper, more demanding, intoxicating.

Her lips were as soft and sweet as they appeared. Lush and inviting, a perfect foil for his own. He found himself swallowed up in her softness, her heat, unable to pull himself away.

She moaned softly, her palm splaying across his chest. He felt the second she relaxed, the moment when she gave in, her wordless gift of sweet surrender.

Somewhere in the back of his mind, he wondered if she understood her full affect on a man or what she was offering. Although her kisses were eager, there was a definite innocence in her reaction to him.

Reality invaded with its cold edge. He was in charge, the Captain of the ship, her employer. It was up to him to curb the situation before it went any further. He was failing miserably.

He groaned. Under a crush of obligation, Grey released her and stepped back, thoroughly disgusted with himself. He half-turned from her, running a hand through his hair and down the back of his neck.

"That was wrong. I shouldn't have...." he started and stopped, blowing out a long breath. "That won't happen again."

Cidra stared at him, flushed, out of breath and astonished by his sudden withdrawal. Her outward composure returned rapidly along with a healthy dose of anger while her mind struggled to catch up.

"Tell me, Captain. Do you always seduce your new crew members?" she snapped, trying to regain some semblance of dignity after her moment of emotional abandon.

He stiffened, his eyes pure fire. "I didn't seduce you. You would know it if I did. I said, it won't happen again."

Cidra blurted out, "And do you always make the rules?" Immediately she regretted letting her mouth work without benefit of her brain.

His eyes narrowed at her. "Are you mad at me for starting the kiss or for stopping it?"

Cidra glared back at him, unsure what else to do. His advance had shattered her self-control and she deeply resented it. On the other hand, she wanted desperately to try it again.

With cold conviction, Grey said, "I'm your employer. Period."

Mercifully, his room comm blared. They stared at each other a second longer before Grey hit the comm. "What!"

"Ah, I'm glad I found you, sir. Barrios and I just broke the code on the holo recording. We're ready to run it," Decker announced with cheerful innocence.

Cidra froze. Finally, answers. Her ire vanished, the past few moments displaced by exhilaration and a new fear. She had not realized until this moment that the answers might not be the ones she wanted to hear.

"We'll be right there." Otherwise distracted, Cidra missed the distinct note of relief in Grey's voice.

"We?" Decker questioned.

Grey cleared his throat. "Cidra's here."

There was a pause.

"Yes, sir!" Decker replied, a little too enthusiastically.

Grey winced and flipped off the comm. It would be all over the ship in minutes. Still he was grateful for the reprieve, and one look at Cidra told him she was looking toward the future again. He was off the hook, at least for now. Gallantly he swept a hand toward the door.

"Shall we?"

* * * *

Decker smiled up at them from the round holo deck table as they entered Grey's office.

Cidra slid into the seat next to Barrios at the table. He patted her hand gently as if sensing her turmoil. She smiled at the only man in the room who truly understood what this meant to her.

Decker addressed Grey, "I didn't even break a sweat on this one, had the encryption key for the holo recording on file. Standard Avion military format. Ages old."

Grey dropped into the chair next to Decker. The holo cartridge's raw data dump scrolled down the display screen. "Find anything interesting in the data section?" Grey asked.

Decker's eyebrows raised. "I sure did and I still can't believe it. Looks like a complete cargo manifest. Serial numbers for almost a thousand ampoules of Ximenes vaccine in the shipment. Do you have any idea how much that's worth? We could all retire," Decker marveled. He shoved Syrus' holo cartridge into the holo deck unit. "OK, here comes the show."

A cylinder-shaped grid surged up from the holo deck in the center of the table to a height of roughly two meters. Cidra's eyes adjusted as the luminous holo recording came alive, filling the grid. A surreal, three-dimensional space battle burst forth, complete with statistics scrolling up underneath. The skirmish was chaotic and it took a few seconds for her to assimilate what they were watching.

"That's one of ours. An Avion freighter," Barrios blurted out, pointing to the largest vessel. "And that's a Kin-sha escort." He pointed to the smaller, silver ships hanging tightly around the freighter. "Four of them."

"Looks like they are under attack by these little fighters." Decker scanned the players as he tried to dissect the players on each side. "Are those Saurelian ships? Nasty little units. There must be twenty of them. Looks like they are swarming and firing on the escort ships." Decker shook his head. "Trying to take out one of those is like trying to swat gypsy wings, there's always more."

Grey frowned. "Decker, what are we watching here? Can you catch some of these stats?"

As the Kin-sha escort was being soundly pummeled, Cidra grimaced. She prayed this was only a simulation. The first Kin-sha escort burst into flames and disappeared from the image. She swallowed, hope shattered.

Decker picked out the details carefully. "The freighter is the Galena. She generated this holo recording from her sensor readings. Left Avion...." his voice faltered. "This can't be right. According to the autodate, this holo recording is ten years old."

Next to Cidra, Barrios' voice was no more than a rasp. "The Galena?"

"Original destination?" Grey asked.

"Got it. My Lord. It's Dakru," Decker said in awe. He stared wide-eyed at Grey. "Are we watching what I think we're watching?"

Grey's jaw set hard.

Cidra looked at Barrios. He didn't move a muscle, but she could see his pulse throbbing at his temples. Another Kin-sha escort exploded and she was riveted again to the recording. She watched the silent, historic battle rage before her. Not a simulation, not a recreation. The destruction of the Avion vaccine shipment bound for Dakru ten years ago. It was raw. It was real. It was the turning point in her life.

Decker continued his commentary. "Their location is just outside Dakru's outer region. So much for the rumor that they never left Avion."

The freighter was fighting back with everything it had, guns blazing unceasingly, scoring some hits, trying desperately to assist the overwhelmed escort. A third Kin-sha ship vanished in a ball of fire. The Saurelian fighters outnumbered the last escort twenty to one. It didn't last long.

Cidra watched in horror as all the attackers turned on the freighter when the last escort was destroyed, bombarding it relentlessly. They were so tight that the freighter couldn't maneuver, couldn't jump to hyperspace. The Galena endured hit after hit.

"They're taking a beating," Decker reported, intent on the statistics. "Systems are shutting down all over."

The freighter slowly rolled left, its port side guns firing constantly. The image flickered strangely before flashing back.

"Hull breach," Decker announced gravely. Cidra knew total destruction was inevitable.

The big guns ceased firing. Internal explosions lit up the Galena. Suddenly, there was a burst of static and the image died.

All four sat in stunned silence for a long time staring into the empty holo grid. The office felt as cold as a morgue.

Decker rubbed his forehead and swore an oath for all of them.

"Well, now we know what happened." It was Barrios who finally said it. "All these years and no one knew."

Cidra closed her eyes. She should be analyzing the situation, but her mind wouldn't cooperate. Someone had deliberately destroyed that shipment and purposely dishonored the Kin-sha, Avion, and her father.

"Why would anyone destroy that shipment?" She didn't realize she'd spoken aloud.

"My question exactly," muttered Barrios. "What do you think Stone?"

Grey stared into the empty holo deck, deep in thought. "Definitely not pirates. They weren't holding anything back. They wanted to make sure there was nothing left to that ship."

"Do you think they knew they destroyed a fortune in vaccine along with it?" Decker asked.

"I don't know," Grey replied. He asked another question. "Do you think they realized a few million people would die without it?"

Barrios groused. "Just what we need, more questions. One at a time. Decker, hand me that cartridge."

Decker ejected the holo cartridge from the holo deck and passed it to Barrios.

"Just as I thought," Barrios commented as he examined the

cartridge. "Standard issue Avion equipment. Manufacture date corresponds with the autodate of the recording."

He held the cartridge up to the group. "You are looking at the original recording media. Has anyone thought about how this recording survived? If the Galena recorded this holo, how come it wasn't destroyed with the freighter?"

Decker voiced his thoughts. "Even if there was another ship around, it couldn't have been transmitted off. According to the stats, their external transmissions were being jammed from the very beginning. They couldn't even communicate with the escort."

Grey folded his hands in front of his face. "It's a long journey from that freighter to Syrus' box. So how did it happen?"

Decker shifted in his seat. "Add it to the list of questions. But I have one answer for you. I know who attacked the shipment. The Saurelians. I can positively ID those ships. From what the Galena could gather, I'd say they were identical. Probably pulled right off the production line. Looks like they were state of the art at the time." Decker shook his head in admiration and regret. "Those Saurelians make good killing machines. They know how to fly them, too."

"No," stated Cidra.

All eyes turned to her in surprise. She straightened and looked to each one in turn.

"That may be their fighters, but I can tell you, those weren't Saurelian pilots. I've studied every alien battle strategy in this sector. It's not their style to deploy twenty fighters to take out five ships. They enjoy the battle too much, and they love flying their own ships. Saurelians prefer even odds, makes the game more interesting."

"This," she waved a hand toward the empty holo grid, "was too easy. Whoever sent those fighters out there wanted to make sure that shipment wouldn't make it to Dakru."

She looked over to find Grey regarding her intently over his hands. He turned to Decker. "Run it again. Half-speed this time. Let's see if we can get some answers."

By the third viewing, Cidra had the entire monstrosity engraved in her memory. Barrios was right. It only raised more questions.

Who was flying the fighters? Why would anyone want to destroy a humanitarian shipment? How did they approach the cortege so easily, apparently undetected? How did the holo cartridge and an actual vaccine ampoule get off the Galena and into Syrus' hands?

And the most important question of all. Grey couldn't deny her mission any longer, not with the evidence before him.

"So Captain, do we have a mission?" Cidra asked with a calm secured by vindication.

Grey was slow to answer. His quick-silver eyes met hers with cold clarity. "We have a mission. A non-profit mission. In case you hadn't noticed, I have an entire crew to pay." He leaned back in his chair, watching her. "I set the rules and timing. We'll look at it until we get to Vaasa. Then it goes on hold for as long as it takes to find the Mask of Teran. Understood?"

Cidra glared at him. "Can't you see how important this is?"

Grey glared back. "I don't need to explain my reasons to you. You just have to live with them."

Cidra opened her mouth to say something but closed it instead. She wasn't going to win this battle. Not today. There was always tomorrow. Patience. She knew all about patience. She took a deep breath, letting go of her anger. "Of course, Captain. So where do we begin?"

Grey narrowed his eyes at her. She smiled back brightly.

He began warily, "Ten years ago, someone purchased twenty Saurelian fighters. That should narrow down the source. I've got some people I can contact on Vaasa. We still need to figure out how this holo cartridge and the ampoule got off that freighter. That's a huge piece of the puzzle."

To Decker, he said, "I want you to get all you can out of this recording. Every stat, every development, in sequence. The answer to the recording's survival is there, but we're missing it. Look for anything unusual. Also, start digging around in the archives and external sources for everything you can find on this shipment. Be creative."

Decker nodded and grinned. "Always. That's where I do my best work."

Grey glanced around the room. "In the meantime, if anyone comes up with any brilliant theories, be sure to let me know."

CHAPTER FIVE

Making her way down the main corridor with Grey's dinner, Cidra reflected on her first meal on *Calíbre* with dazed amusement. It had been a chaotic, riotous affair with a crew of people all talking, laughing, and cursing at once. Much of the time was spent regaling Cidra and Barrios on a few unsavory adventures involving the Captain and crew of *Calíbre*. She imagined every new member got the same initiation.

Leena had kept her word and introduced Cidra to the rest of the crew. She'd met the infamous Coon. Although she had tried to heed Leena's advice and not give him any openings, the man still managed to slip in some suggestive remarks. He looked the part of a wild man with his crazy eyes, untamed hair, and a few unusual-looking teeth. To make matters even more interesting, he'd somehow found an unlikely friend in Barrios. The two had roared with laughter throughout the entire meal.

The rest of the crew consisted of a delightfully strange coalition of a gunner, mechanic, sweeper, retriever, even a historian and physician. Individually, they would be considered rather eccentric, but together they formed a surprisingly cohesive unit. Grey had managed to collect the perfect crew for a treasure hunting operation.

Cidra was grateful to learn that Mora usually spent mealtimes in the galley. No one seemed to request or miss her company.

Decker was also absent, covering the bridge alone. Before dinner, he'd given Cidra a brief message from Grey. The Captain wouldn't be joining them this evening. Evidently, it was normal for Grey to work non-stop for days at a time researching a find.

On those occasions, someone brought him his meals. Cidra had offered with some hesitation, unsure she wanted to be alone with Grey again. The fervent memory of the kiss in his quarters still lingered, but the opportunity to speak to him about the mission was too good to pass up. At least that's what she told herself right up until she stood in the open doorway of his office.

Grey stared into a display station, fingers steepled in front of his face, studying a maze of star charts. The man had an amazing level of concentration. He didn't even know she was there. Only when she stepped into the room did he gaze up at her in mild surprise.

"I brought you dinner," Cidra started in her most cheerful voice, setting the tray on the desk next to him. "You better eat it before it gets cold." As she spoke, her eyes immediately went to the display. She hesitated for an awkward moment. Then relenting to her curiosity, she moved quietly behind him to get a better view of the charts.

Grey didn't take his eyes off her. "Thank you. I see you survived your first dinner with the crew?"

She smiled at him with genuine delight. "A rowdy bunch, especially Coon."

Grey gave a short laugh. "I'll bet you heard all of his best stuff tonight. He always enjoys breaking in a new crew member or two."

"I could tell." She inclined her head toward the display. "What is that?"

Grey saw the gleam in her eyes. "You really want to know?"

She nodded, leaning over his shoulder to get a better look, her long hair drifting down.

"I'm trying to track down the Lost Mask of Teran. It was en route from Teran to Borkova for an exhibition forty-three years ago and disappeared."

He pointed to a small galaxy on the screen. "Their last transmission was tracked to this sector. So that's where we started."

His voice grew husky as he became acutely aware of Cidra's hair brushing his neck. He was truly amazed that she'd come into his office alone after that scorching kiss. Now here she was, standing inches from him. Either she trusted him more than he trusted himself or she was genuinely interested in the subject. He decided it was wiser to focus on the latter.

"Then what?" she asked.

He cleared his throat and continued. "We began with a long list of possibilities, then eliminated them one by one."

She turned to him with those incredible clear, blue eyes. "Possibilities?"

For a split-second, Grey was caught off-guard. *Just keep talking.* "Something caused that ship to disappear. Mechanical malfunction, crew problems, pirates, enemies, natural disasters. Like I said, it's a long list."

Her hair smelled incredible.

She frowned at him. "How can you eliminate possibilities when the ship vanished without a trace?"

"Research." He could hear her steady breathing in his ear, ignored it and plowed ahead. "We get a complete schematic of the transport ship. Identify previous or possible mechanical problems. Locate a crew roster. Find out if the working crew have a history of difficulties? Were pirates working that sector at the time? Who would have wanted the Mask? Any local meteoric activity, asteroids, comets or other anomalies?"

She frowned even more. "Suppose it was completely destroyed like the Dakru shipment? You could do all this work for nothing."

There was a beat of silence before he finally shrugged. "It's instinct."

Cidra's eyes widened. "That's it? Your entire operation is based on instinct?"

He grinned. "Call it hunter's intuition. I wouldn't pursue the prey unless I felt it still existed. I guess you could call it a gut feeling."

Like right now, for instance. He felt her body heat on his shoulder, and his gut feeling told him to back off before he did something stupid. He breathed deeply, crossed his arms, and leaned forward in the chair.

"That's where most treasure hunters give up. They think the research is too time-consuming and tedious. Not to mention, it doesn't pay particularly well if you don't find what you're looking for."

Cidra was quiet for a minute behind him. "You don't give up easily, do you?"

He wasn't sure if it was a personal or professional observation and decided it didn't really matter. The answer was the same.

"No. I like to think it's one of my most endearing qualities." He turned and smiled roguishly. "Among others."

She raised an eyebrow and indulged him with a playful grin. "Really? Do you have many?"

"A few," he acknowledged, sliding his gaze down to her lips. "Unfortunately, decent apologies aren't at the top of the list."

Cidra blushed and managed a smile. "Lucky for you, I'll accept just about anything."

* * * *

Cidra tossed the micropad on the side desk, rubbed her eyes and stared at the ceiling above her bed. Thanks to Decker, hundreds of stats from the unearthed battle swam in her head. Far too many to absorb at once.

She reached back over the desk and picked up the personal communication unit she had been issued shortly after boarding. It felt cool and smooth in her palm, a perfectly balanced disc of metallic technology. The comm unit, as Decker had called it, provided a direct link to other units or the main communication board on *Calíbre*. She smiled. It made her feel like part of the crew.

Cidra placed it back on the desk. She lay back on the bed and contemplated the first day of her new life. Some of it bothered her even now--the Victor battle over Avion particularly. Some of it was wonderful.

She caught her breath as she remembered the kiss of a lifetime. At least her lifetime. The last time she'd been kissed was by a young man who had fumbled his way through it badly. Grey was no boy and he certainly didn't fumble. Even with her limited experience, she realized it was no ordinary kiss. She closed her eyes with a sigh.

So much intensity in one man, so overwhelming and without warning. But more unexpected was her own reaction to him. The strange warmth that had unfurled deep within her. The wild recklessness that had surfaced, goading her on.

Cidra grimaced at how easily she'd surrendered to his unspoken demands. She would have to be more careful with him. He had a way of destroying her defenses with a single look, a single kiss. She wondered if he had the same devastating impact on everyone else.

* * * *

Grey stretched out restlessly on his spacious bed, locked his hands behind his head and forced himself to close his eyes yet again. Sleep eluded him. Even the strenuous workout in *Calíbre*'s rec center had done little to curb his uneasiness.

This mission was unsettling. Instinct told him there was more to it than they had seen. Something greater was brewing, something that would change his life forever. He knew it with the absolute confidence of a man who had ignored the feeling before and had later regretted it.

At least his plan to deal with Sandor Wex was on track. He smiled in the darkness. As expected, Mora had taken the bait: the final location of the Lost Mask of Teran. Or that's what she thought. Knowing his little spy as he did now, the file would be in Wex's hands the minute they landed on Vaasa tomorrow.

But he suspected the real reason for his restlessness was the distraction of innocence, strength, and stunning beauty he'd picked up on Avion. He could still smell Cidra's hair. He cursed Syrus yet again. The old man had set him up with a woman he could lose a great deal of sleep over.

In the blink of an eye, she had stripped him down to primal, elemental male with a single kiss. A kiss that haunted him relentlessly. A major mistake on his part. He'd tasted the fire in her that hovered just below the surface. For a brief moment, she had unchained it and let it rise. He wasn't sure which one of them had been more surprised.

He exhaled hard. Forget it. It would never work. He already had painful proof that business and ecstasy didn't mix, no matter how tempting or how innocent those blue eyes appeared. He wouldn't tolerate another Mora, wouldn't play the fool again.

Satisfied with his renewed determination and self-control, he concentrated once again on sleep. Even drifting toward it, he realized his body hadn't heard a word.

* * * *

It began as it always did. Oppressive darkness and debilitating horror, a suffocating terror that gripped her to the core. Cold, raw, bottomless fear.

The screaming started, blood-curdling shrieks unleashed from the heart. Cidra was never sure if they were her own. A mother, begging, pleading and then silenced with a brutal blast. A sickening flurry of twisted imagination and snippets of reality. Footsteps thundering, so loud, so close, so fast. Fire and smoke.

Fear choked her, paralyzing her body, freezing her legs. Frantically, blindly, she struggled to escape, her heart pounding out the advance of the faceless encroachers. Confusion reigned, panic clawed at her throat.

Cidra braced herself for the final scene, the inevitable conclusion, there was no stopping it. She waited for the pain that would rip through her, the final blast, the same conclusion to the same nightmare she'd relived over and over again for ten years.

She waited, but it didn't come. Not this time. A soft voice whispered to her. Her father's voice. He was there, in her mind.

Run, Cidra. Slip out as fast as you can, and no one will see you. His voice sounded calm and soothing. She wanted to say something to him, anything. It had been so long. She reached out to him.

The blast finally came and it was over. Cidra bolted up in bed like a shot. Heavy shudders racked her body. She was soaking wet and shaking in the darkness. She yanked the covers off and leapt to her feet, residual energy surging through her.

It had been different this time. Her father's voice, that had never happened before. The spell was broken for some reason; the nightmare had changed. After ten years, it had changed. Why?

She stood in the center of her room, hugging herself. There had to be a reason. What was it he'd said?

Run. Slip out as fast as you can, and no one will see you.

She repeated the words again and again. Suddenly, she stilled, her eyes focusing on the micropad lying on the desk. "Oh Lord. That's it."

Cidra spun around, hit the controls that unlocked the adjoining passage and started knocking on the door. She was about to try the comm unit when the door abruptly slid open.

Grey stood in the doorway, his body poised for action, laser in hand--all warrior.

"What's wrong? Are you all right?" His eyes darted around her cabin checking for trouble.

"A back door," she breathed, her eyes huge.

Low light from his cabin lit her face. Grey's eyebrows furrowed with concern. "Cidra?"

She repeated slowly, "A back door. The landing bay. They slipped out of the landing bay."

He struggled to keep up with her. She was obviously wide-awake, leaving him at a distinct disadvantage. Not to mention that, for a fleeting moment, he'd hoped she just plain wanted him and not to bounce some crazy idea off either.

"Cidra, I hate to break this to you, but we watched that holo recording four times. Nothing came out of the landing bay," he explained patiently, lowering the laser pistol and bracing his other hand above the doorframe.

She gave him a challenging look. "I have one brilliant theory for you."

Grey exhaled and hung his head. "It's late, Cidra. Can we discuss this in the morning?"

Her voice shook. "No. I need to see the recording again." She moved closer to him and placed her palm on his bare chest. "I can't wait until morning. Grey, please."

He sucked in a breath and froze. Her hand felt like fire on his bare skin. He gazed down into those beautiful, pleading eyes. It was the first time she'd ever called him by his first name, and it sounded incredibly sweet. He was aware that parts of him were waking up faster than others. He was also aware with every ounce of instinct in him, without a doubt, he was in big trouble.

"I'm going to regret this," he grumbled.

She withdrew her hand at once and smiled brilliantly. "Let's go."

He raised his head and examined her from the floor up with a slow, thorough gaze. Her gown was plastered to her body, revealing every curve, every movement.

"If you walk around *Calibre* looking like that, I won't be held responsible for the actions of my crew." His voice was low and deliberate.

Cidra drew a blank and looked down at herself. Her eyes shot back to him. For the first time, it dawned on her that he was wearing only shorts. He was still standing in the doorway with one hand braced on the top of the doorway, his lean, powerful body now relaxed.

Suddenly, the only cohesive thought in her head was that he was magnificent. Muscle played over muscle, sinuous and imposing. The contours and hard planes of a superb male physique glowed in the half-light. Broad shoulders filled the doorway. Dark hair sprinkled over his wide chest and down a tapering torso. She skimmed quickly over his narrow hips, watching as his legs flexed, potent and solid under her scrutiny. She had to force her gaping mouth shut.

Cidra drew her attention back to his face. It was an amused, all-male smile that greeted her.

She straightened and lifted her chin. "Point taken. Give me five minutes." The door slid shut.

* * * *

Decker wandered in the office, scratched his head and threw himself into the closest chair. Barrios lumbered in a second later, took one look at Cidra's bright, perky face and growled at Grey, "This better be good."

Grey held up a hand in defense. "I'm just the messenger."

He swept a hand toward Cidra. "It's all yours. Let's hear that brilliant theory that couldn't wait till morning."

Cidra winced. It was going to be a tough crowd. "Decker, please run the recording again, starting about midway through."

Decker grumbled something low and the now familiar image flashed up after the Kin-sha escort was destroyed and the dying Galena began its drift to port.

"Stop." The image froze. Cidra turned to the others. "Can anyone think of a good reason why the Galena would rotate position and try to draw the fighters to the port side?"

Grey leaned forward. "Maybe there was a problem with the starboard guns." He threw Decker a questioning glance.

Decker yawned and shook his head. "Nope, they look just fine at this point. A direct order was issued."

Grey frowned. "Strange order."

Cidra smiled, knowing she had his attention. "OK, let it run. Normal speed." The battle continued on its tragic way.

"Wait ... wait. There. See that flicker?" Cidra pointed as the recording jumped. She pinned Decker. "Any idea what caused that?"

He frowned at the stats rolling by. "No, it doesn't look like a malfunction. Maybe a file transfer or something." His eyes met hers, surprised by his own implication.

She now had Decker's attention, too.

"Slow it down. Speed at ten percent," she said. The battle was nearly over. "Decker, what's the status of the landing bay door on the starboard side."

"That's strange. It's open." He paused. "Why would they want the door open? One laser blast from a fighter would destroy them."

"Anything inside the landing bay?" Cidra was almost afraid to ask.

Decker nodded. "Looks like a couple of transports were docked, but there's very little data on them."

The internal explosions had begun. Just as the final explosion rocked the big ship, Cidra interjected. "Let it finish. Then back up to the last frame of the image."

Her heart was racing now. This was it, the moment of truth. If she were wrong, no one in this room would speak to her for a week.

The final split second of action froze.

Cidra squinted. "Zoom in here." She pointed to the landing bay vicinity.

The focus area enlarged.

"Now cut the glare from the explosions inside and the gunfire outside."

Decker nodded and complied.

Suddenly it appeared. Cidra closed her eyes. It was there. A very faint, very fine line coming out of the landing bay heading into deep space. The distinct trail of a hyperspace vortex.

"I don't believe it," Barrios gasped, his eyes riveted to the image. "They jumped a transport into hyperspace directly off the landing bay deck. That's practically impossible to do."

Cidra relaxed in her chair. Mission accomplished. "Slip out as fast as you can, and no one will see you," she murmured.

Barrios chuckled and rubbed his bald head.

Decker shook his head. "I can't believe they'd take such a huge risk. The chances of that transport getting out of there in one piece were pretty slim."

Grey leaned back in his seat and looked at Decker. "Probably figured they didn't have anything to lose. It was evident they weren't going to make it."

Decker snorted. "Yeah, I guess when you look at it that way, it was downright brilliant. Well, this would explain how they got this holo recording and that one vial off the Galena."

"I'll wager they got more than that off." Barrios hesitated, waiting for their full focus. "It was standard practice for a transport to handle the final leg of each shipment. The freighter generally served as long-range transportation and protection only. How much do you want to bet the entire shipment of vaccine was on that transport?"

Cidra whispered. "Are you saying that whole shipment could be out there somewhere?"

"Impossible," Decker interjected. "They would have had to plan this whole scenario ahead of time. The holo recording transfer, the transport and its crew. Not to mention, the manifest information and no less than a thousand vials of vaccine pre-loaded on that transport. According to this recording, there's no way there was enough time to do it during the battle."

Barrios boasted. "I told you Jarid was a master strategist. He always had a plan for every possibility. I'll bet...." He stopped short, suddenly enlightened, and glanced around the office. "Where's the paperwork we found in Syrus' box?"

Decker withdrew the papers from a drawer and tossed them to Barrios. He shuffled through them furiously until he located one small note. With a satisfied grunt, he tossed the note in front of them. Cidra leaned forward to read it. The message was short and hand-written, scrawled hastily across the faded paper.

PLAN A-664 EXECUTED. DAMAGE ON ESCAPE. COMMUNICATIONS OUT. NAVIGATION SYSTEM INOPERABLE. COORDINATES UNKNOWN. ATTEMPTING LANDING ON SMALL GRAY AND WHITE PLANET. ONE GIANT RED STAR VISIBLE. HOMING POD MANUALLY

RELEASED. CARGO INTACT. ORIGINAL MISSION FAILED.

"It didn't make any sense the first time I looked at it." The optimism in Barrios' voice was unmistakable as he tapped loudly on the note. "It mentions a plan. And the cargo."

Decker opened his mouth to object. Then closed it.

Grey nodded. "It had to have come from the transport crew. Sounds like they sustained some damage when they jumped off the Galena. Maybe an unlucky hit from one of the Saurelian fighters. No wonder we never heard from them again."

"A homing pod?" Cidra was reading the message again and missed Grey's last grim comment.

"It's a very small, unmanned pod with a built-in navigation system and a preset destination," Grey explained. "Not standard equipment for a transport, but it could be a custom addition."

Barrios smiled. "Jarid would have done that."

Grey drummed his fingers evenly on the table. "I'll bet it had a storage compartment big enough for one small vial, a scribbled note, and a holo recording. What do you think Decker?"

"It's possible." Decker brightened and bobbed his head. "Yeah, definitely possible."

"That's it!"

All eyes turned to Barrios. He raised his head to look at them. "And that's how Syrus got them. Jarid would have had that pod pre-programmed to return to Avion."

Decker balked. "Lord knows where that transport ended up. It could have taken years for a homing pod to reach Avion."

"How do we know it didn't make it?" Barrios countered. "Syrus could have recovered the pod anytime in the last ten years."

Cidra turned to face Barrios. "Then why didn't he say something?"

Barrios reached out and clasped her hand. "I don't know. He didn't have many friends in high places by then. Maybe he was afraid no one would believe him."

"I would have," she whispered.

Grey heard the break in her voice and decided to push forward before she lost it altogether. "Since they didn't include their coordinates, they must not have been able to determine where they were. Sounds like they were trying to leave some clues as to where they dropped out of hyperspace."

"So now all we have to do is find them, right?" Barrios grinned at Grey and leaned back in his chair while it squeaked in protest. "I've heard you're the best there is."

"I'll tell you right now, it doesn't sound good," Grey warned. "For one thing, that transport could have dropped out of hyperspace anywhere. In case you hadn't noticed, the universe is a very big place. Secondly, attempting to land on a planet when you've lost most of your systems isn't pretty. Obviously, they never returned to Avion. There's a very good chance they didn't survive at all."

Cidra eyed him shrewdly. "Forget the odds. What does your instinct tell you?"

His mouth turned up. *Too damned perceptive.* His gut feelings were positive on this one, but how did she know that? He was definitely in trouble.

He kept his eyes locked on hers. "I'm going to regret this."

CHAPTER SIX

Plass entered his Supreme Ruler's chambers with the bearing of a man on a death march. The red sunset cast a venomous glow over the sparse contents of the chamber. Tausek occupied center stage watching the evening's entertainment--another savage sunset. The room was silent but for the faint clicking of claws on the black, stone floor as the corvits moved to their master's side. Plass came to a halt behind his ruler.

"You have news for me, Commander," Tausek voiced evenly, not a muscle moved on his broad back. "Proceed."

Plass took a deep breath and prepared himself for the inevitable. Tausek did not tolerate failure well.

"Jarid Faulkner did indeed have a daughter named Cidra. It is possible she survived the initial attack and is now posing as the niece of Syrus Almazan. Her description and approximate age fit. Our sources reveal the niece arrived shortly after we eliminated Faulkner and his family. I am inclined to believe, based on the evidence, that she is Cidra Faulkner."

The only acknowledgment from Tausek came as a twitch in his shoulder. He continued to view the sunset unperturbed. "I see. You will, of course, execute her properly this time."

A prolonged silence drew Tausek around until he faced the

Commander. Plass tried to match Tausek's icy facade in a dismal contest. In the fifteen years he had known Tausek, he had never seen any significant emotion in the man. Every movement, every word, every action was expedient, rationed as if coming from a limited supply. Plass shifted uncomfortably, struggling to find words that would minimize Tausek's wrath.

"When we locate her, we will not fail," were the words he finally settled on.

Tausek's expression grew darker. "Explain."

Plass drew himself up with every ounce of courage he'd earned in his lifetime. "It appears she has left Avion. We are following a promising lead now. I am confident she will be located and terminated shortly."

Tausek remained silent for a few long moments, his black eyes drilling into Plass. Heat began to build under the Commander's uniform.

"Sssss." Tausek hissed between his teeth.

Called to attention, the corvits stepped from their positions toward Plass with ruthless concentration. Plass swallowed, his throat constricting to the threshold of pain. Barely visible in the darkness, they were a nightmare come alive.

"Let us hope you do just that, Commander. I will hold you personally responsible. I suggest you handle this matter as if your very life depended on its success." His eyes burned into Plass.

"Yes sir," Plass managed. "I understand."

He took a resuscitating breath. First message delivered and he was still alive, barely. His eyes flicked over the corvits. Even frozen, they looked terrifying.

Now highly motivated, Plass plowed ahead. "There is one other item. Earlier today, there was an unusual security breach into our primary information system. The only files accessed were for the Avion vaccine negotiations and communications ten years ago."

Plass paused, noting with surprise that his ruler's natural arrogance appeared momentarily compromised. Hoping to head off a second storm, he said in haste, "The files were assigned Level Three security only. I consider this a minor incident. I have corrected the oversight, but I thought you should be aware of it."

The momentary lapse passed and Tausek regained his composure without missing a beat. "You thought correctly. I want a copy of every file accessed in this violation. Then permanently purge those files from the system." His jaw clenched ever so slightly. "Have you identified the perpetrator?"

"No sir, but we will. I have our best people working on it." Plass continued with some trepidation. "It may take some time. The transgression originated off-planet."

If Tausek was breathing, Plass couldn't tell.

"How have you corrected this situation?"

Plass' uniform was burning from the inside out, perspiration carving a river down his back. "I relieved the Head of System Security of his position."

"Terminate him permanently." Tausek's words cut through the air.

Plass blinked once. "Yes, sir. Will there be anything else?"

Tausek turned his back to Plass with a single easy movement. "You will notify me when you identify the source of the infiltration. I will decide what action to take at that time."

"As you wish."

"Dismissed."

Plass glanced once at the motionless corvits, spun on his heel and headed for the safety of his office. He didn't slow down until Tausek's chamber door slid shut behind him. Releasing a full breath, he turned right and headed toward his private office, his footsteps echoing through the empty halls.

He tried to sort through the unusual conversation with Tausek. He'd expected the anger. He'd expected the retribution. What he hadn't expected was the fear that flashed ever so briefly in Tausek's eyes. Any other man wouldn't have picked it up, but Plass had known Tausek a long time.

Tausek, the powerful ruler of Dakru, was rattled.

Plass entered his office and dropped into the chair behind his desk, mindless of the perspiration soaked uniform sticking to his skin. Wedged between Tausek's private quarters and office, this room remained windowless, no violent sunsets for him. They were almost too painful to watch.

He laid his head back, steepled his fingers, and began to ponder each point throughout the conversation for a clue to the uneasiness that now gripped him.

Cidra Faulkner's disappearance had prompted Tausek's anticipated anger. The complete destruction of the Kin-sha and the Faulkner's were an obsession for all Dakruians. By withholding the vaccine, they had killed millions and sealed their own death orders. Considering what they had done to his people, not to mention Plass personally, they deserved no less. He glanced soberly at the still-life holo image on the corner of his desk. The faces of his life's mate and three precious children smiled back at him. All beautiful, all lost in the critical early stages of the plague.

It had been much the same for the rest of the d'Hont units. The plague seemed to hit their forces particularly hard. Few d'Honts died, but they watched their families and friends perish slowly, painfully, bit by bit. Helplessly watching.

D'Hont became his life and his future shortly after Tausek's appointment as ruler of Dakru, effectively replacing the family he'd loved and lost. Plass had been selected d'Hont Commander and right hand to the ruler. In this position, he could guarantee that Avion or the Kin-sha never forgot their intolerable mistakes of the past.

Yes, he agreed with Tausek's anger. Knew its basis, understood its justification.

So that left the other issue, the puzzling security breach. Puzzling because the skillfully executed, unorthodox infiltration had gained access to the entire system. Yet the only files touched just happened to involve the Avion to Dakru vaccine shipment. Tausek's shock, and that's just what it was, confused matters even more. His order to execute the Head of System Security struck Plass as excessive, even for the barbaric Tausek.

The questions started rising, questions he didn't know if he wanted to pursue, but couldn't ignore. Why, after all these years would someone want the Avion vaccine files? Was it pure coincidence that Cidra Faulkner had risen from the dead at the same time, only to auspiciously disappear again? And by far the most unsettling, why should Tausek be so disturbed by such a minor system infiltration?

The Commander gazed into space and drummed his fingers on the desk. If Tausek wanted him to handle this personally, that's just what he would do. He'd copy the files to a micropad and then purge them as directed.

While he obeyed his ruler's wishes, it might not be a bad idea to make a copy for himself. In fact, it might not be a bad idea to take a closer look at all those files. Personally.

* * * *

Grey was running hard on the TrackMat when he spotted Decker enter *Calíbre*'s rec center sporting a wide grin.

"Thought I'd find you in here. Isn't this your second time today? You're going to burn up that TrackMat, you know." Decker stopped in front of him and shoved his hands in his pockets. "Having trouble sleeping or something?"

Grey glared at him. With sweat stinging his eyes, his lungs screaming for mercy, and his legs burning, he was in no mood for any digs from his first officer. His lack of sleep was no one's business but his own.

"Maybe I'll make this a requirement for my entire crew," he stated bluntly.

Decker laughed and folded his arms over his chest. "You'd kill us all."

Grey slowed to a steady run, much to the relief of his lungs and legs. "I assume you're here for some other reason than to watch me sweat."

"I just like to see how some people work out their frustrations. Anyone I know? Maybe a new crew member?" Decker turned and gauged the distance to the door.

Grey shot him a homicidal look and wondered how much frustration he could vent with a fist to Decker's face. "Report or leave," he snapped, slowing his pace to a fierce walk.

Decker held up a hand. "I'm reporting. I used the security codes you gave me and pulled the shipment information from the Avion archives. There's not much more than we got out of Syrus' box. So after that, I broke into the Dakru information system."

Grey stopped dead on the TrackMat, grinding the automatic sensor to a halt. "Find anything?"

"Not much. Not what I expected." Decker shook his head. "I managed to get into the files on the Dakru shipment from Avion." He grinned. "I wonder if they realize how bad their security is."

"If they didn't know before, they do now. You could lead them right back to us," Grey charged.

Decker shrugged. "You said be creative. I figured I might find some answers. Besides, it's going to take them a while to trace it back to us, if at all. I left a mess of false trails."

Grey stepped off the TrackMat and snagged a towel from a side chair. "I hope it was worth it."

Decker winced. "I'm afraid not. If I didn't know better, I'd say someone cleaned up those files already."

"You think someone got there before you did? When?" Grey

asked, wiping the sweat from his face.

Decker shook his head. "Couldn't say. But it seems to me that there should have been more information. I pulled every file relating to that shipment. The contract negotiations were intact, but I couldn't find anything on the delivery schedule."

"Maybe they store those files somewhere else," Grey suggested.

Decker glanced at him righteously. "I blew that system wide open. I could see everything they had. It just wasn't there." He started towards the exit. "I'll send you copies of the files, but I don't think you're going to get much out of them."

Grey tossed the towel over his neck and walked out with Decker. "I'd sure like to know who got to those files before we did."

* * * *

Later that evening, Commander Plass leaned back in his chair to digest what he'd uncovered in Dakru's archives.

The negotiations and communications with Avion for the vaccine seemed completely legitimate. All the proper forms were filled and filed, terms established, contracts signed. Routine, no deviations, no indications of deceit or treachery. Very smooth, very normal, with one notable exception. Tausek had handled nearly the entire affair personally.

That didn't surprise Plass.

At the time, Tausek was the d'Hont Commander and the responsibility of Dakru's security and safety fell to him. What disturbed Plass wasn't what he found; it was what he couldn't find. The front-end existed, the back-end didn't. No reference to the actual delivery of the vaccine, anywhere.

That information would have been highly secured, but it should have existed at some level. Arrangements, no matter how covert, must have been established for the safe conveyance of the cargo. Either those arrangements were never entered into the system, a major oversight, or they were deleted, which brought up a whole new list of questions.

It could have been contractual neglect on the part of Avion, but he doubted it. Dakru would have never agreed upon a contract without a concrete delivery plan.

And Avion had no access to Dakru's system to erase them. A break-in at that time would have been detected in the same manner as the more recent incident. And no Dakruian could delete a file without following an elaborate process. Only the highest-ranking officers had that level of clearance.

Following that, he had reviewed the d'Hont activity for the time period of the alleged shipment. Even if Avion had no intention of fulfilling its obligation, Dakru would have been expecting a shipment, a rendezvous. The records should reflect it, but they didn't. No orders were issued.

Plass dug further and found the usual array of training missions, escorts, and surveillance. Only one other incident stood out during that time period. The elite fighter unit was called out to destroy a plague-infested freighter and a few smaller ships bent on seeking refuge on Dakru. The quarantine policy for the planet forbid any such refuge and was backed up by military force, as was the case here.

Plass snorted. So much for the stringent quarantine policy. The plague had arrived just the same.

As he scanned the records, he noted with pride that it must have been quick work to take out the infested ships. Under Tausek's orders, Plass had supervised the purchase of those Saurelian fighters himself. They were a marvel in engineering, stealth, and ultimate killing prowess. The d'Hont pilots wasted no time in proving that.

As expected, the attack was orchestrated by then Commander Tausek. Odd that the details were so sketchy, so unlike Tausek's thorough style.

Plass rubbed his eyes wearily. There wasn't much to go on. A few discrepancies, missing information and a real nagging sensation that something bigger lurked.

* * * *

She should have practiced more.

"Landing gear down." Cidra's voice sounded distant over the pounding of her heart.

More time in the SymPod.

"Docking site identified and locked in."

More practice landing.

"Quad stabilizers on-line and operational."

Less time flying around. Less time playing.

"Thrusters one-quarter power. Main engines shut down."

Her hands were sweating, her breathing deep and rapid. Panic threatened to strike as Vaasa's busiest port loomed precariously beneath her.

Grey had insisted she land *Calíbre* on Vaasa--alone. The atmospheric entry vector had been smooth, the port controller's approach sequence straight-forward, the docking site satisfactory, and the pilot scared out of her wits.

Grey stood behind the helm station, arms folded and relaxed. He alone seemed undaunted with the idea of a novice attempting such a delicate procedure. Cidra prayed he didn't see her hands tremble while she maneuvered the large ship over the small red landing mark in the corner of a bustling, cavernous landing bay.

The deck crew remained conspicuously subdued and Cidra could feel their concerned glances her way. She was now close enough to see the faces of the ground personnel waving *Calíbre* in. The churning mass of activity parted just enough for them to land.

Cidra tuned every ounce of concentration into the landing, checking and rechecking current status from the plethora of displays surrounding her. After what seemed like an eternity, a gentle thump confirmed touchdown. Cidra shut down all systems with a small sigh of relief.

"Landing cycle completed," she announced while giving silent thanks.

The deck crew chatted freely and dispersed in haste, leaving her and Grey alone.

Cidra gathered herself, stood up and smoothed her jumpsuit trying to act as though nothing momentous had just occurred. "Now what?"

Grey placed his hand on her back and ushered her down the portside corridor.

"I ordered a ground shuttle to take us to my home. It should be waiting. Is Barrios ready?"

Cidra slanted him a smile. "Are you kidding? He can't wait to visit the market. I don't think he cared much for Mora's cooking."

She wanted the words back as soon as they slipped out and threw Grey a conciliatory glance. He said nothing, but she sensed the sparkle slip away into foreboding darkness that accompanied any reference to Mora. Cidra cursed the woman for ruining yet another bright moment.

They exited *Calíbre* in silence and were immediately assaulted with the blunt essence of Landing Bay Number Sixty-two. As predicted, Barrios was busy loading bags into the waiting ground shuttle amid the mass confusion and deafening noise.

Cidra stopped, overwhelmed by the chaos swarming around *Calíbre* and several other large ships in the general vicinity. The walls reverberated in the deafening clamor of massive surging engines, shipping containers being unloaded, voices straining above the discord. The air hung thick with the smell of fuel and lubricants.

The bay bustled with a strange assortment of humans and aliens. Old acquaintances waved and embraced. Information blared from speakers high above the bay, barely discernible. Orders were shouted from every corner. Cidra caught fragments of several languages, voices of various modulations, and a few vulgarities mixed in.

She jumped when Grey touched her arm and spoke directly into her ear over the noise level. "I'll be back in a minute. There's someone I need to talk to."

Cidra nodded, fighting the rush of awareness the intimate gesture triggered.

He squeezed her arm. "By the way, nice landing."

She shot him a brilliant smile.

For a brief moment he froze, his silver eyes intensifying as he stared at her. The smile faltered. Air crackled between them. Without a word, he headed out through the throng of activity. She breathed. *What was that all about?*

Cidra followed his progress to a big man standing under the belly of a massive, black ship. As he approached, the man turned and greeted him sportingly.

"Hey, are you going to help or what?" Barrios yelled at Cidra over the pandemonium as he flung another bag onto their waiting shuttle. She dismissed him with a careless wave and set to work.

As soon as the gear was loaded, the driver gestured in no uncertain terms that he was ready to depart. *Now.* Cidra surveyed the bay anxiously and found Grey still in deep conversation with the other man. She hated to interrupt him, but the driver was becoming downright belligerent. After persuading him to wait a few more minutes, she hurried toward the twosome.

As she slipped underneath the large ship and approached them, Grey pinned her with a stern expression. She stopped cold. Cidra debated turning back until the bigger man spun around and flashed a winning smile. Grey immediately strode forward to meet her.

"The shuttle is loaded. The driver says if we don't leave soon, he'll find another fare," she reported apologetically as he halted in front of her, hands on his hips, his eyes burning into hers.

"Stone, old friend. Aren't you going to introduce me?" The man spoke up from behind him.

Grey threw her a thunderous look and shifted just enough so she could meet his colleague. Cidra grimaced, making a very large mental note never to interrupt him in the middle of meeting again.

"This is Cidra Almazan, the newest member of my crew."

Then he said, "Cidra, I'd like you to meet Rourke Jaccar. An old friend of mine."

Rourke stepped forward. He was even taller than Grey and bigger by a quarter. Long brown hair was pulled back into a tail, revealing a handsome face, an engaging smile and eyes full of mischief.

Cidra shook his hand. "It's very nice to meet you, Rourke Jaccar."

His smile was breath-taking. "Likewise. So what is your position on *Calibre*?"

Before she could answer, Grey interjected, "Pilot."

Cidra glared at him.

"She's excellent," he said, ambivalent to her ferocious expression.

"Of course. Why else would you employ her? You only hire the best." Rourke gave him a half-hearted innocent look that prompted a deep scowl back.

Rourke addressed Cidra. "If you ever get tired of working for this tyrant, look me up. I've been searching for a good pilot myself."

"You better keep searching," Grey said tightly.

Cidra ignored him, too. "Thank you. I'll be sure to keep that in mind if the situation ever arises."

She could almost feel Grey's wrath increase next to her. She didn't dare look into his eyes. It was bad enough she could hear every savage breath. It was his own doing. He needed to learn she was a grown woman and a fully trained Kin-sha who could handle herself.

"We're leaving." He grabbed Cidra's arm and giving Rourke another feral glare, he added, "And don't forget about our deal."

Rourke folded his arms over his chest, his eyes fixed on Cidra. "I think I want to renegotiate my price."

"Too late," Grey muttered as he pulled Cidra across the landing bay, leaving Rourke to laughing.

"Hey, take it easy on your *excellent* pilot. Look, I'm sorry I interrupted your meeting, but it was important. I didn't want to lose the shuttle." Cidra fought to keep pace with him. The relentless heat and noise were wearing on her, to say nothing of the internal commotion Grey created.

"Have you ever heard of being inconspicuous?" he muttered through clenched teeth. "Are you aware that every man in here is watching you?"

"They wouldn't be if you weren't yanking on me like I'm a naughty child." She knew he was furious, but so was she. He had no right to manhandle her this way. The attention they were drawing was downright embarrassing. If she hadn't already promised she'd refrain from using Kin-sha in public, she'd fight it out with him right here and now.

Granted, it wouldn't be easy. He outweighed her, outpaced her, and he definitely had her beat in the unrestrained fury department. So much for Plan A.

On to Plan B: distraction. Besides, she was dying to find out what kind of deal he'd cut with Rourke and if it had anything to do with her mission.

How much angrier could he get?

With all the innocence she could muster, she said, "Rourke Jaccar seems like a very interesting man. Have you known him long?" She winced as Grey's grip on her arm tightened.

"You work for me," he stated sharply.

A primal growl rumbled through him. He'd deal with his *old friend* later. First, he needed to vent some excess energy. Raw, fierce possessiveness raged within. The fact that she could extract such a violent emotion from him so easily infuriated him to no end and only added to the potent emotional mix.

When she had walked through the middle of the landing bay, long hair flowing, blue eyes bright, he knew he was in trouble. *So much for keeping a low profile.* He set his teeth. How was he supposed to protect her when she walked through the busiest bay in Vaasa looking like that?

Somewhere halfway across Landing Bay Number Sixty Two, disgust and common sense finally weighed in. She was right. He was acting downright psychotic. At this stage in his life, it wasn't a pleasant revelation. He slowed his pace and shot a scathing glance around. Any onlookers had the common sense to turn away or steer clear.

Cidra continued, undaunted. "No one can predict what the future holds, Captain. You may decide you don't really need me after all. It's not as if you had any choice to begin with."

They reached the waiting shuttle and Grey shoved her into the cool passenger section next to Barrios. He sprawled into the seat facing her, eyeing her ominously as the shuttle lurched forward.

She thrust her chin up. "What if you found a better pilot? What would you do with me then?"

As Grey's eyes locked onto hers with devastating intensity, Cidra belatedly realized she'd pushed too far and now found herself trapped. Again.

A few tense moments passed before Grey drawled, "Don't worry about it. I'd think of something for you to do." He stated it with exquisite calm and conviction.

Cidra stole a shaky breath and tore her gaze away from him to the scenery whizzing by. She was trembling all over and wondered if she would ever be able to handle the hypnotic impact of Captain Grey Stone's absolute and undivided attention.

Vaasa spread out before her and it didn't take long to discover that this was a planet at ease with itself. Everything hailed of a gracious spirit with its wide tree-lined streets, immaculate homes, and spectacular natural beauty. Graceful domes and arches dominated the architecture and landscape.

Through her extensive studies of the sector's planets and civilizations, Cidra knew Vaasa chose to embrace technology for convenience sake, but still clung to the simpler pleasures for day-to-day living. Vaasa's inhabitants were as relaxed and welcoming as their planet appeared. No false pretenses, no hidden agenda, nothing to conceal.

Conversely, Avion came to mind with its rigid, restrictive society. A society controlled by the privileged few in the Central Consortium, the governing body, who fostered the undercurrent of conduct, superiority, and promotion of Avion to the rest of the universe.

They portrayed Avion as a planet with high standards and morality, sophistication, and righteousness. And enforced that image through quiet coercion, deception, and propaganda. It was a dark secret known only to native Avions. Most accepted it for the chance to shine in the universe. Some, like Cidra, Grey and Barrios, saw it for what it was ... a lie.

They had achieved it by hiding behind the shield of the loyal and highly respected Kin-sha. Although the Kin-sha were not native to Avion, they had been welcomed and promoted aggressively by the Central Consortium.

In hindsight, it had been a grievous mistake for the Kin-sha. The same Consortium, intolerant of those who upset their carefully orchestrated image of Avion, had summarily condemned and abandoned the Kin-sha after the Dakru incident.

Looking back, she realized Syrus had been wise to protect her from the same twisted sense of justice that had allowed the sacrifice of the Faulkner family. As Barrios observed, the Consortium condoned the d'Hont attack by its ambivalence or worse. She hated to admit it, but even Mora's condemnation of Avion had held truth. The Consortium indeed wielded the authority to dictate who received the vaccine. A power they were all too proud to brandish.

The last emotion Cidra felt towards Avion was loyalty, but the fact remained. The redemption of her father, family, and the Kin-sha hinged on the redemption of Avion itself. Like it or not, they were one in the same.

Barrios' loud snoring snapped her back to reality.

She slid Grey a cautious glance. Stretched out fully, his big frame commanded the opposite seat of the passenger section. His eyes closed, arms folded over his chest, legs crossed at the ankles. Although she knew better than to think the hunter wasn't alert or dangerous, in repose he was fascinating and compelling.

Unable to stop herself, she took a slow inventory of him starting with dark, supple boots that rose to his knees. Pants of a similar color fit muscular, long legs and lean hips perfectly. A crisp, white shirt offset the darkness of his pants and the wisp of hair visible in the open collar. He wore the laser pistol and blade, something he'd not done since they left Avion.

Her eyes leisurely settled on his forearms exposed by the rolled up shirtsleeves. Big arms, well defined, strong, and hands that looked like they could handle anything. Capable of anything. She was deep into possibilities before the familiar tingle interrupted her thoughts. She stiffened and looked up to find him watching her with a smug, satisfied grin.

"Don't stop on my account."

Cidra inhaled and collected herself, struggling for a daring, coy smile and utter indifference. "Just checking your weapons."

Grey grinned. "Is that right? Does my equipment meet your approval?"

Cidra could feel her forced smile falter. She held his gaze, all the while accepting the fact that there was just no graceful way out of this. "It'll do."

Admitting defeat via diversion, she nodded towards the window. "Vaasa is beautiful. Have you lived here long?"

He gave her a long look as if he wasn't ready to change the subject. Then relented and settled back to his relaxed position before answering her.

"About eight years, but it's always served as my base office. It seemed a logical choice. *Calíbre* isn't equipped for families or long stretches in space. Most of my crew lives here. It simplifies regrouping." He paused. "Vaasa has some amazing natural vistas if you're interested in a tour."

He didn't move, his head back, his eyes closed.

Cidra blinked, digesting his words, trying to visualize the prospect he'd just laid out. A tour? Did he mean just the two of them? Did she care?

Her brain screamed no, but her mouth mutinied. "I'd like that."

He said nothing, remaining perfectly still, except for the corner of his mouth that kicked up.

CHAPTER SEVEN

Whatever Cidra had imagined Grey's house to be, this wasn't it.

She stood gawking in front of a virtual architectural masterpiece of elegant arches and columns, glistening bone white and impeccable in the Vaasa sun. Flowering vines trailed along two levels of finely-detailed balconies that overlooked manicured gardens and walkways. An abundance of windows forged the symmetry of the front facade. In the archways, hanging baskets of flowers swung in unison in the breeze. It was a work of art unto itself.

For the first time, Cidra realized just how successful Grey's treasure hunting operation was.

"Nice place," Barrios mumbled into her ear while they unloaded the shuttle at the front entrance.

"I love it," she whispered louder than she'd intended.

Hands on his hips, Grey interrupted his quiet reprimand of the impatient shuttle driver to acknowledge her approval. The beleaguered driver seized the opportunity and scurried to his vehicle.

As the shuttle raced away, the front door flew open as a silver-haired woman in a cobalt dress rushed out, her short, plump body moved with surprising agility, graceful and efficient. She greeted Grey with open arms and a juicy kiss on each cheek.

She spoke rapidly with a robust accent. "Oh, it's so nice to have you home. It's been too long. You look tired. Have you eaten? No matter. I'll take care of that."

Clapping her hands together, she turned to Cidra and Barrios.

"This is wonderful. Guests. It's about time. You should have more friends, dear. More company, more fun. It keeps you happy." She admonished Grey lovingly and stepped out to meet her guests.

Cidra could have sworn Grey looked almost sheepish as he introduced her to his housekeeper, Rosa Terranova.

Cidra smiled and extended a hand. "It's so nice to meet you, Madam Terranova."

"Ooh, no, no. Rosa, call me Rosa. What a lovely thing you are." Rosa ignored Cidra's hand and kissed her firmly on both cheeks.

"Don't you think so Grey?" She turned to him.

He gave Cidra a potent smile. "Absolutely."

"But look at you. Ah, too thin." Rosa shook her head and patted Cidra's bottom. "Got to give a man something to hold on to."

Cidra managed a weak smile, blushing to a deep pink.

Grey cleared his throat. "And this is Barrios."

Rosa turned to stand in front of him and planted her hands on her generous hips.

"Well, well, so you're the big shot chef, eh? I warn you now, you stay out of my kitchen." She shook a finger at him.

"And a pleasure to meet you too, Madam." Barrios replied sternly, crossing his arms over his enormous chest. "I have no intention of stepping foot in your kitchen."

"I make good food. Not fancy, not complicated, but good," Rosa continued righteously as she headed back into the house, waving them in. "Come, come."

Barrios bristled. "I make good food, too. I am a certified First Order Chef."

"Eh, chef, schmef." Rosa threw both hands up in the air and disappeared toward the interior with Barrios in hot pursuit, the tirade escalating between them.

Cidra laughed, enjoying the banter. It had been a long time since Barrios had a fitting sparring partner.

"Come on. I'll show you the house." Grey guided her up the front steps, glancing inward where a loud crash emanated from the vicinity of the kitchen.

He shook his head. "Before they destroy it."

* * * *

The performance was truly spectacular. Cidra watched with rapt fascination from the second floor balcony of Grey's house as the night air hummed with activity. Around the perimeter of the courtyard, flashes of yellow, blue, and green lights filled the trees where tiny, unknown creatures weaved a dizzying pattern in the darkness. Vaasa's full moon loomed low and large, a luminous background for the cast of thousands.

The distraction eased the restlessness she'd been experiencing since dinner, due in part to Grey's conspicuous absence. Barrios and Rosa had put forth a valiant effort to fill the void, bickering with varying degrees of determination. Cidra sensed a curious meeting of the minds as their barbs became less lethal and more good-natured. No doubt, Rosa's wonderful meal impressed Barrios, a direct route to his heart if there was one.

She leaned against the railing and sighed. The more time she spent in Grey's house, the more she loved it. It reminded her of a fine sculpture. The all-white walls enhanced intricate, classic details. All the rooms were open and spacious, flowing from one to the other effortlessly. Furniture was comfortable and functional, windows uncluttered and unadorned. The abundance of balconies welcomed and showcased the outdoors with a jungle of plants that created a seamless transition from interior to exterior.

By far, the most interesting part of the house was Grey's seemingly endless array of artifacts. His collection aboard *Calibre* paled in comparison to the vast assortment exhibited here. The house served as an elaborate display case for everything from masks to weavings, jewelry to etchings. She smiled. She had even seen some of Syrus' paintings. It was almost like home.

"Enjoying the show?" Grey appeared silently and leaned on the balcony railing next to her, brushing her arm. She willed herself to remain calm, even though his close proximity raised havoc with her body and soul.

"What are they?" Cidra asked of the intertwining lights.

"Vergon Gypsy Wings. They're native to Vaasa."

"Beautiful," Cidra sighed. "Do they do this every night?"

Grey shook his head. "Once a year."

His voice sounded strained and Cidra turned to look at him. He stared at the lights, his face hard set. The lines on his face were cut deeper than she remembered. His eyes were dark and distant.

"Why only once a year?"

"They're mating. The males are yellow, and the females are blue. The colors mix to green when they mate." He took a deep breath. "Then they lay their eggs and die."

"Really?" Cidra's eyes widened.

"Really. Makes you glad you're not a gypsy wing, doesn't it?" Grey rubbed the back of his neck.

Cidra nodded. "Definitely." She suddenly felt sorry for the little doomed creatures. "Do you think they know what's going to happen to them?"

Grey shrugged. "It's their destiny. They can't change what they are."

Although he stood right next to her, he was far away. She could see his muscles bunched tightly under his shirt.

"You talked to Mora," she stated, not stopping to consider the consequences.

"Yes." He looked straight ahead.

"Are you sure it was her?"

"Yes."

"She was more than just your cook, wasn't she?" Cidra whispered.

He didn't answer her. He was too busy mentally rerunning his heated conversation with Mora. When he fired her, she had been furious, swearing at him and making some nasty comments about his lovemaking skills. The discussion had digressed from that point. He must have been blind to trust her. He had no one to blame but himself. He took her without knowing her and paid dearly for his moment of weakness.

"I'm sorry." Cidra reached out and placed her hand gently on his arm.

His jaw tightened. "Forget it. It won't happen again."

Cidra frowned. "What do you mean?"

"I broke my own rule. Never get involved with a member of the crew," he said bluntly. "Bad for business."

Cidra withdrew her hand as if it were on fire. "We all make mistakes, Grey."

"I trusted her. That's one error I won't repeat."

The message was unmistakable.

Cidra's mouth dropped open. She swung around to face him, indignation lacing her words. "Does that include me? Do you distrust everyone you meet or is it just me?"

His eyes narrowed in warning. "You of all people should know the price of betrayal."

His words struck hard. Anger, deep and swift, shot through her. "Yes, I do. But I won't let it rule my life. I believe most people can be trusted."

"Is that a fact?" With lightning speed he reached out, grabbed her by the waist and yanked her hard against his chest. She gasped at the raw strength, hard muscle and harder eyes. He crushed her arms between them.

His words seared her face, all heat and fury. "You don't even know me, Cidra. How do you know you can trust me?" He pulled her closer, her mouth inches from his.

She didn't fight him. It was obvious he was trying to make a point. Damned if she'd give it to him.

"Syrus chose you. That's good enough for me," she replied, calm and cold.

His mouth twisted into a bitter smile. "Maybe I've changed since Syrus knew me."

If she hadn't been watching, she would have missed the flash of regret in his eyes. Pain so deeply buried, that only someone who knew suffering would recognize it. Her anger seeped away, replaced by sudden understanding and great sadness.

"Something tells me you haven't changed very much since you left Avion fifteen years ago," she said softly.

Grey's expression changed, from anger to surprise to disbelief in an instant. Seconds ticked by, she didn't move, didn't want to tempt the dangerous fire in his eyes. Finally he released her and braced his hands against the railing. He stared out into the still night air.

"Go inside, Cidra. Show's over."

* * * *

Grey stormed into the kitchen, threw himself onto a stool and glared at Barrios who was making the morning meal. How he hated sleepless nights.

Barrios looked at him warily, his eyebrows high. "Sleep well?"

"No." The word was an answer and a warning in one.

Barrios nodded once. Heeding the warning, he busied himself

with serving the meal.

Grey finally broke the tension with a gruff, "Where are they?"

"Who?"

"Not funny, Barrios. Where are Cidra and Rosa?" Grey barked.

"There's a note." Barrios inclined his head toward the message board. The old man chuckled as Grey leapt from the stool to read it.

Boys-

We went to the market early. See you at dinner. Behave.

Rosa

Barrios grunted. "Boys! Indeed. That woman needs a lesson on the difference between boys and men."

It was Grey's turn to raise an eyebrow. Well, well. Wasn't *that* interesting. He scanned around for another note. Nothing from Cidra. She was still mad. And she had every right to be.

He blew out a breath in self-disgust, knowing full well it was his own fault. He had spent the better part of last night reliving the argument and it didn't improve with repetition. How could he have been such a fool? She actually tried to comfort him and he brushed her off. No, he had shoved her off, scared her and practically thrown her out. All in less than a minute. Must be some kind of record. He'd better devote a good portion of the day figuring out how to rectify the mess he'd made.

Barrios set the full plates on the table and sat down. "So, what's on for today?"

Grey took a deep breath. He couldn't do anything about Cidra right now. Besides, he had another serious matter to attend. He sat down across from Barrios and smiled for the first time this morning. "Depends. How are you at spreading rumors?"

* * * *

By the time they broke for mid-day meal, Cidra had decided that Rosa's energy knew no bounds. It manifested itself in effervescent chatter, flurries of animated gestures and a walking pace that would have put Grey to shame. But at least keeping up with Rosa's rapid-fire manner took her mind off the previous night's disaster. She was immensely grateful they had escaped Grey's house early this morning before he arose. She had no desire to endure an encore performance.

"Are you all right, my dear?" Rosa placed her hand on Cidra's arm. "Have I worn you out? It was a busy morning."

Cidra shook her head and smiled back across the small dining table in the crowded eatery Rosa had chosen. "No, you haven't." Then she frowned and said uncertainly, "We are done, aren't we?"

Rosa laughed and patted her arm. "Yes, quite. I think Grey will be pleased with your purchases. Those dresses especially." Her eyes lit up. "He'll like those."

"I doubt that," Cidra muttered and caught Rosa's questioning gaze. "We had a few words last evening. Right now, I don't think he'd look at me if I walked in completely naked."

Rosa waved her off. "Oh, nonsense. He would do more than look. And what are a few words? To your life, they add excitement and energy. Tell you things you did not know. Best of all, they give you reason to make up." She winked.

Cidra shook her head in amazement. The woman was positively unsinkable.

"The words, what were they about?"

Cidra sighed, rubbing her temples. "Trust, mostly. Women, in particular. Mora, specifically. And me, by gender. I don't understand it. I've done nothing to earn his mistrust."

"Then you have no worry. He will come around. Grey is stubborn, yes, but fair. A man who admits his mistakes. Give him time," Rosa stated with confidence.

Cidra could only hope. She hated the cold feeling in the pit of her stomach every time she thought of him. She preferred the heat he stirred so effortlessly.

A server delivered their lunch order.

After he left, Cidra hedged, "Rosa, do you know anything about Grey's family?"

Rosa dove into her lunch and shook her head. "He does not offer. I do not ask. Why?"

Cidra shifted in her chair. "I was just wondering."

"What of your family?" Rosa asked with a smile on her ruddy face.

"I don't have any. Barrios is the closest thing to family I've got," Cidra spoke softly and stared into her plate.

Rosa was silent for a few long moment. Then she gently covered Cidra's hand with hers and smiled.

"Well, now you have us."

* * * *

"Here's to a job well done, my boy." Barrios saluted Grey with his fifth drink and downed it in a single swallow. Coon, fresh off his shift guarding the docked *Calíbre*, gave Grey a big smile with a mouthful of mismatched teeth and shot back his drink in kind. Grey shook his head, envisioning a long night of salutes.

The saloon keeper began setting up another round. Barrios shooed him away. "You'll wear yourself out keeping up with us. Just leave the bottle, we'll serve ourselves."

Then giving himself a self-congratulatory smile, he sloppily poured the next round.

It was bound to happen, Grey thought, as he eyed him. Barrios had finally discovered Oeno and embraced it like a long lost friend. Life would never be the same. Still, he couldn't have asked for a better partner today.

Between the two of them and the deal with Rourke, they had spread the word all over the city that Grey was leaving in two days to retrieve the Lost Mask of Teran. That should give Wex incentive enough to take the false file Mora stole and spend the next several months traveling across the galaxy to the middle of nowhere. He couldn't help but smile.

They drank on, saluting everyone and everything. Toasts to the inventors of Oeno and reverse thrusters. To the visionary of long-legged street molls and horizontal beds. To the short skirts the servers wore. To the inventor of short skirts.

Drinks were raised as Barrios offered the next toast. "To fast ships." Grey drank heartily to that.

"To faster women," Coon said. Barrios drank heartily to that. After a moment, he noticed that Grey hadn't joined the required salute.

"Stone, you're not drinking to faster women." Barrios nudged him, splashing his drink. "Don't you care for fast women? Ah, maybe you prefer the ones that burn slower and last longer?"

Grey narrowed his eyes at him. "Maybe, but I'm not talking."

Barrios roared with laughter. "Son, you don't have to. It's written all over your face. You're in deep trouble, my boy. I can feel her cold shoulder from here. What did you do to rile her?"

"It wasn't my fault." Grey defended himself, although the words sounded feeble even to him.

Coon offered some slurred advice, waggling a finger. "It doesn't matter if it's your fault or not. She'll wear you down. Then you'll...." He nodded wisely. The other two men looked at him expectantly, waiting for him to finish. After a few seconds, it became obvious that he thought he already had.

Barrios turned back to Grey and prodded. "Out with it, Stone.

Cidra doesn't get upset for nothing."

"I can't remember exactly. Something about me not trusting her. I was pretty mad at the time," he mumbled over the rim of his drink.

"You told her you didn't trust her?" Barrios eyes widened. Then he let out a slow, wobbly whistle. "You got big trouble, son. She's spent the past ten years trying to make up for what her father was accused of. I never saw anyone take their obligations as seriously as she does. Cidra's straight up. You should know that by now."

Grey sighed in resignation and stared into the undulating Oeno. "I know. I wasn't thinking of her, I was thinking of Mora." He speared Barrios with a grimace. "Talk about fast women."

Barrios nodded and weaved in agreement. "Myself, I prefer the slow burners. You never know what you'll get when you light up one of those." He raised his glass. "To slow burners."

Grey drank to that. Coon made a valiant attempt join the toast, but instead his head dropped down on the table with a resounding thud. Barrios and Grey regarded him in mild surprise.

"I guess slow burners put him to sleep," Barrios summarized, leaning slightly as he attempted to line his vision up with Coon's horizontal head.

Grey laughed. "It would seem so." Clouds of Oeno were descending around him. He was still thinking about Cidra and grinning like a fool. Definitely not a slow burner. He'd already had a taste of her fire. What he wouldn't give to see her fully ablaze.

They drank the next round in silence. Then Barrios listed toward Grey, his tone serious. "Cidra is like my daughter, you know. She's been through a lot, seen a lot, experienced little." He focused on Grey with a lurch. "I wouldn't want her hurt."

"I won't hurt her, I promise. Keeping my mouth shut should help greatly," Grey muttered.

Barrios accepted that. "If you want her, you'll have to apologize. And you better make it a good one."

Grey nodded. He wanted her. He didn't know exactly when the thought became fact, but there it was. The acknowledgment alone eased the twisting in his gut that had plagued him all day.

Grey raised his glass. "To understanding women."

Barrios' laugh boomed through the saloon. "That'll take more Oeno than they got on all of Vaasa."

* * * *

Rosa and Cidra were sitting at the table when the boisterous pair clamored into the kitchen with Barrios singing at the top of his lungs. They both reeled to a halt, looking all the world like two little boys caught in an act of mischief.

Barrios' whisper in Grey's ear came through as a lilting shout, "Nope, they're not sleepin'. We don't have to be quiet. 'S good thing 'cause you make too much noise." He gently patted Grey's cheek. He winked at Cidra with both eyes. "Hello, love. We were just talking 'bout you, weren't we, Stone?"

Grey wasn't listening. All his senses were focused on Cidra.

Barrios donned a stunned and stupefied expression as Rosa began scolding him. "You. You are a bad influence. I should have known. Grown men. Indeed. Look at you. We cannot leave you two alone for a single day."

Rosa pointed to Grey. "Cidra, you take that one. I will handle the almighty chef myself." She then proceeded to pry the joined drinking buddies apart and pull Barrios towards his room. His playful chiding and her feisty retorts echoed down the hallway until the bedroom door slammed shut behind them.

Grey watched Cidra. Even mad, she was the most beautiful woman he'd ever laid eyes on. He leaned against the counter for support and gave her an unadulterated smile. "Aren't you going to yell at me?"

"No need. Your punishment will take care of itself in the morning." She took his arm and led him down the hall toward his room. "Come on, I'll put you to bed."

"Thought you'd never ask." He smiled wickedly.

Cidra shot him a warning look. "I was under the impression you'd sworn off women."

He stumbled to the side, taking her into the wall with him, capturing her in his arms.

"I've been meaning to talk to you about that," he mumbled in her ear, pulling her firmly against his body. He breathed deeply, inhaling her unique scent. Unique and sexy.

He drew her closer and nuzzled her neck, burying his face in thick, auburn hair. So sweet. He wondered if she'd mind terribly staying in this position forever.

Her gaze flew up to meet his, eyes sparkled devilishly back at her. The mellow, controllable drunk seemed to be sobering up in a hurry, replaced by someone highly amorous and single-minded. His big body wrapped around her, gilding her with his heat, accommodating her curves and hollows. Her body reacted of its own accord, recognizing a truth her mind had yet to admit-- he provided an essential element she craved. Unable to stop herself, she basked in the rugged warmth.

He was mumbling something in her ear, something he wanted, something she didn't even know was physically possible. She swallowed hard and decided it was time to get him to bed before he sobered up any more. She wasn't ready for what he had in mind.

Cidra renewed her efforts, despite the fact he was making it more difficult than it should have been. If she didn't know better, she'd swear he knew exactly what he was doing. His hands always seemed to end up on a few strategic locations on her body.

She managed to get him to the edge of his bed, breathing hard from her exertion. He swayed, looking down at her with a most genuine expression.

"I'm sorry about last night."

"I'm not sure an apology from a drunk man counts." She stifled a smile.

He nodded seriously. "Point taken. I'll give you a real one tomorrow. How about a good night kiss instead?" His eyes gleamed as he slipped his hands around her waist.

She didn't fight him, only lifted an eyebrow. "I don't think I can trust *you* tonight."

"You're probably right." He dropped his hands in easy defeat. Without warning, his gray eyes bore into her soul with lucid intensity.

"But you realize it's our destiny, Cidra. We're like the gypsy wings. We have no choice."

She gasped in surprise at the casual declaration.

Recovering, she smiled wide, placed her hand squarely on his chest and pushed him backward onto the bed. "Sorry, Captain. No green light tonight."

He landed flat on the bed with a grunt. His eyes closed almost immediately. She gazed at his peaceful expression and headed for the door.

"I do trust you, Cidra."

The words stopped her cold in the doorway. She wondered if it was the Oeno talking or the man and just how much trust he was offering. She was sure it wasn't much.

"It's a start," she whispered and walked out.

CHAPTER EIGHT

The thunderous pounding of his own pulse in his head greeted Grey bright and early the next morning.

He gingerly placed a hand on his throbbing head to offer some support. Contrary to what he thought, it was still intact. The previous night swirled back slowly as a blur of conversation and salutes and ... Cidra. He groaned.

What did he say to her last night? What did he do to her?

He struggled to think clearly above the steady quartet of drums beating a hapless tune on his skull. He was reasonably sure he hadn't made matters worse with her, but positive his condition didn't do anything to boost her already shaky image of him.

He was also quite sure he hadn't seduced her. For one thing, he was still fully dressed. Belatedly, he realized she hadn't seduced him either. Smart woman.

For the better, he rationalized. Their first time together definitely would not involve any inebriated parties. He would be in full control. It vaguely occurred to him that the *if* had now become a *when*.

Grey rolled off the bed, stood up, and winced as the drums culminated into a roaring crescendo. He swore under his breath at Barrios and hoped he was suffering a similar fate.

Time to get cleaned up and face Cidra and mend whatever damage he'd done last night, along with the damage he'd done the night before. This was getting downright ugly.

A long soak under the water spray did wonders for the timpani in his head. He walked out to the small balcony off his bedroom and took a deep breath.

Morning on Vaasa was unlike any planet he had ever visited. Exotic flowers opened at dawn filling the damp morning air with a heady mix of fragrances that gradually diminished by midday. It always had a soothing effect on his spirit.

There was movement in the courtyard. He slid around the main column and spied Cidra stepping slowly on the grass. It had been years since he had performed it, but he recognized her carefully orchestrated motions as Kwei, position number five. There were thirty-two positions in all, indelibly engraved in every Kin-sha graduate.

The entire sequence could take a standard hour. Each position strengthened one set of muscles and relaxed another, a balance of mind and body.

Cidra performed the familiar motions with complete concentration, her face relaxed while her body worked. Grey had always thought of Kwei as a means to an end, but she performed the same steps with an alluring grace and sensuality.

She wore a blue skin-tight sleeveless outfit, cut to mid-thigh with a low scoop neckline and back. He studied the intricate muscles in her back, the elegance of her hands, the perfection of her bottom, the contours of her legs. Sweat glistened off her golden skin. Beautiful, flawless, glowing skin meant for touching and caressing.

A flash of desire pumped through him, and he found himself suddenly, painfully aroused. He gripped the railing like a vice. *Definitely feeling better.* As he was asserting some degree of self-control over his body, Cidra suddenly stop mid-step and went still.

He froze. A few heartbeats passed before she spun around and looked up at him.

Caught.

How did she know he was watching her? He was sure he hadn't made a sound. Either it was that crazy sixth sense of hers or she could read his mind. Now that would be a serious problem. She'd be shocked if she had a glimpse of what he was thinking.

She smiled and called, "Good morning Captain. Care to join me? *If* you're up to it, of course."

I'm definitely up to it, he grimaced.

The challenge stood.

"I'll be right down," he responded before he could think it through with the few active brain cells at his disposal. Even before he finished the sentence, he was cursing himself. *Now you've done it.* He'd somehow have to maintain control with her right next to him wearing nothing but that little slip of an outfit.

Self-inflicted torture, that's what it was. Like he didn't have enough of that this morning. Grey braced himself as he made his way to the courtyard.

* * * *

Cidra had known Grey was watching her by the now familiar prickle in her mind, but she wasn't prepared for his undisguised hunger when she turned to face him. For that split second, he exuded a primal appeal that sent a wild, answering frenzy rippling through her.

She prayed she had covered up her initial shock well enough. Too bad it hadn't kept her from opening her mouth. What was she thinking inviting him to join her? Another mutiny. Betrayed once again by her own body.

At that moment, Grey strode across the courtyard toward her wearing only shorts and a smile. She let out a small whimper. He was a beautiful man, long muscles flexing and rolling with every step. Sun played off the planes and valleys of his body as he drew near. Pure male power. She felt like prey--frozen in the face of a terrifying, yet fascinating predator, unable to do anything to save herself.

He smiled when he saw her watching him. Grinning wide, he stopped in front of her and folded his arms across his bare chest.

"So, where were you?"

She blinked, seeing only broad muscles and dark, curly chest hair. Aware that it was her turn to speak, she had to work to get the saliva flowing. "Uh, position six."

Without a word, he stepped next to her in standard partner formation and assumed the starting position. Tamping down the turmoil Grey's entrance had initiated, she forced herself to concentrate on the routine. For his part, Grey also appeared engrossed in the exercise.

Only a gentle breeze, the warm sun, and silence accompanied the intricate dance as it re-commenced.

She could feel them synchronize, moving through the paces. They flowed easily, effortlessly, a perfect match of rhythm and ability. It felt strangely exhilarating, the moving as one, side by side. Each knew the steps intimately, accepting the tempo set, enjoying the pleasure of supple bodies responding to unspoken commands.

Cidra stifled a gasp as a staggering erotic wave swept over her. A carnal surge that started somewhere low in her body and unfurled itself in tantalizing ribbons. Never had Kwei done this to her. Certainly not the many times she'd performed it with Syrus. She had never before appreciated its raw sensuality.

Executing a turn that placed her behind him, she stared at Grey's broad back in motion, gleaming with perspiration. Powerful muscles flowed and bunched, carved and cut.

Moving in perfect unison, the world outside them disappeared.

Bonded together in an ageless art, time lost its dimension and its meaning. Step after step, movement after movement as the ancient performance played out. When the last step was completed, a mutual disappointment descended.

During the cool down steps, Cidra looked at him with a mix of admiration and amusement. "I'm impressed. I didn't expect to see you up and around until mid-day."

He winced. "About last night. I hope I didn't...." He paused and ran a hand through his hair, trying to choose his words carefully. *Didn't grope you like a drunken fool?*

"You didn't," Cidra answered the unfinished question, her blue eyes shining. "But you tried."

He gave her a slow smile. "I must not have tried very hard."

"A respectable effort," she said.

"I want you to know, I don't do that often." Noting her single raised eyebrow, he clarified. "Get drunk, that is. I prefer to be in full control of my mind and body."

She laughed and shook her head. "That's what you get for introducing Barrios to Oeno."

Grey grinned. Perhaps he had said something right last night after all. "How about that tour of Vaasa today?"

He sensed the hesitation, saw the uncertainty light in her eyes and the subtle tensing of her body. *Trust me, Cidra.*

Finally she said, "I'd like that."

* * * *

"I want the bastard dead!" Mora's shrill voice cut through the conversation.

She stood shaking with fury in front of Sandor Wex. She'd been on a tirade all afternoon, storming from one end of his ship to the other, leaving anarchy in her wake.

Hoping her emotional outburst was near it's end, Wex laid his small hand on her shoulder. "Easy, love. I said I would take care of him, and I meant it."

"You should have killed him over Avion. The idiots you employ couldn't hit the broad side of a planet." She shook off the hand and paced Wex's office.

Wex glanced at one of his mammoth idiots, standing silently beside him. Dunkin's thought processes were slow, but it was feasible that he could figure out that she was talking about him.

"I expected him to be alone. You never told me he'd have help in the K12," Wex said carefully, watching for any cerebral activity from Dunkin.

"That woman, that Avion woman. I want her dead too," Mora sputtered as she kicked a chair.

"Now, now. Once Stone is eliminated and I have *Calíbre*, we can do whatever we want with the crew." He moved toward Mora, confident that Dunkin had missed the earlier insult. She glared at him as he pulled her to his wiry body. "I'll even let you decide what to do with the woman."

Mora's sneer turned to a sultry pout. "Promise?" She breathed deeply, pressing her prominent chest against his concave one. Wex nearly disappeared in her red jumpsuit.

Wex nuzzled her neck. "Anything you want, love."

Her eyes focused on a distant dream as he kissed her cheek. "Yes, anything I want."

She shot Dunkin a glare. "You, get out of here."

Dunkin jumped like he'd been shot. Scowling, he lumbered out of his boss' office.

Wex began unfastening the top of her jumpsuit and murmured, "I love it when you give orders."

"So do I," she murmured.

* * * *

Cidra couldn't remember ever being quite so relaxed. She ran her hands along the rim of the big tub, stretched out her long legs and closed her eyes in pure bliss. Warm, soft water lapped around her, offering the kind of comfort only water can give-- purifying, soothing, fundamental.

She could learn to love this place. Very simply, Vaasa took her breath away. Her heart wasn't far behind. The day had passed so quickly. No matter how much of it she tried to commit to memory, the sheer beauty of this planet would never be fully justified in her recollections. Where Avion barely tolerated its wilderness, Vaasa embraced it, gracefully conceding civilization to nature.

A mere blur of rolling hills and valleys, lush forests and vast plains was all she could grasp from behind Grey on his speeder. They stopped for a picnic lunch by a spectacular waterfall emptying into a cerulean lagoon. Cidra could barely eat, her attention drawn to the exotic flora and fragrance.

Blossoms sprouted from every plant, every crevice and, it seemed, from rock itself. Great clusters of flowers cascaded and climbed, crept across the ground, dabbing color in the endless green of vegetation. Feathery breezes carried a potent brew of fragrances, mixing and mingling, fighting for dominance.

She could spend a lifetime exploring each turn in the road. That is, if she survived Grey's penchant for speed that bordered on a death wish. She smiled at the thought, wiggling her toes under the water.

More than once today, she was held breathless when his words said one thing and his eyes said another. Dark, intense eyes that watched her every move, every breath. Although he'd kept his distance from her, she could still feel the strange, transparent strings that seemed to pull her toward him, wrapping and binding them together. It seemed the closer he got, the tighter the strings drew, vibrating to her very bones. There were times lately when she felt she was burning alive. It made her feel reckless and wild. A different woman.

She groaned and dropped her head back on the tub edge. When had it happened? When had she begun falling in love with a man who didn't fully trust her and probably never would despite what he said? What would it take for him to let her in?

She rose from the tub, dried off and slipped into one of her new dresses. All worries lapsed into the background with a quick swirl of the short skirt. Sleeveless and black, it covered little and revealed more than she had bared in public in her lifetime. It brought a smile of anticipation to her lips.

Grey had promised her a taste of Vaasa's night life. She was ready. More than ready, eager, daring, and invincible. So this was what freedom felt like.

* * * *

Cidra found them in the kitchen, the conversation loud and lively. The sound of her heeled shoes on the stone kitchen floor announced her entry, calling the conversation to an abrupt halt. All three stared at her with an amusing variety of expressions.

Rosa nodded approvingly. Barrios' mouth gaped wide open. Grey's reaction was more difficult to define. Somewhere, she thought, between fire and ice.

It was Barrios who broke the silence, a shameless smile spreading across his face. "Stars above. Cidra, you look great." He turned to Grey and slapped him on the back. "Stone, old buddy, you better wear that laser pistol tonight."

With fierce deliberation, Grey skimmed from her long legs to the short skirt of the slight dress that molded into every curve to her hair pulled back loosely with stray tresses spiraling over her bare shoulders.

The eyes that met Cidra's were dark and unwavering. "I was

just thinking the same thing."

* * * *

He didn't wear his laser pistol. Instead, he contented himself with being her shadow.

It wasn't easy. The lecherous glances he fended off were nothing compared to the ones he gave her himself. As his eyes swept over her, he groaned silently. This sudden change in her wardrobe was going to be the death of him. No matter how he looked at it, this little outing had 'frustration' written all over it.

They walked the main avenue, Cidra's arm linked in Grey's, with Barrios and Rosa bickering endlessly behind them. Thendara Market teamed with life, entertainment and lovers. Throngs of people milled around the streets and music reverberated between the buildings. A festival of banners and colored lights swung over the pedestrian streets adding magic to the carnival atmosphere. Brilliant images flashed and fluttered in the night breeze, lending a touch of fantasy.

Cidra felt light as air. Grey hadn't let her out of his sight since they arrived, and she was intensely aware of the dangerous looks he gave her. It didn't faze her. Tonight she was feeling reckless. Maybe it was the dress. Maybe it was the energy of the night life. Maybe it was the taste of freedom. Whatever the reason, tonight was hers. She wanted all that it promised.

She glanced up into the night sky at the grand smattering of stars. A curious grid hanging high between the rooftops of the buildings and over the alleyways caught her eye. As they continued walking past the next building, a similar grid spanned the subsequent alley.

Cidra pointed to it and asked Grey, "What are those?"

He glanced up to where she indicated. "The emergency response system. The city is covered with them, like a net."

He gave her an indulgent smile. "This may come as a shock to you, but Vaasa isn't perfect. We get our fair share of quakes, some of them big. When a quake or some other disaster strikes, the grid lights flood the alleys and streets, a siren kicks on and usually, all hell breaks loose. By design, they're solar-powered, independent from the main power system. Keeps the city out of the dark and the looting down."

He moved closer and whispered covertly in her ear. "But I'll tell you a secret. I watched city maintenance test them one day. You can trigger a grid activation by pressing a button in the center of the first gridhead." He pointed up at the nearest gridhead. Cidra could see it was larger and had a slightly different shape than the others.

"I'll bet you could hit it with a long pole." He winked at her. "It's a great show." He grinned like a little boy plotting a practical joke.

She laughed, pulling him along. "Maybe some other time. I just got here. I don't want to meet the local authorities tonight."

A crowd gathered around the next corner, surrounding an impromptu three-piece band. All the music sounded alien to Cidra, in more ways than one. Avion discouraged music of any kind, in keeping with their 'proper' image. Now she knew why. It made you sway, it made you move, took over your body and freed your spirit. How positively uncultured.

Every corner brought a new sound, a new tempo. Slow and sensual, lively and erotic. It all felt good. Cidra let herself move with the primal beats, matching the audience's energy. More than once, she brushed against Grey, noting he stilled every time. After one particularly heavy bump, he caught her arm and guided them to a nearby crowded establishment.

An eerie blue light permeated the saloon, adding a mystic quality to the wide variety of clientele and bizarre decor. A sturdy gentleman behind the bar smiled and nodded at them. Grey acknowledged the greeting and ushered them to an open booth, slipping in next to Cidra and throwing an arm over her shoulders. Barrios and Rosa wiggled into the bench across from them.

Rosa looked at Barrios suspiciously. "The saloon keeper knows you already. What do you have to say for yourself?"

"Madam, be thankful none of those lovely street molls know me already," he said indignantly, his eyes twinkling. Rosa gave him a swift swat on the arm.

Grey ordered drinks from a voluptuous Saurelian server who effectively ignored everyone else. Her pale green skin shone iridescent in the saloon's blue light.

Cidra watched the girl move a little too close and smile a little too brightly. She thought of Mora and groaned. It was the same feeling she had when Mora spoke of Grey. Jealousy? She shook it off.

Grey smiled back at the girl. He must have said something funny, because she laughed a little too loud. Cidra fumed. Okay, it was jealousy. But it didn't mean anything.

As if catching her thoughts, he turned to her, a sexy smile on his lips. "Having fun?"

Cidra was still working on the jealousy issue and simply stared at him. Even with the noise and the smoke, she could smell him, feel his power. She wanted him in a way she'd never wanted any man. She just had no clue what to do about it.

She eyed him speculatively. "Yes. Are you?" His answer to her question suddenly became very important.

"Don't I look it?" He gave her a puzzled look. Not waiting for a reply, he shifted with a groan. The next sentence he whispered in her ear. "But I'd appreciate it if you would refrain from rubbing that beautiful body of yours against me. I'm a man, not a saint."

She turned quickly to look at him and caught her breath with one look at the shimmering hunger in his eyes.

"Sorry," she apologized quickly but it was not what she wanted to say. She wondered what he would do if she told him what she really wanted.

Drinks appeared, along with a not so subtle come hither look from the server to Grey. He handled her firmly, but kindly, and she walked away with a smile.

The conversation wandered through a litany of stories and recollections from everyone, except Cidra. It struck her for the umpteenth time what a sheltered life she'd led or been forced to lead. It certainly hadn't been by choice. All those years missed, locked away.

The evening sped along filled with laughter and friendly chatter until Rosa and Barrios feigned fatigue and departed.

A quartet started playing and the dance area filled up with a mélange of races cast in a surreal haze of blue light. Cidra could identify each species from her Kin-sha studies, but reality proved far more fascinating. With delight, she watched the fantastic flow of skin colors, features and attire bobbing and weaving to the beat.

The band shifted smoothly into a slow, wicked, sizzling number. The audience heated up in response. The patrons closed ranks, bodies rocking in unison. The female singer's high, breathy voice plunged the room into a lusty cadence.

The rhythm tugged at Cidra, drawing her into the dance. She didn't hear the words, only felt the answering call in her body. For the first time all night, Cidra felt awkward. Desire finally outweighed embarrassment.

"Grey?"

He turned sharply. The strange tone of her voice caught his attention more than his name.

Her eyes were locked on the dancers on the floor, her face drawn. "Would you show me how to dance?"

He knew. She didn't have to say anything else. Another experience she'd missed. He closed his eyes and checked his level of self-control. It was as low as it had been all night. He checked the sensual atmosphere on the floor, hot and steamy. This was probably not the wisest move, but he couldn't bring himself to refuse her.

He rose and held out a hand to her. The sweet look of relief and gratitude she gave him more than made up for any discomfort he was about to endure on the dance floor.

Once on the floor, he pulled her to him, unobtrusively placing her hands correctly and coaxing her into smooth steps. She closed her eyes to the world and let him lead, telling her what to do with subtle prompts with his body.

It didn't take long to fall into the intoxicating dance. It swept over her in a hot wave of vibration straight to her core. She could feel the strong muscles under his shirt, warm breath on her neck, the incredible heat of his arms. She pressed the length of her body to his, absorbing the fluid flow of male strength. He hissed in her ear. His body felt so strong and tight, unyielding against her softness. So hard. Everywhere. His arms, his chest, his stomach, his....

Her eyes flew open. She swallowed, stunned by the raw hunger in his face.

"Don't look so surprised. I told you I was no saint," he growled softly.

Cidra gazed into his silver eyes and gave into that impulse when your heart tells your better judgment, your conscience and your common sense to get lost. She stroked his jaw with her fingertips and said quietly, "I never said I wanted a saint."

That stopped him cold, his eyes narrowed. Was that an invitation? Her face exhibited equal parts of doubt and desire. She needed to understand there would be no turning back. He knew he didn't possess that amount of restraint, not with her, not tonight. The effort would kill him. This wasn't going to be soft hugs and gentle cuddling. This wasn't going to be sweet and gentle. What he had in mind was more of a feeding frenzy. He knew once he started, he would never be able to stop.

The big question remained. Did she feel the same way? He

grinned. Only one way to find out.

He lowered his mouth to hers, the kiss sizzling as hot and heavy as he could deliver it. His tongue flickered by and boldly delved deep into the recesses of her sweet, moist mouth. Deeper, harder, hotter.

In a flash, he found himself too close to the edge.

Strong arms gripped her like metal bands, subtle savagery underlying the sensual assault. The world around her vanished in surging stages as she clung to him. He became her ecstasy and terror at once, heightening, yet devastating her senses. It made his sudden, unsteady withdrawal nearly painful.

"I want you like that." His words labored in her ear. He pulled away just enough for his eyes to burn into her, promising fire. They stood motionless, eyes locked, in the center of the writhing, swirling, sensual mass.

Words refused to form on her lips. His primal intensity sent out alternating warning sirens and cheers throughout her system, all demanding equal time of her limited capacity to think straight.

Grey's eyes narrowed. "It doesn't work unless you say it, too."

It was then that better judgment, conscience, and common sense kicked back into full gear. Panic gripped her. Too much, too soon. He was too far ahead of her. She licked her lips nervously. "I'm not sure."

Grey exhaled hard, closed his eyes, and pressed his forehead to her brow. He murmured, "Wrong answer, but we'll work on it. Either way, it's time to go home. Dance lessons are over for tonight."

He released her then and pulled her off the dance floor.

She raised her eyes to his, expecting anger. Instead, his eyes glittered under the lights at her, shrouded with concern and regret.

Tears stung her eyes.

"I need to visit the lav before we leave," she said huskily and turned toward the rear of the saloon.

Grey watched her retreat. He had glimpsed her uncertainty and embarrassment and silently cursed himself. He'd scared her. It showed in her eyes, in the way she'd tensed in his arms and the speed in which she closed herself up. He let his wild desire rise too close to the surface. It had surprised him before he could check it.

Now she would need time. He needed time, too. And space, from her. If for no other reason than to restore his waning self-restraint. Clearly, he'd have to take it slow. He wouldn't scare her again. She wasn't ready. If he had any doubts of her innocence and inexperience, they were confirmed now.

It shouldn't surprise him. With each passing hour, he realized just how sheltered Syrus had kept Cidra. She devoured each new encounter, never holding back and ready for more. She was well-educated and socially adept, but the rest, the very essence of life and living, had been forsaken. Syrus did what he had to, but it didn't make the thought of ten years of virtual imprisonment any easier to swallow.

It came to him in a heartbeat that he wanted to be the one to show her what life had to offer. He wanted to be there when her eyes lit up and the flush of discovery swept over her. He wanted to hear the excitement in her voice and watch her grow with each new adventure. The very thought of another man revealing the wonders of the worlds to her made his blood run hot.

Quite a feat, considering just how hot he was at the moment.

The cold stab of a laser pistol in his back extinguished that heat in a flash. He instinctively reached for his own pistol. Emptiness greeted him.

"Don't turn around." A harsh voice behind him hissed. "Out the back door. And nothing stupid. I know you don't have a weapon."

Grey clenched his jaw, his eyes surveying the room quickly. No familiar faces, no convenient diversions, no easy escape. The light brush of fabric against his back told him the pistol was hidden from view of any curious patrons. And as his assailant had accurately pointed out, he was unarmed. There wasn't a Kin-sha move faster than a laser shot. He'd have a better chance once they were in the alley. That is, unless his abductor had friends.

With the pistol fitted snugly to his spine, he headed for the door. The last thing he needed was for Cidra to see him. Whatever this turned into, he preferred her as far away from it as possible.

He'd owe her another apology for leaving her. The weapon shoved in his back reminded him that that was the least of his worries.

CHAPTER NINE

Cidra exited the lav feeling more in control, if not thoroughly confused, mortally embarrassed, and absolutely terrified. Running away was not her style. Neither was withdrawing an offer. She didn't want to consider what he thought of her now. It certainly wasn't the reason she found herself racing back to him. Her danger sense was screaming. One quick scan of the room confirmed her worst fear. No sign of Grey.

The notion that he would abandon her flickered by with little impact. Of one thing she was certain, he hadn't left by choice. She glanced toward the front entrance. If not by choice, then discreetly as well. She spun around and rushed to the rear exit.

The alley on the other side of the heavy door was empty, dark, and reeked of rotting food. Something scurried a few meters from her feet.

Her danger sense peaked and drove her forward. She ran left, dodging the mass of containers upended and tossed recklessly along the length of the narrow alley. Another left turn and she stumbled out into main artery next to the bar and right into a big, warm body.

"Whoa, little lady. Wouldn't want you to...." Rourke's eyes widened. A slow smile lit his face. "Cidra, right? Nice to see you again."

Her wild eyes met his. His smile vanished.

"What's wrong?" Suddenly alarmed, he shot a glance over her head towards the dark alley. "Where's Grey? Don't tell me he left you on your own."

"He's in trouble." She grabbed the front of Rourke's jacket so fiercely that he actually flinched. "Big trouble. Did you see him leave?"

Rourke frowned. "No. How long ago?"

"Minutes, I think. We have to find him. He didn't leave willingly." Her voice bordered on desperation. She knew instinctively that every second counted.

The shrill signal of her comm unit in her small bag cut through the tension. Her eyes met briefly with Rourke's before she fumbled frantically to locate it. As soon as she touched the control, voices and sounds came through the unit.

" ... should know, you can't hide from me, Stone. I figured sooner or later, you'd have to leave *Calíbre* and then I'd have you. It's really a shame you couldn't have died quietly in our little assault over Avion. I lost several of my best men in that Victor. You will have to pay for that. Your life will do for starters."

There was a sickening thud, proceeded by Grey's pained grunt and winded retort. "Drop dead, Wex."

"Tsk, tsk. I'm a reasonable man. I am willing to forgive your indiscretion. And it'll only cost you *Calíbre*. Legally, of course. Your crew is entirely too loyal for me to step in without your full support. All I really need is your verbal consent on the transfer card, and you can walk away."

Cidra caught her breath and looked to Rourke. He glared at the comm unit and muttered through clenched teeth, "Sandor Wex."

He pulled the comm unit from Cidra's hand, cut the connection and shoved the unit back into her hand. Cidra gasped. "What are you doing?"

"Trust me. Hail *Calíbre*. Now," he demanded.

She did as he asked and Coon answered the summons. "Hi, Sugar. To what do I owe this unexpected and delightful pleasure."

Cidra cut in. "Later, Coon. Grey's in trouble." She passed the unit to Rourke. "All yours."

Rourke palmed the comm unit and addressed Coon. "Wex waylaid him. Sounds like he brought some friends along and they're working him over pretty good. He's wearing a comm unit. I need a fix on his current location. Fast."

Coon's swearing was accompanied by the sound of fingers tapping furiously. "His standard unit is here on *Calíbre*. He must be using his private unit. Hold on." A few more taps. "Got it." He came back triumphantly. "He's between Cutter and Junta Re about half way down the block."

"Thanks, Coon." Rourke grabbed Cidra and pulled her with him. "This way."

* * * *

Grey hit the dirt hard. That last punch had done its job if the sheer number of stars in his head were any indication. Wex had replaced his lost crew with some real heavyweights. The one bearing down on him now was as big and ugly as they came.

"Stone," Wex taunted him. "Really, is all this necessary? Dunkin here does so enjoy his work. Simply give *Calíbre* to me and you can stay with the living."

Grey staggered to his feet, eyeing Dunkin's malicious smile. Oh yes, he definitely enjoyed his work. Staying alive, regardless of what Grey agreed to, seemed a remote possibility.

"If he enjoys his work so much, what do you need the other three for? Why don't you take a hike, and let me and Dunkin here hash this out? Or don't you believe he can handle the job?" Grey knew the significance of his words had sunk into Dunkin's thick head when a worried crease developed in the middle of the single, massive eyebrow.

But Wex's head wasn't quite so thick. "Now, now. Dunkin is well-suited to his vocation and needs little guidance from me. You'll only incite him further."

However, Dunkin looked bewildered and unconvinced. Wex spent precious minutes speaking to him in quiet, fatherly tones.

A few more minutes, Grey thought. She had to come. He hadn't wanted to involve her, but there was no choice. If she didn't show up, he would die right here in this filthy alley. There was no way he'd give *Calíbre* to Sandor Wex.

* * * *

They nearly ran right past the entrance of the alley. Rourke heard the voices first and grabbed her just in time, covering her protest with his hand and whispering silence in her ear.

He ventured a peek around the corner and could make out the shadows of six men, most of them massive. Wex was easy to pick out with his arrogant stance and slight build. He stood flanked by two giants, one of which was delivering another blow to a hunched over figure being held by two more men. Laser pistols glinted all around.

He winced as Grey absorbed the hit with a painful grunt, his head hanging low. They didn't have much time before he'd be down for good.

He felt Cidra hovering over his back, watching the action. He turned to her expecting to see fear or horror. Instead, her expression was brutally fierce and her body wound tight, ready to launch. All that sweet, feminine beauty had suddenly turned formidable and deadly.

Grey had certainly picked himself an interesting pilot.

Rourke pressed his head back against the front of the building and asked Cidra, "Do you have a weapon?"

"No, but I can take care of myself." Her eyes drilled into him, leaving no doubt to her confidence. Despite her words, he suppressed a curse. He had one laser pistol and an unarmed, albeit, furious female pilot against at least five men loaded with weapons and one beaten hostage. Bad odds, but he'd seen worse.

With Grey, in fact.

He cast one more glance into the alley in time to see Grey absorb another blow and drop heavily to the ground, rocking slowly.

"We'll need a diversion then. Any ideas?"

"Just one." Her whisper brought his eyes to hers immediately, but she was looking past him, straight up into the stars. He watched in puzzlement as she began scouring the ground frantically.

"What are you doing?"

"Trust me." She scooped a handful of stones from a nearby foliage container, walked past him to the edge of the alley and stared up at the grid hanging over the alley. "Cover your eyes and get that weapon ready."

She heaved a small stone at the biggest gridhead with all her might. It missed, ricocheting loudly off the opposite side of the alley.

"What was that?" A single voice echoed through the alley. Another voice rose up. "If anyone finds us here...." Followed by, "Let's kill him now and get it over with." Wex's voice cut in, "Just shut up and find out what that was." One set of footsteps rang out, heading down the alley toward Cidra.

Rourke stood ready. Cidra concentrated on the gridhead, heaved another stone and hit her mark.

Instantly, the grid came to life and blinding lights flooded the darkness while a chilling siren cut through the night air. A chorus of obscenities accompanied Wex's alarmed shout of retreat and the sound of a hasty withdrawal in the opposite direction. Her eyes adjusted quickly to the intense lights, yet she remained motionless.

The approaching footsteps materialized into a startled giant of a man, covering his blinded eyes with a meaty arm and swearing viciously. He staggered to a halt and blinked several times before he realized he was standing directly in front of a very angry woman.

The giant aimed his laser pistol, but before Rourke could pull his own trigger, Cidra delivered a lightening quick kick. The man's gun spun into the side of the building. The next kick caught the giant neatly in the throat. He stumbled back, gasping for air. The third kick connected with the side of his head. His eyes rolled back and he dropped like a stone.

Rourke gaped at the downed giant, at the undischarged laser

pistol in his hand, and then to Cidra. She appeared perfectly calm, glanced one last time at the giant to make sure he was down and took off in a dead run into the blinding, blaring alley.

"Well, I'll be damned," Rourke murmured, then took off after her.

Cidra's heart sank. The alley was empty. They must still have him. She rushed ahead, determined to follow them and nearly tripped over his very still body, curled up on the ground.

She froze, disabled by panic. *No.*

Running up behind her, Rourke knelt down and checked Grey's neck for a pulse. The siren continued to scream overhead. Blood was beginning to pool around his head. He groaned low.

Rourke looked up at her, urgency in his eyes. "He's alive, but we need to get him to a med center real soon. Hail *Calíbre* and get some help."

* * * *

Grey braced himself on the edge of the clinic table, watching as the head medic gave Cidra a lengthy list of instructions. She hung on every word, whispering questions and glancing at Grey with deep concern.

In his blood, a potent painkiller and healing accelerator combined into an intoxicating brew they called Triox. Enough of it could make a dead man walk. In other words, he felt awful but was pretty damned happy about it.

For one thing, he was alive. For another thing, Cidra was here. Watching her proved to be the best painkiller around.

Grey heard the medic's parting words. "The broken ribs will take the longest to heal. Lots of sleep and food. The accelerator will do the rest. He's lucky. Whoever worked him over knew what they were doing. It's a good thing they stopped when they did. Tell him it's time to find some new friends."

With a final word of thanks, she nodded and walked toward Grey. The stress of the long evening showed on her face, and he cursed the fear that clouded her blue eyes.

She slipped closer until her legs pressed against his thighs, their eyes locking. There was too much to say and no words to adequately convey it.

Very slowly, very carefully, Cidra raised her fingers to trace around the cut over his swollen eye and along his cheek to his lips caked with dried blood.

His words came out in a raw, hoarse whisper. "It would have been a lot worse if you hadn't shown up."

Cidra squeezed her eyes shut, shaking her head. "Don't."

With exquisite gentleness, she wrapped her arms around his shoulders and pressed her cheek against the uninjured side of his head. He slid a bandaged hand around her waist and pulled her closer, on the verge of desperation. They held each other, sharing and dissipating the violence of the evening with kindred understanding.

Grey couldn't remember the last time he'd been comforted by someone who truly cared about him, who gave and expected nothing in return, who was scared and worried for him. Maybe never. He didn't want to let her go.

A loud knock on the door prompted an abrupt end to the private healing session. Rourke filled the doorway, looking as apologetic as any man could look under the circumstances. "Sorry for the intrusion."

Cidra turned and smiled warmly at him but didn't move from Grey's side.

Rourke grinned at Grey. "Nice to know you're in good hands. You'll be back to your grumpy old self in no time."

"If you came here to abuse me, you'll have to stand in line," Grey said wearily.

Rourke held up a hand. "No, actually, I have some news for you." He crossed his arms and leaned a broad shoulder against the doorway. "Wex is gone. Mora, too. Took off right after he finished with you. I think Cidra's little surprise gave him a good scare." He flashed Cidra a genuine smile.

"Of course, that doesn't mean he's off your back. He could leave the job of killing you to someone more qualified. I wouldn't want you to get too confident."

Then anticipating Grey's next question, he continued. "And *Calíbre*'s fine. He didn't go near it. He wouldn't dare now. Not when word gets out about what he tried. He's going to have a nasty welcoming committee if he ever comes back here."

He stopped, narrowing his eyes at Grey. "You know, I wish you'd warned me that you gave Coon a laser rifle. He nearly took my head off when I checked around *Calíbre*."

Grey chuckled and winced from the sudden movement. "He's better than any security system I could find."

"The man is a menace. He took a shot at me. If he knew what he was doing, he might have actually hit me," Rourke said indignantly.

"That's what you get for sneaking around my ship," Grey

countered, finding the incident too funny to let go and wishing he could at least laugh about it.

"Yeah, that's what I get for being a friend," Rourke answered with a snort.

Grey grew serious and spoke quietly. "You are. A good one, too. Thanks."

Rourke waved him off. "Forget it. You buy the drinks for the rest of our lives. Besides, I had a little help." He grinned at Cidra.

Cidra blushed and whispered into Grey's ear, "I'll tell you about it later." He grunted an acknowledgment, eyeing Rourke with half-hearted suspicion.

Rourke just smiled broadly and put his hands on his hips. "So, where to folks? You can't stay here all night. I brought a ground shuttle."

Cidra turned back to Grey. "*Calíbre?*" she ventured.

His eyes met hers in quiet astonishment. She already knew him better than anyone. He nodded, fatigue gathering under the heavy cloak of Triox.

Rourke frowned at Grey. "Will you be all right there alone?"

"I'll be with him." Cidra helped Grey off the table and steadied him while he walked.

Rourke only smiled in envy. "You're one lucky man, Stone."

Grey shot him a single look that told him he knew it, too.

* * * *

"Cidra. Don't go yet."

The tired request sounded more like a command. Cidra had just turned down the lights in Grey's quarters after settling him in bed. She had hoped he would doze off quickly, slipping into sleep's blessed refuge, giving the accelerator the time and energy it needed to heal his wounds. Her eyes swept over his big, battered body, filling most of the bed. So much damage in one night.

"You need to rest. Do you want another injection of Triox?" she asked gently, sitting on the edge of his bed and brushing aside a stray curl from his face. His eyes were heavy from the effects of the massive accelerator dose, but his body still shuddered from the aftershocks of violence.

"No. Talk to me."

Cidra pursed her lips and relented, hoping he would eventually wear himself out. That was the problem with Triox. It told the mind that you were immortal. Unfortunately, the body wasn't. She took his uninjured hand and wrapped it in both of hers.

"How long have you known Rourke?"

Grey closed his eyes. "The better part of ten years. We met during a salvage operation that went bad. Nothing like facing certain death together to cement a friendship."

He shifted and groaned sharply, trying without success to find a more comfortable position. Cidra winced at the effort and the vulnerability it disclosed.

"Are you trying to tell me that this happens a lot?"

"Hardly." He snorted. "It's been a while since I've had my ass kicked. Frankly, I wouldn't mind if this was the last time."

He laughed. Immediately his face twisted in a grimace.

"I should let you sleep." Cidra began to move away from him. He grabbed her wrist.

"No. I'm fine, really." It hurt like hell. He was getting too old for this. Then again, those beautiful blue eyes filled with concern sure held a certain appeal. It was almost worth it.

Cidra looked at him doubtfully but settled back on the bed. "What are you going to do about Wex?"

"I put a false trail in *Calibre*'s systems for the location of the lost Mask of Teran. And just as she did for the last two finds, Mora stole the file. They will spend the next several months on the other side of the galaxy heading to coordinates in the middle of nowhere. Enough time for me to get the Mask myself."

Cidra smiled wide. "Maybe Wex will think twice about stealing and spying."

Grey smiled weakly. "I hope so. He'll have to learn to do it the hard way like the rest of us." Grey paused. "I'm glad you approve."

Cidra ran her eyes over his battered body again. "He deserves whatever you gave him."

Grey yawned, admitting depletion at last.

Cidra watched as he peacefully slipped into the blissful haven of sleep with a smile still playing on his lips. His breathing turned even and deep, denying pain any more torment tonight.

Only then did she reach out to him, her hand hovering over his bare chest above the bandaged ribs, close enough to feel the heat build between her body and his. Delicious heat rose and gathered until her hand felt on fire. That's what their lovemaking would be like. Fire, consuming and glorious. And she had almost lost the chance forever. It was a mistake she wouldn't repeat. She couldn't. She loved him.

Cidra withdrew her hand, stretched out next to him and fell

asleep watching the even rise and fall of his chest.

* * * *

A man entertains strange dreams with Triox coursing through his veins. This one promised to be a real winner.

In the fertile fields of his mind, he could smell her hair, feel the heavy silkiness of it against his face. She lay spooned against him, her back to his chest, his heavy arousal pinned to her firm derriere. *One hell of a dream.*

His hand rested over one soft, warm breast. When he slid his thumb over the tip, it tightened and she stirred. *So real.*

He moved his hand along the curve of the breast and over her ribcage, committing every inch to memory. She wore that little dress from last night. It made sense it would be in his dream. It would probably be in every dream he had for the rest of his life.

With only a vague awareness of pain lurking in the background, he flattened a hand against her slim waist and pulled her tighter against him. Then his fantasy exploration continued in earnest.

Her hip swelled under his touch, followed by a bare, smooth thigh. He groaned. *Damned best dream he ever had.* He should go back and thank that medic.

His fingertips slid to her inner thigh and began to trace the incredible softness. Up, up, seeking heat.

Her gentle but firm hand halted his progress.

"I see you're feeling better," she purred.

In an instant, dream became reality. Her presence swamped his senses. She was there. Real and warm and soft against him in his own bed. His eyes flew open. Pain rushed in, compliments of last evening's cold violence.

Another fact emerged.

Reality hurt.

Rolling onto his back with a deep, heartfelt moan, he squeezed his eyes shut, but pain's floodgate stood wide open.

Cidra scrambled to her knees beside him. "Grey?"

"It's not you," he gritted out. That said, he concentrated on controlling the sudden influx of discomfort. At least today he could distinguish the specific parts of his body in agony. Unfortunately, it proved to be pretty much everything.

"I'll get the Triox." Cidra hopped off the bed.

Grey clenched his teeth. He hated the drugs, hated the fact that he needed them. But he had no choice. He had work to do. They were going to locate that lost shipment. He'd made up his mind sometime in the blur of last night after Cidra saved his hide. It had become his number one priority. The Mask of Teran would have to stay lost for a while longer.

He gazed at her as she finished administering the Triox. In the haze of pain, she looked like a divine apparition. He captured her wrist. "I never thanked you, Cidra."

She stilled and tears welled up without warning, dropping like molten fire to his body. She blinked them aside furiously and turned away.

"Cidra?"

With her back to him, she planted both hands on the side table and lowered her head. When she finally spoke, her voice shook. "I've never been so scared in my life. Not even the night the d'Hont came to my house or the nightmares that followed."

"Cidra, come here." The Triox hit him like a wave, making his world a much more pleasant place. Until he saw the shattered look on her face when she turned around.

"I'm sorry," he offered.

"You could have been killed," she whispered, her face reflecting memories of the past.

He held his voice steady. "Thanks to you, I wasn't."

She rubbed her arms and stared at the floor in silence, her mind clearly at work. Then her shoulders seemed to drop in defeat.

"Grey, I've been thinking about the Dakru shipment. Whoever attacked the fleet...." She stopped and looked directly at him. "It's too dangerous. I don't think we should continue."

Her train of thought stunned him. It took him a moment to comprehend what she meant. She was willing to give up Syrus' last wish, live with the burden of her past, accept the loss of the Kin-sha and bury her own dreams, all to keep him safe. The strength that took, he couldn't imagine. The unselfish gift she offered, he couldn't accept.

"I don't think that's necessary." His voice was quiet, masking increasing alarm. "We'll be very careful from now on. Believe it or not, I don't usually get into this kind of trouble."

She gave him a long, skeptical look and shook her head. "The price is too high. It's not worth dying for."

"You can't live the rest of your life not knowing what happened, Cidra. It'll eat you alive," he insisted, fully waged in a battle he did not dare lose: to keep her close.

"As opposed to losing you which would kill me all at once?" Anger flashed in her eyes.

Powerful satisfaction warmed him. "I didn't think you cared."

Cidra clenched her fists and stared back at the floor. "Just because I lost my nerve on the dance floor doesn't mean I don't care." Then she drilled him with a stern look. "And don't try to change the subject."

"If I only could," he muttered, but secretly, he was ecstatic. The warrior had re-emerged. Now all he had to do was point her toward the battlefield.

"What about the Kin-sha and Syrus' last wish? What about your father's name and your family's honor and Barrios? Not to mention the millions who died on Dakru. Don't they figure into the equation?"

Her jaw tightened. She looked away but not before he saw the impact of his words. There was more at stake here than all the points he'd brought up. Her very sanity was on the line. And his. For the first time he realized how much he needed her. He pushed forward, driven by one thought: to keep her tied to him as long as possible. For that, he was prepared to fight dirty.

"Whoever did this it still out there, free to terrorize other worlds. They proved they can kill without conscience and not leave a trace. They're good, Cidra, deadly, fast, and dangerous. I, for one, want them neutralized."

She struggled for an out. "It's been ten years. Maybe they aren't even around anymore."

"There's only one way to find out."

She took a deep breath. "All right, but we'll be careful. Very, very careful. No unnecessary chances. And from now on, you don't make a move without me. Deal?"

He suppressed a triumphant grin, his world in order once again. "Deal."

* * * *

Barrios' bulky form filled the doorway of Grey's office, casting a long shadow across its occupants. Grey, Cidra, and Decker turned to him in unison from their positions around the holo deck table. Decker nodded a greeting and returned to laying in a program for the holo deck.

Cidra smiled at her old friend. He was the last crew member to board *Calibre* before their scheduled departure for Saurel. Barrios looked happier than Cidra had ever seen him.

"About time you got here. How's Rosa?" Cidra asked. It was a gratuitous question. The sparkle in his eyes said it all.

Barrios beamed. "She's just fine." He hitched his head toward

Grey. "And she's been worried sick over you, Stone. I can see why. You look like death."

Grey smiled grimly. "You should have seen me two days ago."

Between the Triox and Cidra's care he felt much better than he looked. And with the way Cidra had been eyeing him lately, he felt invincible. She watched his every move, painstakingly tracking his recovery. He had the distinct feeling she was keeping her distance until he healed. He had more motivation than he knew what to do with.

"You missed all the excitement," Grey drawled, prompting a grimace from Cidra.

"I'll say. Anyone we know?" Barrios frowned.

Grey barely nodded. "Remember the ambush over Avion?"

Barrios grunted and shook his head. "Persistent bunch, huh?"

"You have no idea," Grey muttered.

"I think I'll head to the galley and start the evening meal," Barrios said with enthusiasm and disappeared.

Decker spoke up. "Here we go. Program loaded and executing."

On impulse, Grey reached for Cidra's hand under the table. He slid his fingers through hers, linking them together. She glanced at him in surprise, but he was completely focused on the holo deck rising from the center of the table. The grid fluttered and filled with a full-dimensional star map of the galaxy. Frame after frame, the holo image zoomed down to a specific sector. Then an opaque cylindrical cone materialized horizontally, overlaying the sector.

"It's a cone," Cidra observed, her eyes glued to the image. It started at one tiny point and ballooned into a three-dimensional wedge that continued to the edge of the star map.

"Correct." Decker tapped keys and gave the computer verbal instructions. "I integrated the precise coordinates of the Galena's battle scene into the actual star charts."

"So the Galena is the small, starting point," Cidra noted.

"Right again," Decker acknowledged. "Then I calculated the exact position of the Galena's landing bay doors when the transport escaped. The white area represents all possible vector paths of the transport. It starts out small, expanding over greater distances. Therefore, the cone shape." Decker grinned. "And before you ask, yes. You are looking at the galaxy as it appeared on the day of the attack."

Grey said, "Everything within that cone is a possible target. We are lucky the transport was pointing at the outer spiral arm of the galaxy and not through the galactic nucleus. Makes the job easier."

Cidra noted with dismay the massive target area displayed. It extended out into infinity since they had no way of knowing where the transport dropped out of hyperspace. The task of picking through thousands upon thousands of systems one by one seemed indomitable.

Decker must have sensed her despair. "Don't worry, we'll narrow it down."

Grey concurred. "He's right. Now we play a game of elimination and see who survives the cuts. You'll see." He glanced at Decker. "Are you ready?"

Decker nodded.

Grey's eyes gleamed. "First cut, all systems without red giant suns and white or gray planets."

Realization dawned on Cidra as some areas in the ghostly wedge turned black. He was using the information in the note from Syrus' box written by the original transport crew. She turned to say something to Grey and inhaled sharply. He looked like a hunter, his eyes piercing and his full attention on the quarry.

"Out of those left, keep only the systems where the red giant and the planet would be visible together with the naked eye." His eyes narrowed.

Decker worked feverishly and more systems blacked out.

Grey continued his instructions. "Good. It's probably safe to eliminate systems with unusual characteristics that the crew of the transport didn't mention. Additional visible planets or moons, nebulas, asteroid belts."

Decker said, "I'm also removing any systems with volatile or destructive natural forces."

Cidra's hope soared as isolated pockets of white became distinct. She squeezed his hand.

Grey's eyes never left the display. "Better. Now eliminate systems with advanced civilizations capable of space travel. They would have detected the transport and either rescued or destroyed it."

Grey smiled at the greatly diminished search area and turned to Decker. "That's more like it. Load the remaining possibilities on a micropad. I'll take a look at them in my quarters." He released Cidra's hand, stood up and stretched his healing body.

"That's it?" Cidra asked and glanced back at the holo image. "But look at all the systems left. How do you know which one it is? Don't we have to check them out? Don't we have to...." Her next question was cut off by a sizzling kiss that blanked her mind.

When she opened her eyes, Grey was smiling down at her. "You'll have to trust me, Cidra."

He straightened, took the micropad from a clearly amused Decker and walked out of the office.

Cidra stared in his wake, the kiss still burned on her lips. She wanted to jump up and run after him. Wanted another kiss more than her next breath.

She suddenly realized that Decker was still grinning at her.

Rising on shaky knees, she told him, "I'll be in my quarters if you need me." She paused. "On second thought, I'll be in the lounge. I think I need a drink."

* * * *

Commander Plass stood ramrod straight outside Tausek's quarters, staring at the door. He'd lost track of how long he'd been there and didn't care. He dreaded his impending task. Dreaded the answers to the questions he had. Answers that could shatter his steady, routine world.

Yet duty called as it always did and he stepped forward into the door's activation field. The interior lay flooded in red like a bloodbath. Plass shivered, he'd seen enough blood to last him a lifetime, many lifetimes.

Tausek stood in his customary position by the bank of windows viewing the crimson sunset as Plass approached him. The corvits watched him come to a halt with morbid interest.

"I expected you yesterday, Commander."

Plass frowned. The icy greeting did not bode well for the tone of the meeting.

"Yes. Our sources on Avion had a difficult time gathering information," he answered succinctly, determined to push this encounter along as quickly as possible. "Apparently, Syrus Almazan was well-liked and well-protected. However, the information is guaranteed reliable. Cidra Faulkner left with a man by the name of Grey Stone. He is a successful treasure hunter and most likely a Kin-sha since he was reported to have resided with Almazan for some time."

Tausek kept his back to Plass. "Did your reliable sources tell you where they are now?"

Plass winced at the acerbity. "A search has been launched beginning with his home base planet of Vaasa. I expect to locate them shortly."

"Find her and kill her, Commander. I don't care how you do it or who you take with her."

"I understand, sir." Plass nodded and braced himself. "I also have information on the security breach into our primary information systems. I am told it was an unorthodox method originating from Stone's ship."

Tausek didn't respond.

Plass continued, choosing his words carefully. "I have no idea why they would be interested in the Avion shipment negotiations."

"Neither do I, Commander." Tausek's voice sounded slightly off.

Plass pursued his course. "As you requested, I have personally reviewed those records myself. The only incident in that time frame was a strike on a refugee ship per your orders. The official records appear incomplete. Do you recall anything unusual about that incident?"

"I have reviewed those records, Commander. They *are* complete. The action was routine and necessary at the time," Tausek answered abruptly.

"Of course, sir."

A painful silence descended as Plass wrestled with his next move.

Unexpectedly, Tausek spoke first. "Under the circumstances, I think you should personally handle the elimination of Cidra Faulkner."

The Commander shifted uneasily. "I am."

"I want you to be present to identify her body and deliver it in time for the annual Celebration." Tausek words hung in the air as thick as blood.

Plass narrowed his eyes. "But my duties here?"

"Can be handled by Lieutenant Stoll," Tausek cut in.

Unable to think, Plass simply stared at Tausek's back. "As you wish."

"I wish," Tausek answered tightly. "Dismissed."

Plass departed with the distinct feeling that he was being dismissed--permanently. It was evident he had crossed the line and would pay for his curiosity with his position or worse. It was the latter that motivated him. Before that happened, he'd make sure he found out exactly what happened ten years ago.

CHAPTER TEN

Cidra watched the planet of Saurel fill the K12's viewport as they approached. It dangled in black space as if suspended by an invisible string, girdled and attended by nine smaller moons. As planets went, it offered little in the way of aesthetics, lacking significant relief from a monotony of gray. Even as the K12 drew closer to the surface, the terrain remained flat and barren, all but dead.

Few lifeforms could withstand the broiling heat induced by the planet's twin suns. Saurel and its tiny moons were destined to bake in a tight, vertical looping orbit, pawns in the gravitational battle between the dueling stars.

The race who inhabited this scorched, desolate world did so for a singular reason: consistent underground temperatures. The Saurel race had outgrown their original home planet and founded a new home here. With the twin suns heat evenly distributed over the entire planet, the rock beneath maintained an unvarying, unwavering warmth. The planet was custom-made to regulate the volatile body temperatures of the Saurelians and protect their fragile skin from sunlight. Below the planet face, they thrived.

Private residences, businesses, factories, schools were hewed from the bedrock beneath the scalded surface--a world connected with tunnels and shuttles. The Saurelians developed the technologies they needed to forge and support their enterprises. Their very existence was an engineering marvel and so were the unrivaled fighter ships they produced. Ships that could shift the balance of supremacy, guarantee outcomes, and reign in absolute terror.

Still, Cidra suppressed a shudder when she looked at the planet. To say the Saurelians were a male-dominated society would be an understatement. Females were looked upon as little more than slaves and servants, granted negligible rights and freedoms. Only when they married and bore offspring were they considered of any value.

"You're quiet." Grey interrupted her thoughts as he sat comfortably at the helm of the K12.

She slanted him a meaningful glance. "Just wondering how many brilliant minds had been wasted because they happened to be in female bodies."

Grey raised an eyebrow. "I assume we are talking about Saurelians."

"You assume correctly," she said. Cidra leaned back in the co-pilot seat and crossed her arms over her chest. "How do you feel about Saurelians and their male-dominated nation?"

He eyed her with the same respect he'd give a loaded laser pistol. "I think it's the way they run their society."

"Coward."

She said it with a smile and he chuckled. "That's right, but since we are on the subject," he spun his seat around to face her, "are you familiar with the roles we need to play on Saurel?"

She narrowed her eyes at him. "You're going to enjoy this, aren't you?"

He gave a mock look of shock. "Having you at my absolute beck and call? Serving my meals? Obeying my every wish without question?" He shook his head solemnly, but the smile remained. "No, I won't enjoy that at all."

"I could strangle you."

His laugh filled the small cabin. "Don't worry, I won't get used to it." Then he turned serious. "But it is necessary if we want to get any information from Bohr."

Cidra sighed deeply. "Yes, it is. I'll do my part. It's just that I have a problem with virtual slavery in any form."

He nodded. "So do I. Let's hope Decker located the right Saurelian seller of those fighters. I don't want to stay here any longer than we have to."

As they made their final approach, a massive, protective cover dilated open and exposed the landing bay pit. Saurel was dotted with thousands of such circular covers. They served as a defensive strategy and an environmental necessity. The covers were virtually indestructible and immune to attack. They could also be tightly sealed to preserve Saurel's supply of manufactured oxygen underground and were a critical part of Saurel's survival. No self-respecting spacecraft or living being could survive the blazing temperature of the surface.

Under Grey's expert hand, the K12 descended and landed with a thump. Overhead, the cover contracted shut, plunging the landing bay in darkness. A bank of lights flashed red and a steady hissing sound denoted the replenishment of oxygen in the

landing bay. Slowly the hissing stopped. The lights flashed green
and then off. Oxygen levels had stabilized to acceptable levels.

It took Cidra several minutes to adjust to the dim lighting. The
large, circular landing bay was earthen and empty. Several large
entrances were carved into the smooth walls and softly
illuminated. Markings on the walls were unreadable in the faint
light.

"Apparently, they don't want to waste energy." Grey struggled
to discern his surroundings. When his eyes had adjusted fully, he
stood up and headed for the rear hatch. "They should be waiting
for us at the main entrance of the bay. Let's get on with it." He
shot a pleased look over his shoulder. "And don't forget. Try to
look like you worship the ground I walk on."

She rose to follow him and let out a dramatic sigh. "The
sacrifices I make for Avion. I'll suffer through it."

He laughed. "Maybe you'll get a commendation."

Then he spun around and pulled her into his arms. "There's
one more thing." His mouth descended over hers with all the
pent-up passion he'd stored up over the past few days. Cidra
threw her arms around his neck. Her fingers slid up his neck and
into his hair, gently pulling him closer.

Heat roared through him. Her immediate response
momentarily dazed him. He had been expecting hesitation,
uncertainty. She gave him neither. Instead, she met his desire
equally, fueling an already wild fire. He knew if they continued,
he'd take her right here in the K12. Grey broke off the kiss,
breathing like he'd just run for this life and pressed his forehead
against hers.

"Cidra." He couldn't think of another word for a few moments.

Under tenuous control at best, he raised his hands to cup her
face and gazed into the clear blue of her eyes. "Saurelians have a
very sensitive sense of smell. That's to let our host know that
you belong to me."

Cidra searched his face. "And that's the only reason?"

"No, but it'll have to do for now. We can't keep our hosts
waiting." He dropped his hands to his sides, but there was
resolute promise in his eyes and undisguised hunger in his body.

"Then lead the way, Captain," she said with a sudden smile.
"It's a nice view from back here."

* * * *

Cidra's first impression of Bohr was that the man had huge
feet. She stood behind and beside Grey with her eyes lowered in

customary fashion while he introduced himself to Bohr. The women were ignored until Bohr's blunt introduction.

"This is my mate, Sil. She will provide you with anything you require." He hissed through his teeth. He addressed Grey. "You may introduce me to this female."

Cidra felt Grey tense beside her.

"This is Cidra. My mate."

The message was unmistakable. Apparently, Bohr didn't hear it. The Saurelian stepped up and abruptly lifted Cidra's face with a scaly finger under her chin.

Grey bit off every word, "She is unavailable."

"Pity." Bohr released her.

Cidra dropped her eyes back to the ground, stunned. It had only been a few seconds, but what she saw left her thunderstruck. The Saurelian's eyes held greedy lust. For her.

Physically, he was bigger and stronger than she had guessed. Probably a real prize by Saurelian standards and he knew it. Like the rest of his race, a deeply grooved fin-like ridge ran along the top of his hairless head. His eyes were golden slits, his nose two narrow dimples. A triangle-shaped space formed between his upper and lower unlined lips for the flicking tongue.

He was dressed in conspicuously embellished attire, a sharp contrast to the simple garb worn by his mate. Cidra guessed him to be Grey's height, but much heavier, more muscled. His demeanor was superior and cruel. The blatant, arrogant way he'd sized her up told her something else. Like a spoiled child, he was used to getting what he wanted.

She could hear Grey's deep breathing next to her, feel the anger simmering in him. It was only in deference to their mission, her mission, that he tolerated Bohr's treatment of her.

"Sil will show the female to your chambers. You and I have business to discuss." Bohr nodded once to Sil. Properly cowed, she led the way through the massive entrance and down the main corridor to their residence.

Cidra could feel both sets of male eyes upon her as she followed Sil. Once out of view, she raised her head, drawing her first real breath since she exited the transport.

As they walked side by side, Sil glanced up at her and smiled sadly. "You get used to it."

"Never," Cidra said with more bitterness than she could suppress. "I would never get used to it."

Sil nodded and turned down a side corridor. "If you had no

choice, you would."

Cidra assessed the woman unfortunate enough to have been chosen by Bohr. She was very lovely and walked with quiet grace. Her gentle voice held a heavyhearted kindness. Her Saurelian features were classically delicate, well-bred and refined. The complete opposite of Bohr and probably the reason he selected her. Cidra couldn't imagine what Sil's life must be like.

"I'm sorry. I didn't mean to offend you. We come from such different worlds," Cidra apologized.

Sil led her down yet another unidentified side corridor. Cidra struggled to keep her bearings. She realized all the hallways looked identical. All upward and downward orientation was gone.

"No offense taken. You are correct. Our paths are different. Perhaps we are not so different in other ways." Sil glanced at her. The flicker of fire in her eyes caught Cidra by surprise. She smiled. Apparently, there was more to Sil than met the eye.

As they turned into another corridor, Cidra slowed to study the intricate details on the walls more closely. Every surface consisted of rock and was decorated with patterns cut directly into the stone itself. A deep, diagonal design covered the walls and ceilings. A patchwork pattern decorated the floor. The craftsmanship was exquisite, especially considering the sheer volume of the extensive corridors.

"The carvings are beautiful," Cidra said in awe.

Sil smiled. "Yes, aren't they? Our cutters are the finest. They have to be. Our entire world is down here. They get a tremendous amount of practice."

"I'll bet," Cidra agreed. Looking around, she was forced to admit that she was hopelessly lost. If the corridors were set in any pattern, she had been unable to detect it.

Sil finally stopped in front of a smooth, metal door. It opened obediently. Sil ushered Cidra into the guest chambers with a low bow.

"I hope you find everything to your liking. We rarely have the pleasure of guests. Please summon me if you require anything. Dinner will be served within the hour."

Cidra smiled warmly at her. "It's lovely. Thank you."

Sil bowed again and backed out of the room without a sound.

Cidra surveyed the spacious room with amazement. Every inch of it was carved out of solid rock, but it was different from the stone in the corridors. It sparkled. Cidra took a closer look. Flecks of light emanated from the stone itself. She realized that this entire room had been cut from a vein of precious stone. She grudgingly admitted that Bohr must be very successful. Only wealthy Saurelians could afford such prized property.

She flattened her hand against the wall and found that everywhere she touched, the temperature was the same. The furnishings were functional, simple, and slightly larger than standard human size. There were no windows, but ambient light cascading from the high ceiling lit the entire room evenly. Technology gleamed conspicuous against the natural materials.

Her eyes finally came to rest on the lone, large bed occupying center stage. Glancing around quickly, the significance sunk in. She should have realized this would happen. He couldn't very well sleep on the floor. And there was no reason to.

Cidra drew a deep breath. She would not back down again.

* * * *

As the guest chamber door closed behind him, Grey glanced around the room for Cidra and could hear her in the lav. He threw himself into a chair and noted the one bed. He blew out a long breath. He was in no mood to deal with that issue right now. He leaned his head back and closed his eyes, preparing himself for what promised to be a torturous evening.

The short time Grey had spent with Bohr had reinforced his intense dislike of the man. Bohr was little more than a child, his manners crude and his demeanor overbearing. There was no doubt that Decker had picked the right seller for those ships. Based on Grey's brief observation, the man would cut a deal with anyone with credits. Forget the ethics, honesty or integrity.

He had spent the last hour showing the Crystal Zemi to Bohr, guaranteeing its authenticity and exalting its value. It was one of the most valuable artifacts in his collection on Vaasa, but its monetary value meant little to him. He'd give up more than that for the name of the Saurelian fighter buyer.

Although the greed had been evident in Bohr's eyes, if he didn't bite, this trip would be a complete loss. They had to find who purchased those ships. He wanted it for Cidra. She was counting on him. If he failed, the questions would haunt her forever. The guilt would haunt him longer.

The lav door slid open. Grey looked up quickly. He was about to tell Cidra about his meeting, but the words never came out. She stopped just outside the doorway, stunning in a sleeveless, silky azure sheath dress. The subtle lighting glowed across her bare shoulders down to the scoop neckline. Her auburn hair flowed down her back.

But it was the material of the dress that caught Grey's attention, a shimmering, glowing fabric that seemed to move of its own accord. He gripped the arms of the chair fiercely.

"Rosa insisted I purchase this." Cidra hesitated. "Do you think it's appropriate?"

Grey launched himself out of the chair and covered the distance between them in a few long strides. Cidra's eyes were huge as he stopped within inches of her.

He reached for the fabric at her hip and rubbed the silky material between his fingers. It was gazar, a fine weave of silken threads, a product of the ethereal world of Mimos. Against human skin it felt cool, petal soft, and all but alive. It was practically an aphrodisiac for the male species and he was no exception.

He searched her face. Did she know it could drive him wild? Was she deliberately baiting him? All he could see in her eyes was apprehension and confusion. It suddenly occurred to him that this was Rosa's doing. He could almost hear her rich laughter ringing in his ears. The woman was incorrigible.

"Grey?" Cidra whispered with concern in her voice.

"It's fine." He ruthlessly curbed his passion.

Under his intense scrutiny, Cidra's breathing had increased to match his. She was acutely aware of her breasts rising and falling inches from his chest. She was unsure what to say next. The dress was obviously having a profound impact on Grey.

He slid his arm around her waist and held her firmly in place. "But I should warn you. I may not be able to keep my hands off you tonight," he growled low, his eyes dark.

Cidra could feel his heat through the thin fabric separating them as he pulled her to him and crushed her mouth under his. Cidra gasped at his masculine power and hunger. It was the same riveting, raw, dangerous, and utterly exciting kiss he'd given her on the dance floor. He possessed her, his breathing deep and savage.

Her body reacted instinctively, melting against his. Grey groaned. His tongue invaded her mouth, exploring deeply as she returned it with reckless abandon.

Grey moved his hands across the dress, sliding it over her soft body, the silkiness commanding his senses. He had to stop soon before he was pulled too near the edge. They would be summoned for dinner any moment. He hated Bohr all the more for it.

On cue, a gentle chime announced company. Cidra's head pulled back.

"The door," she whispered, regret in her voice.

There was a moment of silence before the chime rang again. Grey released her. "You better get it." Feeling the full ache in his lower body, he added, "I'm in no shape to greet our hostess."

He smiled grimly and sunk onto the bed. Cidra turned and headed for the door, hastily straightening her dress. The door slid open. Sil stood on the other side, her head bowed.

"I hope I didn't interrupt anything." Her yellow eyes met Cidra's, woman to woman.

"Not at all. We were just ... resting." Cidra smiled lightly at Sil while trying to calm the pounding of her heart.

"Very well. Dinner is prepared. Kindly join us when you are ready." Sil bowed and left.

The door slid shut. Cidra turned and rested back against the door, her body struggling to recover from the intimate assault. Grey sat quietly on the edge of the bed, his elbows resting on his knees, his hands relaxed.

"Cidra, just how isolated were you on Avion?"

She looked confused. "What do you mean?"

"Did you see anyone?"

Cidra blinked at him. "Of course."

"Men?"

She turned ashen and then angry. "Why do you want do know?"

"Because I don't want to hurt you," he persisted.

Cidra's mouth went dry as the full meaning struck her. He meant when he made love with her. She looked away quickly and then straight at him. "Syrus wouldn't allow anyone to get close to me. He felt it was too dangerous. Does that answer your question?"

He nodded once. "Must have been lonely for you."

Cidra tilted her head back against the door, watching him. "Very. But you know all about lonely, don't you?"

Grey looked up at her in surprise. "I know lonely."

"How?"

"I was an only child. My mother died shortly after my birth." His eyes never left hers. Cidra knew she was about to hear something he'd probably never told anyone except maybe Syrus.

"And your father?" she whispered.

"Lied to me." The words were so sharp and bitter that Cidra gasped. His gaze burned into her, through her to somewhere long ago.

"He told me she died giving birth to me. Every day of my life he reminded me that I was responsible for her death. And I believed him. Until the day I broke into Avion's archives."

Cidra's eye widened. She had heard of Avion's secret archives. An information system of sordid details, confirmed or otherwise, all documented meticulously. Juicy, potentially destructive tidbits with which to control their citizens and intimidate neighboring worlds.

"That's when I discovered that she had died long after my birth. Beaten to death. The attacker was never found. The whole incident was covered up and forgotten." Grey's fists were clenched tightly, white and bloodless.

Cidra stopped breathing. Oh dear Lord. No wonder he didn't trust anyone.

"When I went home that night and confronted my father with the truth, he beat me for the last time. I left and never returned."

Tears burned her eyes. "I'm so sorry, Grey." The hushed words sounded wholly inadequate. Her heart went out to the child and the man, wanting desperately to take back the past and make it right. She couldn't do anything about the past, but she could do something about the future. She could help him heal.

"Don't be. It's history." He looked at her as if he finally saw her standing there. "I consider it a lesson."

Cidra sucked in air. "Don't say that. You can't go through your life believing that everyone will lie to you."

He snorted. "Why not? It's worked pretty well so far."

Cidra touched the center of her chest. "Because, its not good for your heart."

Grey stared at her and for a fleeting moment she saw the longing. Then his eyes hardened and he stood up abruptly. "Let's go. I want to get this over with."

* * * *

After more than two hours, Cidra conceded that the dinner was not going well. It was obvious that Bohr wanted the Crystal Zemi badly. He was willing to pay any price for it except the name of the buyer of those Saurian fighters. He flatly denied any knowledge of the sale at all. The fact that the mere name was so highly safe-guarded even after ten long years sent chills down her spine.

Grey was a capable and patient negotiator, but Cidra could feel his frustration growing. They weren't going to get anywhere this way. Time for a more direct approach. Time to find Bohr's office.

Cidra politely excused herself from the table, using the auspice of a lav trip to freshen up. She was fully aware of Bohr's lecherous gaze as she walked out. He had barely concealed his carnal desire all evening, staring exclusively at her breasts. Sil seemed unaffected by the blatant conduct, obediently holding her silence.

Grey was another story. Only Bohr seemed ignorant of Grey's extreme displeasure simmering just below the surface. Cidra suspected, under different circumstances, Bohr would find himself in serious trouble.

Silently, Cidra headed in the general direction of Bohr's office. The hallways were a maze of walls and doors, with no apparent pattern. Between the dark, earthen walls and sporadic lighting, it was nearly impossible for her to see anything.

It didn't take her long to realize that her chances of finding Bohr's office were small. Just as she was about to turn back towards the dining hall, she froze. Her danger sense triggered. She spun around to find Bohr staring icily at her.

"Are we lost?" he asked with a lewd smile, his green skin dark and menacing.

"I must have missed a turn. The lighting is very dim." She obligingly lowered her eyes and managed a faint smile with all the humility she was willing to give Bohr--which wasn't much.

He suddenly stepped forward and trapped her between him and the wall, his tongue flicking around her furiously. She backed up instinctively, stunned by his swiftness. But disgust and anger followed with a vengeance. She glared directly into his glowing eyes, throwing humility to the wind.

"I've always wanted to claim a fiery human female," he said leering down at her cleavage. His luminous, yellow eyes slitted. "I shall thoroughly enjoy this." He grasped both her arms tightly with amazing strength and moved closer to her. A wave of repulsion swept over her when his tongue flicked over her, tasting the bare skin of her breasts.

She spoke crisply. "Let go of me *now*."

The corner of Bohr's reptilian mouth raised in amusement.

"Back off, Bohr. She's mine."

Bohr's head snapped around. Cidra saw Grey standing behind him, a dark, looming figure backlit by the distant dining hall.

The Saurelian stared at him for a long moment as if gauging his opponent's size and strength. Finally, he said, "She's only a female. You humans trade females all the time."

Grey's face was deep in the shadows, but his voice came through low and deadly. "Not this female."

"Not even for a name?"

Cidra's eyes widened. *The name.* He would give them the name for her. A sickening shiver rolled through her.

Her eyes flashed to Grey. Even in silhouette, she could tell he was furious, on the threshold of explosion. Fists clenched, body coiled, and much, much too still. Looking back at Bohr's cocky grin, she realized the Saurelian had more arrogance than brains.

"Not even for a name. Release her." Grey took a step forward. Bohr didn't move. War was declared.

Cidra made the decision. Grey was still healing. She had no doubts he'd win a brawl with Bohr. But at this rate, she'd never get her hands on the man.

Without hesitation, she brought one knee sharply up into Bohr's groin with enough power to lift him to his toes. He released her immediately and crumpled to the floor, groaning all the way.

Grey stepped into the light, crossed his arms, and leaned his shoulder against the wall. "You're lucky she got to you before I did. I wouldn't have stopped there."

Cidra made no move, leaving Bohr rolling helplessly on the floor between her and Grey.

"Did I ever tell you about Saurelian law, Captain? Civil law, rules of claim, penalties, and punishments?" Cidra glowered down at Bohr as he fought to breathe.

"No, I don't believe you did," answered Grey, playing along. The fierce rage that had gripped him when he saw Bohr's tongue flick over Cidra began to dissipate. He could have killed the man with his bare hands. The bastard didn't know it, but he owed Cidra his life.

Cidra continued as if no one was writhing in pain at her feet. "It's very interesting. Females on Saurel have little power, however, once she is claimed by a male, total commitment is required by both parties. If a male is caught claiming another female, the law is on her side."

Bohr's head shot up. He stared wide-eyed at Cidra.

"While he is sleeping or otherwise occupied, she can make sure he never claims another female as long as he lives. It's usually quite a surprise for the husband--one minute he's a male, the next...." She grinned in satisfaction.

Grey kept his gaze steady, fighting a flinch any red-blooded male would have made. "Sounds extremely painful, not to mention depressingly permanent."

Bohr looked at him with desperation. "You won't tell Sil, will you? She'd do it tonight. I know her. And she'd enjoy it, too."

Grey only raised his eyebrows. "Cidra does carry your scent now, and she does have a witness." He shrugged in mock resignation.

Bohr scowled at him. Then at Cidra and finally slumped in surrender.

"What do you want?" he mumbled gruffly.

Grey and Cidra exchanged a triumphant look.

"You know what we want."

Bohr muttered, "Information." He took a deep breath. "The name of the buyer was Plass. I never met him or heard from him again. We conducted all our business over subspace."

"Was he working alone or for someone else?" Grey questioned, hoping for a more recognizable name.

Bohr shrugged. "I don't know. He never mentioned anyone else. In fact, he didn't say much at all." He painfully staggered to his feet, leaning against the wall. "That's all I have."

"It's enough. Appreciate your cooperation, Bohr." Grey slid over to Cidra's side.

"I have your promise, not a word to Sil, right?" Bohr begged.

"I always keep my word. By the way, if you're so worried about Sil, may I suggest you give her the respect she deserves. You might sleep easier. Extend our thanks for a lovely meal. I think we'll call it a night. And stay away from Cidra. She won't save you next time."

Ignoring Bohr's baffled expression, he took Cidra's arm gently and headed back to their chamber.

Cidra smiled up at him brightly. He could feel the satisfaction of their victory flowing through her, see the exhilaration in her eyes but the man in him saw something more. He saw a woman's hunger. The hallway felt like it would never end.

Finally he escorted her through their chamber door. Once inside, she pulled away from him and headed directly for the lav.

Grey stood empty-handed and confused.

CHAPTER ELEVEN

"Cidra?"

He heard water running in the basin. She re-appeared with a wet cloth and began rubbing her arms with it. He watched the trail of water glisten on her skin, heard the blood thrumming through his veins.

Glancing up at him, she explained. "Bohr's scent. I can still smell it." Then she paused, wondering if Grey would find that fact disgusting. Her eyes searched his face, but the only emotion she found made her want to melt. Looking down, she continued to wash her arms.

She didn't realize he'd moved until he gently pried the cloth from her hand.

"I'll do that." His voice was husky and heavy. The heat from his body wrapped around her, drawing hers out, mingling and sinuous.

She watched in detached fascination as he started with her hands. He swabbed a finger with the cloth and pressed the clean fingertip to his lips. Cidra drew a shuddering breath as each finger enjoyed the same treatment. Then he wiped and kissed each palm and moved up her arms. Long, lingering, hot kisses followed the cool wet trail of the water. By the time he reached her shoulders, she was leaning back against the wall for support.

Cidra closed her eyes. Moisture skimmed along her throat and across her collarbone. She thought steam would surely rise. Gentle kisses followed, his warm breath sending shivers down her spine.

Then he stopped. She opened her eyes to find the cloth in his fist hovering inches from her throat and over her breasts. His eyes were dark, fathomless, and locked onto hers. She knew what he was doing--giving her one last chance to run.

"There'll be no going back, Cidra." It was little more than a raspy warning.

The slow smile that touched her lips gave him all the sanction he needed. Lucid thought evaporated.

Grey squeezed the cloth. One drop at a time rolled down her

chest and disappeared between her breasts. A soft moan escaped her lips as he laid the cloth to her chest and followed the water's trail.

Holding the cloth in place, he reached for the fastener in the back of the sheath dress she wore. Blue gazar slid lazily to a puddle on the floor. She stood before him wearing only white silky panties. He couldn't move, couldn't think at all.

Her deep breathing lifted her breasts to him. With intense concentration, he drew the cloth down and circled each nipple, calling them to hard attention. His hands shook as he passed the cloth over one tip. Cidra gripped his wrist tightly, her fiery eyes met his, demanding and turbulent.

No longer willing nor able to prolong the game, he pulled her roughly to him and closed his mouth over hers. The cloth dropped to the floor, forgotten. She met his ravenous hunger with her own, opening her lips for him in a frenzy of blind desire.

He sucked in air when she slid her arms around his neck, tangled her fingers in his hair and pressed her body against his. A low growl escaped his lips. This time she was ready for him. He hadn't expected so much passion. Heat roared through him like a supernova. Her unexpected urgency fueled the fire, igniting a deep, rumbling groan.

Reveling in her effect on him, she slid her hands down his strong neck and across his broad shoulders. There was so much of him. She wanted to explore it all.

His kiss took on new urgency while his hands moved over her, possessing and claiming. She dug into his shoulders, demanding more, need conquering fear. Grey's warm fingers glided down her back and rested firmly on her bottom, pulling her against his burning arousal. Stunned by his size and hardness, she trembled in anticipation and want.

She had always been in full control of her mind and body, but suddenly she felt swept up in a violent whirlwind she couldn't begin to conquer.

Grey's kisses deepened as his hands moved up to her breasts, cupping them gently in each large palm. Sliding his mouth down, he whispered against her throat. "Be mine, Cidra. Be my mate."

She tipped her head back, struggling to get a decent breath of air under his onslaught.

"Yes." It was a gasp of surrender. He was right. There was no other choice. This was their destiny. Unstoppable, unavoidable, inevitable. Just like the gypsy wings.

Grey knelt, wrapped his arms around her waist and pressed his face to her stomach. He lifted her straight up and carried her to the bed. Laying her down, he covered her completely. She felt his unconcealed desire straight to her bones. She needed more. *Now.* She arched her soft body against his hard body and heard him swear.

Cidra fumbled to unfasten his shirt. He brushed her hands aside and yanked it off impatiently. Her hands stroked his bare chest, reveling in sleek muscles and hard planes. When she kissed his throat, a soft growl erupted deep in his chest. He rolled off and rid himself of his pants.

Grey came back to her and slipped one strong leg between her thighs. He moved his mouth down to a delicate nipple and sucked gently, his hot, rapid breath enflaming her skin. Distracted by the sensation, she jumped when his hand reached down to the silken panties and tugged at them. She was in no condition to help him. Frustration finally won out as he tore them off. Moving to her other breast, he mumbled something to her about another apology.

Whatever he said, she missed it. Those masterful hands were on the move again.

Grey heard Cidra's gasp as he explored the fine, soft tangle of hair between her thighs. He pressed his head to her breast, momentarily stunned by the wetness and heat. She was ready for him and it threatened to send him over the edge. Clamping down on his own runaway desire, he forced himself to continue with the scene he had replayed in his mind a thousand times in the last few days.

Cidra closed her eyes, lost in the wealth of sensations rushing through her. His mere touch left wild fire in its wake. A chaotic flow of heat and passion fused together in strange union.

"Grey!" she called as fire burned from very her core, coiling and tightening to an unbearable point.

"Let it take you, Cidra." His mouth returned to hers while his fingers continued the gentle assault, pulling her towards her climax.

Unable to stop it, she allowed the moment to vanquish her self-control, crying out in a half-sob. Pressure unleashed with frightening force in wave after wave.

His control near its limit, he slipped between her legs and

positioned himself against her, waiting for her to recover.

"Look at me Cidra," he demanded softly. She opened her eyes dreamily and startled at the raw, animal desire in his face.

"I promise this will be the last time I ever hurt you." With that he surged into her and stopped. She was more stunned by the tightness than the pain. He felt so large inside her, she was afraid to move.

"Breathe, Cidra. Relax. Trust me."

His big body shuddered with the effort. Sweat glistened over his entire body. She could feel the leash he held onto, loved him for the struggle it took. Cidra finally exhaled, allowing her body to relax. She trusted him, with her life, with her love.

She softened her fierce grip on his shoulders and heard the release of his own breath. Cidra felt him tremble as he began to move slowly, thoroughly, beautifully.

She closed her eyes and concentrated on his heat, the smell of him, the power in him. He was pure male muscle and strength. Anticipating his rhythmic thrusts, she pulled him into her with increasing enthusiasm. The coil tightened again. This time she welcomed it, her cry filling the chamber.

Although he heard her, he was blind to the world around him, connected body to body, soul to soul. If he could capture this moment in time, he'd die a happy man. He finally let loose the last remnants of restraint and buried deep inside her one final time as his body screamed in liberation.

* * * *

Commander Plass stood still and silent in the thunderous grip of dejá vu. Although the ship had changed and the crew's faces were different, the view was the same as it had been over ten years ago. The planet of Saurel sat squarely in his ship's main viewport.

Expunger was a superior d'Hont espionage starship, capable of camouflaging itself to its surroundings and negating any scans that might detect its presence. Plass always preferred to study his quarry before taking action. It was a strategy that served him well and kept him alive.

Before leaving Dakru, Plass had commandeered the ship and hand-picked the crew. He now worked for himself. He was determined to uncover the truth, the reason why Tausek lied and then dismissed him. Locating Grey Stone's ship in orbit around Saurel confirmed his suspicions.

He recalled standing in this exact spot ten short years ago, negotiating a contract for twenty Saurelian fighters with a broker named Bohr. Plass had chosen the man based on his willingness to sell to a client he had never and would never meet. The transaction had been covert with no hard documents to support it. Just the way Tausek had ordered it.

They just happened to be the same ships used in Tausek's attack on the refugees. The same refugee attack that coincided with the Dakru shipment. The same Dakru shipment detailed in the files accessed by someone on Stone's ship. The same ship Plass had tracked to Saurel. Plass hadn't become the d'Hont Commander by believing in luck, miracles or coincidences.

The footsteps behind Plass jarred him back to the present. He turned to face his First Lieutenant.

"Commander Plass." The officer addressed him with a perfect salute. The boyish face looked out of place inside a d'Hont uniform.

Plass nodded once. "Report, Lieutenant Fiske."

The young officer squared his shoulders. "We have confirmed that Stone and Faulkner are meeting with Bohr as you suspected. The tracking device has been attached to Stone's K12 jet. We should be able to follow them even at hyperspeed. Do you wish us to detain them?"

"That won't be necessary. We need more information before we take that step." Plass' attention turned back to Saurel.

"Yes, sir. Will there be anything else?" Lieutenant Fiske asked.

Plass nodded. "Inform Major Berman that I would like to speak with him immediately in my private quarters. That will be all."

The young Lieutenant acknowledged the order and departed.

Plass clenched his jaw. Stone knew about the ships. That was the only explanation for his meeting with Bohr. Treasure hunters had no need for Saurelian fighters. If he knew about the ships, he probably knew who purchased them by now. The only connection between those ships, that refugee attack, and the Dakru shipment was Tausek. Directly or indirectly, he was the common denominator.

Plass stared at Saurel one more time before heading to his quarters, wondering what else Stone knew.

* * * *

Cidra felt the weight of oppression lift as the K12 breached Saurel's atmosphere. They had bid a hasty farewell, with Bohr more than a little anxious to be rid of them. Cidra noted he never left them alone with Sil for even a moment. The thought of Bohr shaking in his boots over a mere female finally prompted a huge grin.

Grey glanced up from the transport controls curiously. "What's so funny?"

"I think Bohr has a whole new respect for females." Cidra didn't try to hide her victory.

Grey shared her shameless grin. "I couldn't have done better myself."

She blushed at his open admiration. He believed in her, respected her abilities. "Thank you."

A long silence filled the small cabin while Grey set the K12 on autopilot to rendezvous with *Calíbre*.

Grey folded his arms across his chest and stared out into space. "What are you going to do once we find the missing shipment and clear your father's name?"

Cidra's eyebrows raised. "My, so optimistic." She smiled sweetly. "You make it sound easy."

Grey shrugged. "It's only a matter of time. It always is. I want to know what your intentions are once we've completed this mission."

His sober expression suddenly alarmed her.

"My intentions? I work for you, remember? Don't you want me to stay on?"

Grey didn't take his eyes off the expanse of deep space in front on him. "I more or less forced you to come with me. I'm giving you a choice now. You're strong enough to take care of yourself. You don't need anyone to watch over you. I have a right to know what your plans are."

Cidra stared at him incredulously. "Are you serious? Do you really think I'd have agreed to come with you if I didn't want to? I already made my choice, Grey, whether you realize it or not. I'm not leaving unless you throw me out."

Grey swiveled his seat around to face her, his expression serious, his voice ominous. "I'd never have the strength to throw you out, love."

"I'm more than your lover. I'm your mate or have you forgotten?" Cidra clipped, unable to curb her rising indignation.

His face hardened. "I haven't forgotten. I meant every word. I just wanted to make sure you understood what it meant."

Cidra threw her hands up in the air, admitting defeat. "Then tell me Grey, what does it mean?"

"It means you're with me," he said in a low, steely voice. "This is my life, my livelihood. I'm not going back to Avion. I'm not settling down on Vaasa or any other planet. We're out here, together. If you choose to stay, everything I have is yours. The good, the bad, and everything in between. No more, no less. Now do you understand?"

Cidra sat in silence, dazed. "Grey, don't *you* understand? I have no choice." Her voice dropped to a whisper. "I love you."

Cidra watched Grey's stunned expression with utter surprise. He acted as if he'd never heard those words before. Maybe he never had.

His anger melted, his arms reached for her. He pulled her out of her seat and across his lap, taking her face in his hands. He nuzzled and kissed her gently. Cidra knew he hadn't said the words, but she could taste them on his lips. It was another step toward trust. For him, love and trust were tied together. He couldn't give one without the other.

She felt the fire build with every kiss until it was all passion, all heat, all Grey. His hands moved up and down her spine, around her bottom, up her waist, finally resting under her breasts. His thumbs slid across her nipples, tugging at the passion deep within her. He opened the front of her shirt, baring her breasts to his plundering. The kiss deepened in quiet charge. His hand slipped down between her thighs demanding entrance. She gasped as his other hand snagged the fastener of her pants and released them deftly.

"Uh, Grey?"

"Yeah," he mumbled distractedly, his breathing becoming rough. He lifted her slightly and tugged her pants down her legs.

"I don't think the K12 was designed for this."

He nipped her jaw. "It was designed by a man."

She blinked several times, struggling with his logic and laughed. "Are you telling me that all men think about is one thing?" Her voice broke as he lifted and spread her legs to straddle him. She almost didn't hear his reply when he plunged his fingers deep into her heat.

"No, but it's a close second to everything else," he murmured against her throat.

Her breathing increased to match his as she slid her hands down his taut abdomen to where his pants strained. She loved this honest reaction from him, reveled in her own power. She traced the bulging outline with her fingertips, enticing a low, feral growl from him.

His fingers flicked and taunted her relentlessly. She almost purred. "I see it's a close second for you, too."

He raised his head, meeting her eyes straight on with trapped fire. "When you're around it's the first thing on my mind."

He punctuated the statement with a possessive, lingering kiss as he single-handedly freed himself. Recklessly, he impaled her on him while she threw her head back and moaned.

He gripped her hips and set them in rhythm, losing himself in the wonder of her body. Deep space formed the backdrop behind her with *Calíbre* glinting in the distance. He realized his world was perfect.

* * * *

"How did you get Bohr to give up the buyer's name?" Barrios squeezed himself into a chair at the table in Grey's office.

"Cidra used her people skills." Grey winked at Cidra, who smiled back, flushing slightly.

Barrios frowned. "I thought Saurel was a patriarchal society. Women are barely permitted to speak."

"Believe me, it wasn't her words that spoke for her." Grey laughed and shook his head.

Barrios gave Grey a confused look and shrugged. He leaned back in the chair, pushing it to its limits. "Plass. That name sounds familiar, but I just can't place it."

"I can." Decker stood in the doorway. "And you're not going to believe it."

All eyes turned to him as he sauntered over and settled himself into one of the chairs with a graveness that filled the room. Grey knew Decker to be well above theatrics. From the look on his face, his sources had come up with something big.

"Plass is the Commander for the d'Hont. He reports directly to Tausek. Always has." Decker shot Cidra a glance. "He keeps a very low, very discreet profile. He is Tausek's eyes and ears."

The room took on a suffocating silence while each occupant digested the discovery.

The first wave of emotion through Cidra was disbelief. "That can't be right," she gasped and turned to Grey. "Bohr must have lied to us."

Grey ran a hand through his hair. "I don't think Bohr lied. He was too scared."

The second wave of emotion was shock. "That could only mean that Tausek arranged the ambush himself." She nearly choked on the horror of her own words. "Why? What could he possibly gain?"

"Power," Barrios spoke stoically. "He engineered a plan certain to make himself a hero and Dakru's next ruler. I don't know why I didn't see it before."

Decker wondered aloud. "How did he get his men to destroy the vaccine in the first place? It was their only chance to stop the plague from killing millions of their own people."

Barrios shook his head. "I can't imagine they would. Unless they didn't realize the cortege was carrying the vaccine. Who knows what Tausek told them? He was the Commander then, he gave the orders. They would have followed him anywhere."

Grey nodded and rubbed his chin thoughtfully. "It makes sense. He would have known precisely where the Galena would be dropping out of hyperspace. All he had to do was sit and wait. They never knew what hit them."

The third wave of emotion was indescribable. A foul wrenching in her gut. The truth was more horrible than she could have imagined. When she finally spoke, her words were deadly, laced with fury. "It all comes back to Tausek. He ambushed the shipment. He persecuted my father. He killed my family. He condemned the Kin-sha. He blackened Avion. He destroyed *everything*."

Grey addressed her warily. "Don't get any crazy ideas, Cidra. We're all in this together, remember?"

"I'm getting a few crazy ideas myself," Barrios spat.

"Look, we'll deal with him, but we need to work together to do it," Grey ordered. "Is that clear?"

Cidra closed her eyes, fighting for self-control. Grey had a point. They needed to do this right. There was no other way to get to Tausek. He was too well-protected. She would have to be content to let the truth convict him.

Still, there was always a chance. Hope welled up inside her. There was always a chance he would make a mistake, leave an opening. She glanced over at Barrios. If the opportunity ever arose, she knew they'd be standing side by side to destroy Tausek.

"Perfectly clear, Captain," Cidra replied for both of them.

Grey's eyebrows raised at the use of his title. The formality of her answer surprised and worried him. How one woman could be so full of passion one minute and so deadly the next was beyond him. He wasn't about to let her run loose.

Decker cleared his throat conspicuously. "What next, boss?"

"Next, we find that shipment. If we can recover even part of it, we'll have all the evidence we need to go after Tausek."

Cidra eyes widened. "You know where it is?"

"I think so. It's the only place that feels right," Grey said with an easy smile. "Ever heard of a planet called Courf?"

* * * *

Commander Plass sat behind his desk in the center of his private quarters and awaited Major Berman's arrival.

The Major had been with the d'Hont when Tausek had turned the average military unit into a formidable, deadly force. Berman had lost most of his family to the plague, surviving that living nightmare and dedicating himself to the d'Hont. It was a history that tied and knitted the d'Hont force tightly together. A bond joined in blood.

Berman's conviction and excellent flying record had earned him the command of the d'Hont airborne fleet. It was one of the reasons Plass had chosen him for this mission. The other reason was even more compelling.

Major Berman just happened to be part of the mission that destroyed the plague-laden refugee ships ten years ago.

Plass glanced at the time. The Major was apparently in no hurry to obey Plass' summon and he knew why. The entire *Expunger* crew knew a Faulkner was within reach. Each felt the overwhelming pull of revenge. He knew he had his hands full keeping that vengeance at bay.

As if that wasn't enough, Plass had a direct order from Tausek to find and kill Cidra Faulkner no matter the cost. He raised a corner of his mouth. It was an order he had every intention of carrying out, but Cidra Faulkner would die only after Plass had his answers.

The door sensor chimed and admitted a cavalier Major Berman. Plass held back a smirk. Despite the gray hair and growing paunch, the Major hadn't lost any of his brashness to age. He walked with the arrogance and confidence of a seasoned military man.

"Have a seat, Major Berman." Commander Plass motioned to the chair on the other side of the desk.

The Major scowled but said nothing as he seated himself.

Plass raised his eyebrows at the blatantly disrespectful display and steepled his fingers before him.

"Is there something you wish to say, Major?"

Major Berman shifted in his chair. "No, sir. Just wondering when we are going to see some action. I understand the Faulkner woman has been located. I eagerly await your orders to move in."

Plass leveled his gaze at his subordinate. "My order will come when the time is right."

The Major jumped to the edge of his chair. "My fighters are ready, sir. My men and I can take out Stone's ship in minutes."

Plass placed both his hands on his desk and leaned far forward. "If that is the decision I make, you will be the first to know." He could see the frustration simmering just below the surface and continued, "That's not the reason I've called you here. There's been some discrepancy in our information files. I need you to clarify a few details for me."

The quick diversion seemed to take Major Berman by surprise. He loosened his death grip on the arms of his chair.

Plass leaned back in his chair. "Ten years ago, you were a pilot on an attack of a plague-infested refugee ship that attempted entry into Dakru. Do you recall that mission?"

Major Berman frowned slightly. "Yes, sir. The mission was led by then Commander Tausek. There were twenty of us altogether. We took out the enemy without incident."

Plass asked, "Was there anything unusual about that mission?"

The Major rubbed his chin thoughtfully. "Not really. The orders came directly from Tausek. We never had any communications with the refugees. I believe Tausek ordered all transmissions blocked."

"How was the attack initiated?" Plass asked calmly, hiding his increasing curiosity.

The Major dropped his hands back to the armrests. "We waited for them to drop out of hyperspace."

Plass' heart thumped in his chest. "You knew they were coming?"

The other man shook his head. "We didn't. Tausek did. He gave us the exact coordinates. We set up an ambush and attacked them the second they dropped out of hyperspace." He smiled. "They never knew what hit them."

"How many ships in the convoy?" Plass inquired quietly.

"One large freighter and four small fighters." The Major paused, drawing on his memory. "I was somewhat surprised that a bunch of dirty refugees could secure such advanced equipment. They did manage to give us quite a fight. I wasn't anticipating that. Tausek must have known. Otherwise, he wouldn't have used so many of our men."

"Yes." Plass kept his voice steady under a crush of emotion. "That is surprising."

Oblivious to his superior's state, Berman boasted, "The only other item I can add is that there wasn't a trace of those refugees or the plague they carried when we finished."

Plass sat stiffly. "Very efficient indeed, Major. I know your pilots are the best, the pride of the d'Hont. Your loyalty is unquestioned, as is your execution of orders. I fully expect that performance to continue throughout this mission."

Silence hung heavily between the two men.

"You have my word, Commander."

Plass smiled a humorless smile. "We won't lose her again, Major."

"Will that be all, Commander?"

"Yes. Dismissed."

The Major stood, turned on his heel and walked out the door.

Plass sat and stared after him, his mind racing. The pieces were clicking into place. He was now positive the convoy destroyed was not a bunch of ragtag, plague-infested refugees.

There was only one convoy destined for Dakru that could have matched the description given to him by Major Berman. Only one way that Tausek could have known precisely where they would have dropped out of hyperspace. There was only one reason why Stone would have accessed the Avion to Dakru shipment files. Only one purpose for Cidra Faulkner to come out of ten years of hiding and expose herself to certain death.

All the clues pointed to a single inevitable, terrible conclusion. Tausek had destroyed the Avion vaccine shipment bound for Dakru. It finally made sense.

Realization hit him in a wave. Tausek had arranged the destruction of the shipment, orchestrated the slander of Avion and the Kin-sha, ordered the cold-blooded deaths of Faulkner and his family, and stood by as millions of Dakruians died.

Anger and rage built in Plass as he gripped the arms of the chair. It had all been a lie. Tausek alone had handed down the death sentences of countless innocents.

Plass clenched his teeth and brought himself under control. As much as he wanted to head back to Dakru and face his illustrious ruler, it would be a foolhardy effort. Tausek had sent him away for a reason. The truth was at hand and Tausek had felt it. But it would take more than accusations to bring him to justice.

First, Plass had to verify his hypothesis. Then he would need evidence. Irrefutable evidence and enough of it to convince even Tausek's most loyal supporters of his atrocious deed.

He spun his chair around to face the floor-to-ceiling viewport in his quarters and stared into deep space, pulling his thoughts together. The Faulkner woman was the key. She had launched the events into motion. Plass nodded absently, he would have to capture her. Alive. That would be quite a feat considering how much this crew wanted her dead. But he needed to find out what she knew. Obviously, she was aware of the Saurelian fighters. She must know more.

All Plass had to do was keep her alive long enough to find out what.

* * * *

Grey studied the information on a micropad in his private quarters, grateful for Cidra's offer to collect dinner. He found it increasingly difficult to concentrate when she was around. He caught himself smiling.

When his room comm chimed softly, he reached over and activated the link. "Yes, Decker."

"Sir, I have a subspace communication for you from Rourke Jaccar. It's coming through on a secured link." Decker sounded concerned.

Grey frowned and prepared to give the ensuing conversation his full attention. Rourke rarely took those kinds of precautions. "Send it through."

Rourke's voice boomed through the comm. "Hey, Stone. How are you feeling these days? Still in good hands?"

"You have no idea." Grey grinned.

Rourke laughed on the other end. "I can just imagine. I'll bet it's been really tough."

"Why the secured link, Rourke?"

"I've got some information for you," Rourke began. "You may not even want your crew to hear this, especially Cidra."

"What kind of information?" Grey already had a pretty good idea.

"Word on the street is that the d'Hont are looking for Cidra. There's no explanation going around other than they want her badly--dead or alive."

Grey didn't reply.

"What is going on?" Rourke prodded. "Why would the d'Hont

be looking for Cidra? From what I can tell, the woman is a saint."

Grey ran a hand through his hair. "She is, but you're still better off not knowing what's going on."

"Then you knew about this?" Rourke asked in disbelief. "They know who you are, Grey. They know she's with you. Do you have any idea what the d'Hont will do when they find her and you?"

"I'm afraid I do," Grey said grimly.

"Maybe you should hide her for a while until this blows over," Rourke offered.

Grey shook his head, even though he knew Rourke couldn't see him. "Not a chance. She's staying with me. She's my mate."

A long, low whistle came through the comm.

"I never thought I'd see the day." Rourke chuckled. "You couldn't have picked a nice, quiet Vaasa girl, huh? Leave it to you to find the most wanted woman in the galaxy."

Grey couldn't let that one go. "Sleeping alone, by any chance?"

Rourke laughed outright. "Yeah I'm sleeping alone, but I'm alive. Can't say the same for you if the d'Hont find you. Is there any place you can hide *Calíbre*?"

"Can't do that either," Grey came back. "But this does move up my timetable a little. I appreciate the warning."

Rourke waited on the other end and finally asked, "Stone, what have you gotten yourself into?"

"You wouldn't believe it if I told you," Grey mumbled. "Don't worry. We'll be all right."

Rourke grunted. "I have my doubts about you, but I know Cidra can take care of herself. She took out one of Wex's giants with two kicks. If I were you, I wouldn't make her mad."

"That's the plan," Grey agreed. "Thanks for the update, Rourke."

"I'll keep my ears open for you. If you need any help or somewhere to hide, you know how to find me. And give Cidra my best. I want to stay on her good side." Rourke laughed.

"Got it." Grey cut the communication and closed his eyes. It wasn't a surprise, but he hadn't expected the d'Hont to close on them so soon. He hit the comm unit and hailed the bridge.

"Decker here."

Grey lowered his voice. "I want you to make the hyperspace jump to Courf as soon as possible."

There was a pause.

"Trouble?" Decker asked in an equally low voice.

"The worst kind," Grey admitted. "If we don't get out of here now, we're going to have company. The d'Hont are breathing down our necks."

Decker swore on the other end. "Sorry about that. They must have tracked my break into the Dakru computer systems."

"Could be. But somehow I doubt it. Just get us into hyperspace. Then we need to make some contingency plans for the rest of this mission." Grey paused. "One more thing. Lock out the K12 so no one can use it."

Decker balked. "Why? Who would steal it?"

Grey stared at the door to his quarters thoughtfully. "Just a hunch. Humor me."

"Yes, sir." Decker signed off.

Grey leaned back in his chair and rubbed his face roughly with both hands. He wasn't looking forward to telling Cidra about this latest obstacle. He already knew what her reaction would be.

They were so close he could feel it. Courf was the right place, he was sure of it. He felt the pull of the hyperspace jump just as Cidra appeared at the door.

CHAPTER TWELVE

Cidra stood motionless holding the dinner tray and staring at his somber expression. "We weren't supposed to jump until tomorrow."

Slowly he rose, walked to her, and took the tray. After placing it on a table, he wrapped both of her hands in his. Cidra watched with growing dread.

"We have a problem." His mouth was set in a hard line. "The d'Hont know about you. They were looking for you on Vaasa."

Her mind frantically worked over the implications. She drew in a deep breath and nodded once in acceptance. "Then they know about you, too. And *Calíbre*."

"Probably. I have a feeling they're close. That's why I moved up the jump."

Cidra gazed into the beautiful face of the man she loved, memorizing every feature. His hands squeezed hers. She closed her eyes, remembering what wondrous pleasure those hands could reign over her body. She would miss him. Her life would be empty without him. Her heart shattered but there was no other choice. She had to leave or they would all die. Grim resolution replaced sadness. She opened her eyes and tried to pull away from him.

As if he had expected it, his grip tightened, and he pulled her against his body. "You're not going anywhere, Cidra."

Her anger flashed. "Don't you realize what this means? How can you put your crew in danger for my sake, Grey? Don't you care what happens to them? You know if the d'Hont find us, they'll kill you all because of me." She tried again to yank her hands free. "I won't allow it."

"You have no choice. I'm not letting you go," he said as she struggled in earnest. The battle was waged. He couldn't help but smile. She'd give him a fight.

She wrestled a hand free and shoved him with it.

Grey fended her off. There was no way she was leaving him now. They were too close and he needed her too much. He spun her around and trapped her in his arms from behind, careful not to hurt her.

Cidra had no such reservations as she growled in frustration, fighting for freedom.

He spoke into her ear. "There's no way off the ship. The K12 is locked out."

"I don't believe you." She jammed her heel onto his foot and with a grunt Grey released her. Cidra lunged for the door, but he tackled her to the floor. She squirmed and wiggled under him as he positioned himself over her, face to face. He pressed down on her with his full weight, throwing his legs across hers. Then he snagged both her wrists and pinned them on either side on her head. Kin-sha or not, he could conquer her by sheer weight, muscle, and bulk alone. They were both breathing hard, eyes locked, neither willing to give in.

"I said, you're not going anywhere, and I meant it."

After a few more futile attempts, Cidra dropped her head back on the floor and closed her eyes in defeat. Her words came out in a series of shudders. "Grey, please. Don't do this to your crew. Don't do this to me. I can't bear it."

Grey gave silent thanks, knowing he'd won this one. He shifted to lighten his weight on her. "I'll keep the crew safe. I give you my word that I will take every precaution."

"And who's going to protect you?" She opened her eyes, her

voice breaking.

"You will." He smiled down on her. "You took out Wex's hired help. I couldn't ask for better protection than that."

Cidra rolled her head from side to side wearily. "Wex's hired killer isn't the same as facing the d'Hont, and you know it. You've never seen them in action." Her voice caught. "They are ruthless and cruel. And more than that, they are very, very good at what they do. Two Kin-sha aren't going to be any match for a ship full of d'Hont."

While she spoke, Grey rained gentle kisses over her face and down her throat. He'd heard what she said and knew she was right. But there was no way he was going to let her face the d'Hont alone. He raised his head and looked into her eyes. "Let's hope it doesn't come to that. All we have to do is find that shipment and get back to Avion. Then it will be over. You'll be free. The Faulkner name will be cleared."

Tears spilled down the sides of her face. "I don't want you to die because of me, Grey."

The tears caught him off-guard, ripping at him, clawing at his throat. He closed his eyes and pressed his forehead to hers. He could barely get the words out. "I won't. And neither will you. I promise."

* * * *

"Commander, they've jumped to hyperspace." The Lieutenant's report rang out moments after *Calíbre* disappeared in a streak from *Expunger*'s main viewport. Plass smiled. The chase was on thanks to the tracking device attached to their K12 jet.

"Track and follow them, Lieutenant. Stay back a discreet distance." Plass noted the confused faces of his deck crew. They didn't understand his reluctance to seize Cidra Faulkner. He sighed and headed off the bridge. *Expunger* launched into hyperspace in a spectacular matrix of starlines that lit up the viewport behind him.

He would not offer them any explanation until he had Cidra Faulkner, until he possessed the irrefutable evidence he needed to bring down Tausek. For now, he was the Commander of the ship. The crew would obey his orders. He acknowledged there could come a point where that might not be enough.

If he couldn't convince the crew of Tausek's guilt, his life would be worth no more than hers. Over time, Tausek and the d'Hont had virtually become one entity, linked by blood and death and revenge. Plass saw clearly that the alliance was Tausek's absolute manipulation, giving him the force he needed to achieve his goal. They had been used. He had been used.

It was his responsibility and duty to expose Tausek for what he was. He only hoped he could do that without destroying the d'Hont as well.

* * * *

Decker groaned to no one in particular. "That's one mean, cold rock."

Accessed from the archives, a three-dimensional, miniature scale projection of Courf occupied the holo deck in front of him. Underneath, the slowly rotating planet scrolled its environmental, physical, and chemical properties.

"No wonder it's uninhabited. Not exactly paradise," Grey agreed. The statistics were not encouraging. He glanced at Cidra to see if she grasped the situation.

"According to the galactic chart records it has a minimal atmosphere. Oxygen is nil. Mainly gaseous carbon dioxide in the form of ice fog," Decker muttered. "I hate ice fog. Forget a visual search."

Cidra remained silent, studying the statistics somberly.

Grey kept his eyes on her. "They probably died on impact or shortly thereafter. It wouldn't have taken long."

She nodded in understanding, but the blue eyes that met his were brimming with unshed tears and the shadows of more death. A reminder that this entire affair had taken far too many lives.

Decker rattled along, totally oblivious. "It's going to be a challenge to find a crashed transport under all that fog, even for Coon. This planet is rough. Rilles, mountains, caverns, fissures." He shook his head. "It'll be a miracle if we find it at all. The only good thing is that it should be preserved exactly the way it was ten years ago. In cold storage."

Cidra paled. Grey changed the subject. "Can we get by with the survival suits?"

Decker nodded. "I think so. You're not going to be able to move real fast and whatever you do, don't puncture a hole in it. You won't last a second on that hunk of ice. Not even long enough to make it back to the K12." He did look at Cidra and immediately amended his blunt warning. "But the suits are pretty tough."

When she didn't respond, he cast Grey an apologetic look.

Grey hitched his head toward the door. Decker nodded and stood up. "If you need me, I'll be on the bridge." He walked out.

Cidra nodded automatically, her thoughts well beyond the current discussion. The transport crew was dead. Until now, she had held out a glimmer of hope that they had found a planet that could support life. That they had found a way to survive until someone could rescue them. One look at Courf and those hopes were dashed.

Grey didn't like the look on her face.

"It's going to be cold down there." He smiled at her. "We could share a suit."

Cidra's eyes focused on him with a start. Then she smiled as if she'd just seen him. "Let me guess. They were designed by a man?"

"How'd you know?" His smile grew. She was back and she was his.

She laughed. "I'm beginning to detect a pattern here."

"Actually, I think it's a matter of imagination and variety."

"Getting bored?"

Grey was already making his way around the table to where she sat.

"Cidra, we've barely begun." He pulled her into his arms, tilting her head back for a sizzling kiss that left them both breathless and wanting.

The room comm unit chimed. Once. Twice. Then one long, insistent chirp.

Grey broke off the kiss and growled, "I'm going to fire whoever that is." He reached around Cidra and activated the unit. "What!"

Decker cleared his throat. "Sorry, Captain. I thought you'd want this transmission. Rourke Jaccar. You can blame him for bad timing."

Grey stared wistfully at Cidra's lips. "Put him through."

A second of static preceded Rourke's cheerful voice. "Stone. Hope I interrupted something good."

"You did, you bastard. You owe me." Grey snagged Cidra's arm as she tried to leave and give him some privacy.

"You aren't going anywhere," he whispered in her ear.

Rourke gave a hearty laugh. "Ha. You should thank me for helping you pace yourself."

"My pace is perfect, thank you." He winked at Cidra. She gave him a slow smile and dropped back down into her chair.

"Well, you might want to speed it up a little, Stone. I just heard from a friend on Saurel that the d'Hont were keeping an eye on you."

All smiling stopped.

"They were on Saurel? When we were there?" Grey kept his eyes locked on Cidra's.

"I don't know if they were *on* Saurel, but they were detected off-planet. Far off-planet, running surveillance in a Class One cruiser. You've got your hands full with that ship." Rourke didn't sound optimistic.

Grey leaned against the table while his stomach did a tight pitch and roll. "Just one?"

Rourke choked. "Just one? Do you have any idea what those ships can do to you? Yeah, trust me. They only need one of them."

"Are they still there?"

"That I don't know, but I'll check into it," Rourke said. "I wish you'd tell me what is going on. I could help out."

Cidra shook her head emphatically. Grey held up a hand to agree.

"Sorry, Rourke. This game's a little too rough." Grey came back. "I'll let you play the next time."

"You are one stubborn bastard," Rourke grumbled.

Grey smiled. "I have my moments."

* * * *

"I don't like it a bit, Captain," Decker grumbled. "Not one bit."

"Neither do I." Barrios glared at Cidra. She refused to look at him and instead concentrated on her meal as they all sat around the dining table in *Calíbre*'s lounge.

"Those are direct orders," Grey stated. "Cidra and I go after the shipment in the K12 once we get to Courf. If the d'Hont show up, you take off. You won't do us any good if you are destroyed."

Decker slammed a hand on the table and silverware jumped. "They are going to kill you no matter what we do. We're not going to just fly off and leave you."

"You better." Grey's voice rose. "It's my ship. It's my call. With any luck, they will follow you."

"And if they don't, you'll be target practice," Barrios stormed.

Cidra piped up. "There is no other way. We have to use the K12. How did you think we were going to get the shipment in the first place? We have to go down there."

Barrios turned on Grey. "Exactly how close are the d'Hont, Stone?"

Grey dropped his fork on his plate, giving up on trying to eat. "Close. Word is they were just off Saurel at the same time we were. If the d'Hont wanted us dead, they had their chance then. A single Class One cruiser was sighted."

Decker grimaced at that bit of news and suggested, "Let me and Coon take the K12 down."

Grey shook his head. "This is our mission, not yours."

Decker frowned. "How did they know we were at Saurel to begin with?"

"Maybe it was a parting gift from our little spy," Grey said through clenched teeth. "Mora must have seen the schedule before she left."

"Well, they can't possibly know we're heading for a chunk-of-ice planet in the middle of nowhere," Decker said.

Grey blew out a breath. "I'm not taking any chances. Until I'm certain we lost them in hyperspace, this is the plan. At least if they find us, you can get help."

Barrios snorted. "What for? There won't be anything left to help."

Grey ignored the comment and gave Decker a hard look. "Don't even think about taking them on yourself. *Calíbre* is no match for a d'Hont cruiser. Just get out of there as fast as you can."

Cidra nodded and finally met Barrios' eyes. "You still have enough evidence to take back to Avion. At least enough to launch a full-scale investigation. If anything happens to you, the truth will never be told. That's all that matters."

"Forget it," barked Barrios. "Dead is dead, whether it's today or tomorrow. We'll never be able to get help in time to save you. Forget the whole thing. I don't care about any of it."

For the first time in her life, Cidra raised her voice to her old friend. "Well, I do care, Barrios. I can give you ten years worth of reasons why I care." Her last word rang out, leaving the dining room in an uncomfortable silence.

Barrios slumped back in his chair, emotions warring across his face. Cidra silently cursed herself a hundred different ways. "I'm sorry." She placed her hand over Barrios'. "Just promise me, you will see that the evidence gets back to Avion."

He stared at her hand, pursed his lips and nodded.

"It's settled." Grey resumed eating his cold dinner.

"Yes, sir. If that's all, I have work to do." Decker rose abruptly and exited the dining hall.

* * * *

The lav's water spray drizzled over her like a fine, misty rain. Cidra stood cocooned in a fog of steam. Taking advantage of *Calíbre*'s rec center had been a good idea. A hard run on the TrackMat was just what her body needed, but the solitude had given her mind too much time to think.

Tomorrow they would reach Courf. It was the end of the line. The entire mission came down to this.

If--Courf was the right planet.

If--they could find the transport.

If--the evidence was intact.

If--they could get it back to Avion before the d'Hont caught them.

If--anyone would listen.

It was still a long way from here to there. She sighed and did the only thing she could do--she pushed the doubts aside.

The water slid in rivulets down her. A body awakened. She let the spray stroke her, luxuriating in its intimate caress. Grey had done this to her, unchained the woman within. Touching her, tasting her, and drawing the heat from her very soul.

She washed up, skimming lightly over areas where Grey had lingered and worshipped with his warm hands, his devoted mouth, and adventurous tongue. There wasn't a spot on her body he'd missed in the past few days. She smiled a slow, satisfied smile.

He loved her. She could see it in his eyes, feel it in his touch. Someday he would say it to himself and to her. She only hoped they both lived long enough to hear the words.

A great sadness crushed her warm thoughts. Her hands stilled. He would die for her, there was no doubt in her mind. Die defending and protecting her, die fulfilling his promise to Syrus.

Sudden, painful tears mixed with the spray. The d'Hont were close. Grey wouldn't admit it, but his preparations were obvious. He sensed it. There was a very good chance that tonight might be their last night together. It drew a gut-wrenching cry from her. It had all been too short. Anger at the injustice surged through her. Not that she believed in justice, but just this once, she wanted to believe it existed. Wanted it for Grey, for herself, and their future. There was still so much she wanted to do.

She deactivated the spray and dried off quickly. She had to be with Grey. That single thought energized her as she dressed. She paused as another thought invaded, wondering if she had the courage to go through with it.

Cidra finished dressing and smiled all the way to his office. The door slid open. She stepped inside.

"I have a question for you."

Grey glanced behind him as Cidra's voice interrupted his study of the Courf's miniature scale projection in the holo deck. He had been too absorbed in the details to notice she had entered his office, never heard the door slide open and shut. The room was silent except for the subtle hum of equipment.

He wondered how long she'd been standing there watching him.

He straightened his back, rolled his shoulders, and turned to face her. "What question?"

She moved in closer, running her gaze over his body. "The night Rourke and I were looking for you on Vaasa, you were wearing a comm unit. Coon said it was your personal unit, but I never saw one on you." Her eyes met his with marked curiosity.

Grey smiled broadly. "That's because it's not on me. It's in me."

When her eyes widened, he laughed. "It's surgically embedded. That way I don't forget to put it on in the morning."

"Then how do you activate it?" Cidra asked, fascinated.

"That's a secret."

Cidra narrowed her eyes at him. "Where is it?"

He folded his arms over his chest. "That's a secret, too."

Cidra knew a challenge when she heard it. "Really. I'll bet I can find it."

Grey knew an opportunity when he saw it. "I'll bet you can't."

"You're on. Winner gets breakfast in bed tomorrow morning," Cidra laid down the stakes.

Grey smiled. Cidra in his bed. He was a winner either way. He shoved off the table and stood in front of her, his hands on his hips. "Deal. Search away."

Cidra smiled back. She began circling him slowly, scanning him from head to toe as if plotting her strategy. Her blatantly erotic appraisal had him rock hard in a flash.

"You'll tell me when I'm getting close?" she asked in a lazy, sultry voice.

"I'll tell you."

He watched her circle him again, watched as her eyebrow

raised at his unmistakable arousal. She stopped in front of him and went to work on his shirt, releasing the fasteners and tugging it off. He drew in a deep breath as her hands slid over his shoulders and smoothed down the fine, dark hair covering his arms. Retracing her path, she spread her fingers wide across his chest, raking the flesh lightly. Grey sighed and congratulated himself on his brilliant maneuver.

Her palms slid over the ridges and planes of his torso, her eyes shrouded in concentration. It wasn't until she ducked her head and licked one dark nipple that he understood who was really in control. His pulse quickened as his mind dulled.

"Am I close?" she murmured against his chest, kneading his pectorals with her fingers.

Grey's voice was husky. "Not yet." He felt her hum softly against him as she kissed and licked her way across his chest to the other nipple.

"Now?" she asked innocently, her warm breath feathering the sprinkle of chest hair. His breath caught when she nipped him lightly.

"No."

"Hmm, this could take some time," she said sweetly. Grey grimaced. She'd kill him for sure.

Her hands continued their delighted torture over his body, reveling in the splendor of the male form. Soft skin over hard muscle. She would never tire of it, never tire of the way he felt under her hands. Never tire of her own body's reaction and that wicked, wonderful hunger for him.

Cidra raised her head and kissed him full on the lips, her hands sliding around his waist. When Grey tried to slip his hands around her, she brushed them away. "No help from you. We had a deal remember," she whispered. Grey swore and deepened the kiss in frustration. Cidra moaned low in her throat.

Her hands traveled down his bare chest and slipped inside his pants. Grey sucked in air. Before he knew it, she had his pants undone and was pushing them down his legs. He dropped his head back and groaned aloud. He was definitely in trouble. A steamy sweat broke out all over his body.

Cidra felt the sudden change in him. He kept his word, giving her free run of his body, but it was costing him dearly as he battled for control. Raw desire shimmered from his body into hers. Her own control waned when she exposed the hard evidence of her effect on him. Wild fire raged within her even as she fought to dampen it.

Cidra tugged his pants to the floor. He stepped out of them without a thought. He couldn't think if he tried. She was kneeling before him, caressing his calves and legs with her hands and mouth. His breath hissed through his teeth, his body straining with urgency. He didn't know how much more of this sweet torment he could endure.

"Nothing here," she commented calmly against his thigh.

" 'Scuse me?"

Cidra laughed softly at his strangled response. "No comm unit yet."

He had beautiful legs, she thought as she traced the tense, steely muscles. A hunter's legs, full of stamina, endurance, and power. Cidra heard his succinct curse as she slid higher up his thighs. She could feel his heat, see his desire looming beside her. More than anything, she loved the way he wanted her.

Her hands moved up and gently captured him, stroking the engorged length of him. Grey's hands balled into tight fists. When she took him into her mouth, he growled as he braved the wet flames that licked and burned him. Every muscle in his body was pushed to the limit, trembling and twitching. Each breath expelled forcefully through flared nostrils. Her technique was unskilled and excruciating. Heaven help him, she learned fast. Experienced or not, she reduced him to a base sexual animal like no other woman.

"Am I close?" She rubbed her cheek against him.

Grey clenched his teeth. "No, but I am."

He reached down and hauled her to her feet. Her eyes were hooded, her curve of a smile sexy and languid as he undressed her in the same order she had disrobed him. Only much faster, much rougher. His face was dark and fierce, his motions jerky, his control lost. As soon as the last of her clothes were shed, he gripped her around the waist and set her on the edge of the table with the planet of Courf spinning behind her.

He pushed her legs far apart and thrust into her, a feral growl curling his lip. Cidra clung to his shoulders as he drove into her again and again. She wrapped her legs around him, pulling him closer, deeper. Raw, naked, powerful lust took them. Her climax was an explosion that careened through her body. With one final, violent lunge he buried himself in her and shuddered, ravaged mercilessly by his own release.

Slowly, the room came back into focus for him. He became

aware of the translucent glow of Courf's holo image and the low hum of equipment. Became aware of the smell and taste of his own sweat dripping down his face. Aware of the incredible woman whose legs wrapped around him, her head resting on his shoulder. She was tracing one of his earlobes with her finger. He hadn't died after all.

"You're close," he murmured in her ear.

He felt her smile against his neck. "I know," she whispered back. "Decker told me it was behind your left ear."

There was a beat of silence before Grey doubled over laughing.

CHAPTER THIRTEEN

"Last stop. The middle of nowhere. Thank you for flying *Calíbre* Starways," Coon joked.

Grey shielded his eyes against the brilliant light of the star lines that flooded *Calíbre*'s main viewport and bridge as they slipped out of hyperspace. After a few disoriented seconds, the galaxy appeared with its familiar star-sprinkled, black palette before them.

"Any company?" Grey asked.

"Scanning." Coon crisply tapped the console. "Nothing. We are all alone as far as the scanners can reach."

Grey nodded. "Good. I want to know the minute we are no longer alone." He shot Coon an all-business look. Coon smiled back wanly, his orders perfectly clear.

"Is that Courf straight ahead?" Cidra asked from behind Coon.

"That's it, sugar," Coon acknowledged. She smiled at the endearment. The man just grew on you.

"Pretty," she said. *Too beautiful to be a grave*, she thought. It was more crystalline than the holo image had portrayed and perfectly formed, almost artificial. The giant red sun behind it gave the planet a rosy, healthy glow--clever camouflage for its deadly environment. The forbidding, darkside facing them revealed the planet's true nature.

Coon's long whistle cut through the silence on *Calíbre*'s bridge.

Grey pulled his eyes away from the planet of Courf filling the main viewport and walked over to Coon's station.

"What's up?" Grey leaned over, looking at the displays on Coon's console. Courf's solar system appeared in miniature, hovering above the bridge's holo deck before them.

Coon chuckled softly and shook his head. "This is your lucky day, Captain. Would you believe there's a ship down on that rock that's emitting a weak but persistent distress signal?" He turned to Grey and smiled. "Looks like you did it again. I locked the coordinates into the K12. We can be out of here before dinner."

Grey didn't smile back. He didn't even blink. Coon tracked his eyes to holo image. "See something?"

"I don't know." Grey pointed to a section of miniature the solar system. "I thought I saw a shadow of some sort, a ghost. Then it disappeared."

Coon tapped the controls frantically, changing the filters and adjusting the frequencies to full capacity. He spoke as he worked. "In my experience, there's no such thing as ghosts. I can't see a thing. I don't like it."

Grey straightened. "Neither do I. That ghost just happens to be on the other side of the planet and conveniently blocked from sensor range. I don't suppose there are any transmission stations around here that we could bounce a signal off and get a look at it?"

Coon looked mortally wounded. "Don't you think I'd have done that by now? I'm not an idiot."

"Sorry," Grey apologized absently, deep in thought. "How long would it take for a surveillance probe to check it out?"

"Too long," Coon muttered. "At least twelve hours."

Grey shook his head. "You're right. Too long." He paused, fighting down the common sense that told him to retreat until they knew what was going on. "After Cidra and I depart, I want you to take *Calíbre* out of orbit above us. Hang back so you get a good view of any spacecraft rounding the planet."

"And what if we come face to face with a ghost?" Coon's voice raised an octave.

"Try not to get blown to bits before you jump to hyperspace," Grey replied.

Coon's mouth dropped open. "And just leave you here?"

"Hopefully it won't come to that. I may have found a way to shake them up." Grey smirked. "Maybe we can get them to follow one of our own ghosts."

"How do you plan to do that?" Coon asked.

Grey frowned at the holo image. "The same way they followed us here. Get Decker for me. There's a tracking device somewhere on this ship and I want to know where it is."

* * * *

Major Berman stood tall and defiant in the doorway of Plass' quarters.

"Why are we hiding from the Faulkner woman?" Berman demanded, his face pinched in anger.

Plass leaned further back in his chair and breathed deeply. The confrontation was inevitable. His time had run out. Actually, he was surprised Berman had held out this long.

"Major Berman, please sit down," Plass replied in an even voice.

Berman scowled as he stepped inside and took a seat as ordered. Plass eyed him. The man looked positively explosive.

Plass leaned forward, taking a few long moments to gather his thoughts and let Berman squirm. Unfortunately, Berman squirmed about as much as Tausek.

Finally, he looked the man in the eye. "We've been together for many years, Major. In all that time, have you ever known me to lie?"

Berman blinked at his superior officer, stunned by the unexpected question. "No, sir."

Plass nodded. "Have you ever known me to be irrational or unreasonable? To take unauthorized liberties with my position? To do anything that would compromise the d'Hont?"

Berman shifted uncomfortably in his chair, his initial anger dissipating rapidly. "No, sir."

"Good. Keep that in mind, Major. I have an interesting story to tell you." When Plass stood up, Berman arose.

"Sit," Plass snapped as he walked to the viewport and stared at Courf's giant red sun. Plass drew a deep breath and clasped his hands together behind his back. He heard the rustle of uniform as the other man complied.

Satisfied with the shift of power, Plass paused and contemplated his existence against the eternity of space. His entire life would be judged by a single day. The balance of this mission lay before him as he took the biggest risk of his life. He was about to gain an ally or lose his command.

"Ten years ago, Dakru and the d'Hont were betrayed," Plass started.

"I know what happened ten years ago Commander." Major

Berman interrupted impatiently. "I was there. Jarid Faulkner abandoned us and a million Dakruians died including my mate and children. You don't need to remind me of that."

Plass gazed out into the stars. "You're wrong, Major. Jarid Faulkner did not betray us." He spun around and pinned the Major with a look. "You did."

"I did no such thing," the Major growled, rising from his seat in a furious rush.

Plass stared down the giant of a man and took a steady step toward him. "Jarid Faulkner sent that shipment as agreed. You and nineteen other d'Hont pilots destroyed it."

Major Berman's eyes widened. His face grew red with rage. "That's impossible."

"It's true," Plass continued as he walked slowly to the desk, placing it between him and the Major. "That was no refugee ship bound for Dakru. The fleet you destroyed carried the vaccine shipment from Avion. You were lied to. Jarid Faulkner did not betray us. Tausek did."

The words hit Major Berman like a fist. He looked stunned. His eyes were wild with confusion, disbelief, and enough speculation to keep Plass hopeful. Then Berman's eyes narrowed dangerously at his commanding officer.

"How do you know this?" he hissed.

Plass smiled grimly. "You described the Avion fleet to me yourself. Tausek was the only one who knew the exact coordinates of the Avion shipment. Tausek alone directed the attack."

"Why would Tausek do that?" he growled.

Plass sidestepped the question with one of his own. "Do you think Tausek would be ruler of Dakru if it were not for the Avion incident? Do you think he would have risen to power so quickly if half the government body wasn't decimated and the planet in chaos?"

"What does that have to do with this?" Berman demanded.

"Think about it, Major. Before the incident, the d'Hont were an average military unit and Tausek, an average military man. What do you think his chances were to change that?"

Berman scowled at him but the point was given grudgingly.

"That's all you have?" Berman accused. "Perhaps you are simply jealous of Tausek's power." He crossed his arms over his barrel chest, warming up to his subject. "Thinking you can topple the ruler with a few accusations and circumstantial evidence?"

Plass hesitated to add his own gut feelings and suspicions. They weren't exactly hard proof. Bluffing seemed the logical choice. "I have additional evidence. When we capture Cidra Faulkner, I will have even more. That's why we need her alive."

The Major held him in lethal scrutiny, evidently deciding whether or not Plass was fit to command. Before Berman could make a final assessment, Plass made a final, shrewd point. "Either way, we will have her. If she has nothing to offer, we can kill her as planned. If we kill her now, we may never uncover our real enemy."

Plass waited. There was nothing else he could say or offer. The seeds of doubt had been planted.

Berman drew himself up to his full height, bearing down on Plass. "Very well. We will capture her alive. You will have one hour to obtain any information from her. After that, *I* decide her fate."

Knowing it was the best offer he would get, Plass nodded.

Berman turned and left without another word.

Plass stared at the door, contemplating his next move. Major Berman covered *Expunger*'s aircrew and Plass now had Berman's tenuous word of honor, as well as his unconcealed warning. Plass shook it off. At this point, his only real fear was failing himself.

Next on the list of allies would be Major Holtz, his Security Chief in charge of the ship's crew. As with all the high-ranking personnel Plass had hand-picked for this mission, Holtz's integrity was absolute. Not only was his service record impeccable, he was reasonable as well.

Plass steepled his hands. Yes, securing Major Holtz's support and cooperation would be the next order of business. With both forces supporting him, he would at least be able to keep Faulkner alive long enough to find out what she knew.

* * * *

"Sure you don't want to share a suit?" Grey asked as he grinned and leaned against the landing bay wall watching Cidra fight an opponent she couldn't beat--an uncompressed, integral-environment survival suit.

Cidra shot him a scathing look as she struggled inside the massive bulk of the apparatus.

"There's enough room in here for the whole crew," she muttered, trying to locate her hands in the meters of crisp, white material. "Now, I can believe it was designed by a man."

"Hold still," Leena said from somewhere behind her. "You won't be very comfortable if this doesn't shrink right."

"Are you sure about this?" Cidra looked down skeptically at the metal collar around her neck. "This thing is going to protect me down there on that ice rock?"

"Trust me. It will. I've done this lots of times." Leena straightened suddenly, her hair swinging around her head. "When activated, the collar will radiate a force field over your head like a helmet. Invisible. You won't even know it's there, unless something comes in contact with it."

Cidra frowned at her. "Then what happens?"

Leena shrugged. "Depends. If it's another force field, they merge together. If it's not, the force field will act like an ordinary solid helmet."

Remembering Decker's earlier comments, Cidra hedged, "What if the suit tears?"

"I've never seen that happen." Leena shook her head, her hair bobbing away. "We use these all the time on finds. You wouldn't believe the beating they can take. Not only that, the suit is self-healing. If it detects a tear, it will compress around it, sealing it off."

Leena checked all the gages and settings on the outside of the suit one last time. "OK, here goes. Whatever you do, don't move until it's done."

Cidra froze as the thermoform survival suit began to hiss and growl, squeezing excess material snugly around her. It was then she wondered how it knew when to stop. After a few uneasy minutes, it halted, apparently happy with its final form.

Leena gave it a quick check and smiled proudly. "Perfect. You're all set. Try walking around."

Experimentally, Cidra stepped forward, pleasantly surprised at the lightness and flexibility of the custom-fitted survival suit. She squatted and straightened. Leena was right, the suit fit perfectly. "Amazing."

Grey smiled at her. "Congratulations. It's yours now. Every crew member has one."

Cidra grinned back at him. "It's a dream come true. Really."

Grey laughed. "That's exactly what they all say."

"Can anyone join this party?" Barrios walked into the landing bay toward the trio.

Cidra smiled at him. "You just missed all the fun. Maybe you should get one of these."

"No thanks. Besides, I don't think it would do much shrinking around me," Barrios joked, but Grey noted his heart wasn't in it.

Grey said something softly to Leena. She nodded and turned to the group. "I have to run. Cidra, if you have any trouble with the suit, let me know." With that, she left.

Grey pushed off the wall and made a conspicuous trip into the K12, leaving Barrios and Cidra alone.

Barrios watched Grey enter the K12 and turned to Cidra, taking both her hands in his beefy fingers. "You're leaving soon."

"Yes. As soon as we take position over Courf." It broke her heart to see him so grim, knowing full well that it was her fault.

Barrios nodded for a few moments, working on his next words. "The d'Hont are close."

"I know." Cidra smiled sadly at his downcast expression. "You can't worry about it, Barrios. We have no choice."

He squeezed her hands. "I know." He raised his red-rimmed eyes to meet hers. "In my heart, you are my daughter. No matter what happens, always know that I love you."

Cidra felt the tears burn behind her eyes. She threw her arms around her old friend's shoulders. "I love you too, Barrios. I would never have made it this far without you, but I can't quit now. I owe it to everyone who ever loved me."

She backed away from him and smiled, feeling Grey's presence behind her.

Barrios looked at him over Cidra's shoulder and ordered, "You take care of her down there."

Grey gave the older man his pledge. "I'll do my best." *Or die trying.* The words went unspoken, but understood.

Barrios kissed Cidra on the cheek, turned, and walked out of the landing bay.

* * * *

From one hundred meters above, Courf's exterior didn't resemble the beautiful polished stone Cidra had seen from deep space. Between dense patches of ice fog, the darkside loomed ominous and terrifying just below them. The K12's searchlights revealed a surface that was tortured and scarred with criss-crossing ridges and slashing canyons. Courf endured a painful existence.

She gave silent thanks to the crashed transport's crew for having the foresight to set the distress beacon on.

"We're almost there," Grey said gruffly.

Cidra cast him a sidelong glance. He looked large and imposing in his survival suit. He also looked irritated. He had hardly spoken since they'd entered the K12. Even though the transport was still on the darkside, he had insisted they suit up immediately and locate the shipment. It was an unexpected risk, but he had refused to answer her questions about it. His expression was as icy as Courf itself.

Grey adjusted the angle of the searchlights. He was still angry with himself. How could he have missed it? Decker had found the d'Hont tracking device on the K12. It was now safely aboard *Calíbre* in a space pod, ready to be launched at a moment's notice. A convincing diversion, he hoped. It was his only trick left.

As it was, the d'Hont now knew his exact position. He had led them straight to the shipment. His ghost had come alive in the form of the d'Hont Class One cruiser. As much as he hated searching for something in the dark, they had no choice. Time was running out. The d'Hont were waiting. He wondered what they were waiting for.

"It should be dead ahead and within visual range. There." He pointed to a distant ridge lit up by the K12's probe light.

Cidra tried to pick out the shape of a transport as the clouds of ice fog swept along the jagged surface. Then she saw it and breathed a sigh of relief. Not only was it visible, it appeared intact.

Grey maneuvered the K12 in close, landing on a relatively flat patch of ground with a thump. Silence, fog, and incessant night encased them. He left the K12's engines running in the even they needed to make a quick liftoff. He turned to Cidra with a faint smile. "Ready?"

She gave him a haunted look that turned his stomach. He pulled her with him as he stood up. Framing her face in his hands, he kissed her gently. "I'll be there with you."

Cidra gazed up into his eyes with a longing and relief that pumped him full of desire. He wanted nothing more than to forget this death mission and get her out of that survival suit.

"Let's go." His voice was husky while he activated her survival suit. It droned low. She flinched as he tested the suit's force field around her head by tapping on it. Hard and hollow sounding. Perfect.

He activated his own, tapped on the force field, and headed to the back of the K12. He pulled a few tools from a storage locker and handed a rod to Cidra.

"What's this?" She turned the rod over in her hands.

"A heater torch." Grey activated his own torch to show her. A faint blue light fanned out from the tip of the rod. "It will thaw whatever it's pressed against. We'll probably need them to free the cargo." He punched a control on the chest unit of both suits that activated a wide beam of light, released the K12's outer door and stepped out.

Cidra followed without hesitation but once outside, stopped dead. She cast a look around. Courf looked sterile. No life, no movement. White clouds swallowed them up. Beyond the K12's beam and the survival suit's lights, there was nothing but fog and shadows. Ice vapor undulated and swirled in endless formations. Suddenly, she felt a low moan that emanated from somewhere deep within the planet. Around and beneath her, the ground hissed and popped reminding her that Courf was a world that lived in perpetual torment as its frozen carbon dioxide surface was alternately heated by the giant red star and cooled on the darkside.

She fought back a chill that sliced through her, turning her focus to Grey's retreating form. Ice crackled under her feet as she hurried to catch up with him.

The transport lay directly in front of them. Its nose was buried in a pile of ice boulders, its body scratched and scarred black. He circled the small ship once, searching for identification markings. There were none.

"That crew did a remarkable job landing her." Grey's eyes assessed the condition of the transport.

They approached the ship's outer door. With some trepidation, Cidra stood by as Grey tried to activate the external manual release. After his initial attempt failed, he pulled out the heater torch and pressed it against the release mechanism. Cidra watched in fascination while the area around the release glowed to a soft pink. Grey pulled the release again. The hatch popped open without protest except for the gasp of escaping air.

He smiled triumphantly at her. "We're in."

Using both hands, he pried the door fully open and stepped inside. The interior lights had long since lost their charge, but the K12's powerful beam lit up the interior of what appeared to be the cargo hold. Cidra stepped in behind Grey as he stooped to examine an unmarked squat container resting atop a hover pallet.

"This could be it." He looked around. "I don't want to open it here. Let's see if we can find some identification on-board first."

"Stay here." He stood up and walked toward the open doorway to the front crew section.

Cidra followed him and was immediately sorry she hadn't heeded his direct order. She stood frozen in place just inside the doorway. In the glow of her suit light, two very still crewmembers sat with their backs to her, facing forward. Ice crystals covered their bodies. Silent sentinels to the truth.

"I told you to stay in the cargo area," Grey said as he worked his way around the small cabin. He pulled out the heater torch and pressed it against a handle on center console until it glowed pink. Then he pulled a short cylinder out of the console board by the handle.

"Memory core?" Cidra's voice sounded raspy.

He nodded. "Most likely contains the same data as Syrus' holo recording. I'm taking it with us."

"This is it?" she gasped. "You're sure?"

Carrying the core, he guided her back through the doorway to the cargo hold. "The crew members are wearing the Kin-sha crest on their uniforms."

Cidra's stomach rolled over. Grey tossed the core on top of the large cargo container and bent to check the controls on the hover pallet. He seemed completely unaffected by the presence of two dead crewmembers. She, on the other hand, was shaking uncontrollably.

Grey tapped the controls several times. The hover pallet hummed to life. He blew out a long breath and thanked the stars above. There was no way the two of them could move this heavy container back to the K12 alone. Luckily, they didn't have to. He programmed the settings. The pallet under all that vaccine rose steadily off the floor, hovering a half meter off the floor.

"We're done." With a gentle push, he began guiding the huge container out the cargo door.

Cidra clenched her fists. "I'll be there in a minute."

Grey shot her a hard look. "This is no time to mess around, Cidra. We have to leave."

She didn't back down. "I have to do something first."

"Fine. Make it quick." He maneuvered the hover pallet through the door and toward the K12.

Cidra watched him push the pallet along. After taking several deep breaths, she turned toward the front crew section.

After securing the container aboard the K12, Grey stormed

back to the transport. She still wasn't back. He was going to chew her out good when he got hold of her. He stomped into the cargo hold. No sign of her. He caught the glow of her suit light in the crew section. *What was she doing?*

Whatever he was going to say was completely forgotten when he stepped foot inside the front section. She had used the heater torch to thaw two blankets that she was placing over each of the dead crewmembers. He watched her tuck and smooth the blanket with the gentle care. She glanced up at him with a bleak expression. Her hands went still on the blanket.

"They looked so cold," she said in a fragile voice. Her gaze skittered away as she resumed her task.

He stood watching her for a few seconds, all the anger draining out of him. This was tearing her apart, but as always, she did what was necessary. Despite his wrath and her own aversion, her compassion had won out. She had more heart than anyone he'd ever known.

"Cidra."

She slowly lifted her eyes to his. He almost choked on the thick emotion in his throat. He extended a hand to her. "Come on. Let's get out of here."

CHAPTER FOURTEEN

Cidra was still trembling as they cleared Courf's atmosphere and headed into space. It was the kind of trembling that went so deep, it felt like it would never stop. She wasn't sure if it was fear or excitement or grief. The emotions were too close together.

"Keep an eye on the long-range scanners, Cidra." Grey interrupted her thoughts. "I don't want anyone sneaking up on us."

He appeared grim as he piloted the K12. Not grim, she corrected. Worried.

"Why is *Calíbre* so far off planet?" She drew her attention back to the displays.

"I ordered them out further. I wanted them in a better position to watch for unexpected company," he murmured, all his energy focused on the scanners.

Cidra stared at him while all the pieces clicked into place.

"They're here, aren't they?"

Grey didn't answer her, hailing *Calíbre* instead. "Decker, do you see anything?"

Decker replied back instantly, "Nothing yet. Just you heading toward us. Can you kick that thing up a notch? This place is giving me the creeps."

Grey pursed his lips. Cidra heard him mumble, "Unprotected, with a long way to go."

"Launch the pod now, Decker," Grey ordered.

Decker replied, "Pod jettisoned."

"What pod?" Cidra asked as she watched a streak escape from *Calíbre*'s side portal heading into deep space. "Hyperspace?" She turned to Grey. "What's going on?"

He didn't answer her, his eyes locked in the direction of the jettisoned pod.

"Grey?"

"Diversion." He glanced at her. "I hope."

* * * *

"Commander, they've just jumped to hyperspace. Shall we follow?" Lieutenant Fiske's voice carried across the bridge.

Plass walked to the Lieutenant's station and studied the star map. It showed the tracking device moving away from the planet at a projected trajectory of ninety degrees to their original location.

Plass frowned. It didn't fit. To access the planet, they had to use the K12 with the tracking device. According to his information, it was the only vehicle aboard *Calíbre* capable of handling the brutal terrain and conditions of Courf. So why would they come all the way out here and then leave without even landing on the planet?

Plass contemplated the game. There was only one explanation. If he was wrong, Major Berman would not be pleased.

"No, Lieutenant. Round the planet at maximum speed, all systems on high alert," Plass ordered.

The Lieutenant turned to him. "But they're gone, sir."

"You have your orders. Follow them," Plass snapped. "Order Major Berman's pilots to their fighters."

Fiske nodded and proceeded to lay in a course. *Expunger* leapt forward toward the darkside of the planet at full speed.

* * * *

Decker's alarm came through loud and clear. "Captain, incoming! High and hot. One d'Hont cruiser, Bearing 180, Mark

060. We're heading in to cover you."

Cidra's heart jumped in her chest. It was like a nightmare unfolding its hideous cloak. She frantically checked the displays. *Calíbre* and the d'Hont cruiser barreled toward them. It would be a race--to the death.

"The bastards didn't bite on the tracker." Grey's hands moved quickly over the console. Cidra could see he was trying to get more speed out of the tiny K12. She watched the blips close in. Then a number of new, smaller blips swarmed out from the d'Hont cruiser. The K12's detection system verified her worst fear.

"Grey, they've launched a dozen fighters. Saurelian."

* * * *

The transmissions between *Calíbre* and the K12 came through *Expunger*'s bridge. Plass listened intently. Captain Stone was aboard the K12. He didn't hear Cidra Faulkner's voice or her name called from either vessel.

"Fighters away as ordered," Lieutenant Fiske announced. "Visual on."

Commander Plass turned his eyes to the main viewport. Stone's ship was closing on the K12 transport jet much too fast to bring it aboard. The two ships passed by each other. *Calíbre* took a defensive position to protect the escaping K12 from the oncoming attacking fighters.

Interesting, Plass thought. There must be someone or something very valuable on that transport jet for Stone's small ship to take on a fleet of Saurelian fighters alone. He had a decision to make. The chances were far better that Cidra Faulkner was aboard the larger ship, but his instincts prevailed.

"Order the fighters to surround and guide the K12 back into tracker beam range, Lieutenant."

Lieutenant Fiske turned to him. "What are your orders for *Calíbre*?"

"Inflict enough damage to render them harmless and immobile." He was not taking any chances. He didn't want to blow up Cidra Faulkner if his instincts were wrong.

* * * *

"Get out of range!" Decker yelled over the comm unit.

"Remind me to retrofit a hyperdrive on this ship tomorrow," Grey growled as he pumped the K12 for more speed. At this rate, the Saurelian fighters would be on top of them in no time.

"*Calíbre* is taking multiple hits. Too many fighters for our gunners to handle," Cidra reported. "The cruiser is opening up on *Calíbre* now. Direct hits. Move that bird, Coon."

As if Coon heard her, *Calíbre* dipped and rolled over the top of the massive d'Hont cruiser. Her guns were firing incessantly, but causing ineffectual, surface damage only. Compared to the giant ship, *Calíbre* looked like a pesky, little insect.

Suddenly, a Saurelian fighter swooped over the K12 and filled the main viewport. Cidra manned the guns, shooting at will. The first fighter slid dangerously close on the portside. Another fighter took up the flanking side, snuggling up to the K12.

"Hold your fire," Grey warned. "They're too close. If they blow, we blow."

Cidra detected six ships closing in formation around them. "They're blocking us in."

"At least they're not firing," Grey noted. He didn't have the time to wonder why.

He slammed the K12 in reverse. The Saurelian fighters shot out into the distance without them, but not for long. Another group took up the vacated positions, tightening their grip and completely surrounding the tiny K12. As the formation slowed, Grey was forced to slow with them or impact on one of the fighters.

Cidra watched helplessly. There were just too many of them and they flew superbly. Under different circumstances, she would have been impressed.

She glanced at the displays. A new threat loomed. "The d'Hont cruiser is heading toward us."

Abruptly the fighters peeled off, splitting formation. The K12 shuddered violently. Grey's hands stilled on the controls.

Cidra looked at him. "What was that?"

"Decker, get out of here," Grey ordered over the comm unit as he began to shut down the K12's main engines before the tiny ship was torn apart.

He couldn't answer her immediately. He had failed her. He turned to Cidra, his eyes dark. "Tracker beam. They've got us."

Decker cut in. "We aren't leaving you."

In the background, Cidra could hear the shouts of the crew and alarms blaring aboard *Calíbre*. Checking the displays, she could see they were now trying to outmaneuver the full contingent of fighters. They would be lucky to get away at all. Visions of the final moments of the Galena's demise flashed through her mind.

Grey slammed the comm unit on. "I said, escape while you still can. That's a direct order."

As Decker began swearing, Grey shut off the comm.

Cidra watched as *Calíbre* fired a few more times and executed a stunning maneuver to shake the fighters. Once clear, *Calíbre* shot off into hyperspace.

Suddenly, the battle ceased. The Saurelian fighters began filing back into the bank of landing bays on the starboard side of the big ship. The d'Hont cruiser now filled the K12's main viewport as they were being drawn toward a landing bay. For the first time, Cidra took a good look at the cruiser. The ship resembled the shadow of a giant knife, slicing through space. Unbroken black covered the cruiser's exterior. No lights, no markings, no seams. Nothing to warn unsuspecting victims of its deadly presence.

"Would it do any good to fire on that thing?" she asked quietly.

Out of the corner of her eye, she saw him smile grimly. "If it would make you feel better, be my guest."

Silence followed. Cidra's eyes filled. The words came out in a whisper, "We're done, aren't we?"

"If they wanted us dead, we'd already be dead."

The uncontrollable shiver came through her voice. "Maybe what they have planned for us is worse than death."

He couldn't argue with that. It was the only explanation for why they were still alive. He turned to her and gathered her in his arms.

* * * *

"They jumped, sir," Lieutenant Fiske announced

"Note their trajectory, but let them go." Plass turned and walked off *Expunger*'s deck toward the lift. "Order Major Holtz to send a security team to Landing Bay Number E-11 to greet our guests. I will be there shortly."

"Yes, sir," Lieutenant Fiske answered, highly pleased. The entire deck crew fairly hummed with victory as Plass passed them.

Only when he was alone in the lift did Commander Plass relax. He gave his destination to the lift computer. As the lift engaged, he began to rehearse the next part of his plan. He knew Stone was aboard the K12, but he didn't know if Cidra Faulkner was with him. His brazen decision to capture the K12 instead of *Calíbre* had been purely instinctual. If she wasn't aboard that ship, he would at the very least lose his command.

* * * *

Trapped. He hated being trapped. Grey glanced over Cidra's head to the contingent of rifle-wielding guards outside the K12. He frowned. They looked professional and well-trained. The tracker beam had deposited them in the very center of a large landing bay with the K12's nose facing the massive landing bay door. The closest cover was a stack of containers fifty meters to their left. The exit was probably behind them.

From his limited vantage point, he estimated that twelve guards surrounded the jet. He mentally checked off the armament on board. A couple of laser pistols and the K12's forward guns. There was no way he and Cidra would make it to the exit alive with just the pistols.

He contemplated the closed landing bay door. From the outside, it was nearly impenetrable. However....

He glanced down at the survival suits they were still wearing and calculated how much oxygen they had left. The plan solidified. He kissed Cidra on the head and placed her back in her seat. She stared at him in bewilderment.

"Don't ask, just listen." He began to warm up the K12's guns. The d'Hont security team outside donned surprised expressions in unison at the whining sound emitted from the transport jet.

"Activate your suit. Set the weight regulator to maximum. Grab your weapon. Go back to the exit hatch and wait for me," he spoke rapidly and without emotion.

Cidra's eyes widened in comprehension as she watched him enter the firing sequence into the K12's weapons board. She opened her mouth to argue with his decision, but he stopped her. "We don't have a choice, Cidra. You know that. Besides, it's going to take a few passes for the K12's guns to breach the bay door. If those guards have any brains, they'll be gone by then."

Cidra glanced at the guards backing away from the K12 and sighed. He was right. She prayed they had brains as she headed toward the back of the jet.

Grey finished setting up the sequence and touched the controls to lock the K12's landing legs to the landing bay floor. The last thing he needed was the K12 spinning around the bay in weightlessness, shooting indiscriminately. Dodging twelve laser rifles was enough excitement for him.

Then he swiveled the K12's guns toward the landing bay door and fired. The opening sequence disabled the containment field barrier designed to hold back cosmic space when the door was open. Closely spaced blasts drilled into the middle seam of the heavy door in explosion after explosion. The security team scattered as the bay filled with smoke and fire. Ricocheting blasts and sparks flew in all directions. The noise was deafening and the reverberations sent shock waves through the floor. Several guards turned their weapons on the K12. Cidra jumped at the bursts that rocked the tiny ship.

Grey locked the automatic firing mechanism and released the exit hatch in the back. He had his suit activated and his laser pistol in hand by the time he was standing next to Cidra.

"The guns should breach the door any second now." Grey concentrated on the gunfire battering the doors. He had a clear view from his position in the back of the K12.

He turned suddenly to Cidra and grabbed her around the waist. There was sharp sizzle and pop as the survival suits' force field helmets meshed for his kiss. Cidra gripped him in quiet desperation. For a fleeting moment, she could almost forget the world of danger surrounding them.

The absence of explosions broke off the embrace. Grey looked down at her, his eyes silver and glittering. "Do you trust me?"

Cidra nodded without hesitation.

"Good. Then do what I tell you. No questions asked." He glanced out the front viewport. The K12's barrage had ruptured the door, the pre-programmed firing sequence shooting harmlessly out into deep space. Now fully decompressed, the landing bay lay in eerie silence.

He pushed Cidra behind him and opened the exit hatch. The K12 decompressed with a hiss. With his laser pistol raised high, he listened for any activity over the steady pumping of the K12's guns.

"Wait here." He stepped out of the K12 slowly. The effects of walking in weightlessness were neutralized by the survival suit's max gravity setting. Still, the going was slow as he circled the K12. Red warning lights flashed along the walls. The absolute silence was eerie and alien. After he was sure it was clear, he motioned to Cidra and resealed the K12's hatch behind her.

She quickly scanned the strange, morbid spectacle. Everything in the bay was in slow motion--even the frozen bodies floating about. She shuddered, hoping that at least some of the guards had escaped before succumbing to the frigid vacuum of space.

After making a thorough visual sweep of the dead bodies, Grey reached up and snagged one out of the air.

Cidra gasped. "What are you doing?"

Grey spun the dead man horizontal toward them.

"Getting his security pass. We'll need it to move around the ship." Grey relieved the dead man of his authorization card and laser rifle. He grabbed Cidra's arm just as she headed to the exit doors that led to the cruiser's interior.

"We're not leaving that way." He pulled her toward the battered landing bay door, circumventing the K12's incessant gunfire.

Cidra stared at his determined expression. "We can't stay here. There's no way two of us are going to hold off the entire crew of this ship."

Grey grinned at her. "I don't plan to be here when they come barging in that exit door."

"The K12? You know the tracker beam will just pull us back in," Cidra prodded as Grey stopped them in front of a wall display screen.

He scanned the display quickly, getting his bearings. Then he began working the controls to bring up different views of *Expunger*'s layout.

"We aren't going to use the K12 either." He slipped the dead man's security card into an authorization slot. As he entered commands, a grid of boxes lit up on the wall display. Suddenly the damaged heavy landing bay door groaned and opened, giving a glorious view of deep space. More lights flashed on the wall display, blinking red and green.

"Perfect." Grey withdrew the card from the slot and turned to Cidra. "Set your boots on magnetize. We're going for a walk outside."

She took one long look at the gaping bay entrance and the expanse of endless space. Fear crept into her voice. "You can't be serious."

Grey stepped to the edge of the bay. "I don't have time to argue. This is the only way out of here. This bay is going to be crawling with d'Hont in a few minutes. We only have to go down one level. I figure about thirty meters." He casually peered far over the edge of the great abyss.

Cidra held her breath as he reached out and drew her along with him.

"I can't do it," she choked out, closing her eyes at the absolute void before her.

Grey wrapped an arm around her waist and led her out onto the exterior skin of the cruiser. "You have to. Now look down at the cruiser's surface. If we lose contact with the ship, we'll become a permanent part of the universe."

His casual warning forced her eyes wide open. The stars were a brilliant backdrop and crystal clear like she had never seen before. It didn't seem real. She looked down at her boots firmly planted on the vessel's exterior. They were already outside.

"Shouldn't we use a tether?" she suggested desperately even as Grey was dragging her with him.

He smirked. "We should definitely use a tether. But I don't want to leave any clues how we escaped. Besides, they'll figure we'd have to be insane to try this without one."

Cidra clenched her teeth and took another reluctant step forward. "Little do they realize we *are* insane."

Grey's only response was a wide grin.

The effort of walking in fully magnetized boots was more than she could have imagined. The boots clung stubbornly to the metal skin, making it difficult to advance.

A dreadful thought overwhelmed her. "How are we going to get back in?"

Grey kept her moving with one boot at a time clamping tightly to the cruiser's skin. "I opened all the landing bay doors on the ship. Hopefully no one will notice it until we are inside again."

Cidra glanced at him, her face white. "Hopefully? What happens if they close the doors?"

Grey kept his eyes down. "We pray they don't jump to hyperspace."

* * * *

Commander Plass stepped out of the lift at Level E and into the throes of a high alert status. Long, narrow light bars along the corridors flashed red, the distress siren wailed and bands of security guards raced past him. He could hear the echoes of guards shouting and automatic warning messages ringing through *Expunger*'s passageways.

Something was very wrong.

He returned to the lift and addressed the onboard computer. "Locate Major Holtz."

A sterile female voice replied, "Major Holtz is in the Security Center."

"Take me there."

The short journey gave him a chance to get his displeasure under control. He had no doubt that the prisoners had escaped and that Major Holtz's forces had failed a simple task. It was a failure Plass planned to exploit fully.

The lift halted and the doors opened onto Level B. Commander Plass marched down the corridor and into the Security Center, the heart of *Expunger*'s defense system. The mood was urgent. The dark circular room hummed with activity as human and computer-generated voices buzzed. Harsh lights illuminated anxious faces of the officers at their stations around the perimeter.

The professional female voice recited present systems status. Plass listened to the rundown to orient himself with *Expunger*'s current condition.

In the center of the room, a full blown, detailed schematic of *Expunger* floated in a massive holo deck. The transparent replica displayed the current status of all systems aboard. Plass noted the red areas lit throughout the ship. Trouble spots.

Major Holtz appeared and gave his Commander a stiff salute. "Sir, we have a problem."

Plass' eyes narrowed at the man. "So it would seem. First, explain the situation. Then you can tell me why I was not notified immediately."

Major Holtz was a tall man, lanky and lean. Brutally short white hair held a direct contrast to his ruddy complexion and wide-set blue eyes. A careful and thorough officer, his dissatisfaction with their predicament showed on his face.

The Major reported to his superior officer crisply. "There has been an incident in Landing Bay Number E-11. The landing bay doors have been destroyed and containment breached. Every member of the security unit assigned to the area is dead. And the captives have vanished."

Plass glared mercilessly at him. "Define *vanished*."

Major Holtz cleared his throat. "My men have scoured the entire bay. There is no sign of them. They could not have entered the corridor outside the bay. Our secondary security units were already on their way. They would have been spotted. We think they may have been expelled from the bay during the rapid decompression."

Commander Plass didn't believe that for a minute. "How many prisoners?"

"We visually identified at least two--a man and a woman."

Plass suppressed a smile. His hunch had paid off. She was here. "What about their transport?"

Holtz reported grimly. "Still in the bay. That's how they

destroyed the bay door."

Plass cursed himself. Apparently he had underestimated his foe. How else could two virtually defenseless prisoners have caused so much trouble?

"Were there any other spacecraft in the bay?"

The Major shook his head. "No, sir. The bay was empty."

"Lock out all the aircraft on board. I don't want them escaping in one of our own ships," Plass ordered. "You have a search plan in place?"

Major Holtz replied, "Yes. The landing bays are first on the list." He paused. "There is one other unusual item. According to the ship's computer, the Lead Security officer in charge of the prisoner's escort issued some peculiar orders during the incident. Doors and exits throughout the ship were opened randomly including the majority of landing bay doors. The on-board lighting and communications systems have been reset. Several secondary systems were shut down. Since the Lead Security officer was among the dead, we are treating it as a systems malfunction."

Plass stilled as the swirl of confusion and facts began to settle. "Did this Security officer still possess his authorization card when you identified him?"

The Major looked momentarily stunned. "I don't know."

Plass continued, eyeing *Expunger*'s schematic. "Are the landing bay doors still open?"

"Well, yes." Major Holtz sounded surprised. "We were about to override the command and close them."

"Don't override," Plass cut in. "Not yet. Lock out all the internal exits of every landing bay surrounding Number E-11. Send security teams," he pinned the Major with a warning. "*Competent* security teams, to wait outside the exits for further orders."

Major Holtz looked confused. "Yes, sir. But why only those bays?"

Plass ignored his question. Let the man figure it out for himself. "After the security teams are in position, close the bay doors and flood the bays with audio stun bursts. That should bring our guests to their knees. Then open the exit doors and send the teams in. Remind your men to capture the prisoners alive and unharmed. Maximum restraint, Major."

Holtz's face reddened. "My units already have those orders, sir."

Plass took a step closer to his Chief Security officer. "Then tell them to get it right this time."

CHAPTER FIFTEEN

Grey added a shower to his wish list as he helped Cidra back inside the lower landing bay of the d'Hont ship. Sweat slicked the inside of his survival suit, evidence of the tremendous energy it had taken to scale the cruiser's exterior. His legs were shaking from exertion and he was still trying to get his breathing back to normal. It had been the most grueling thirty-meter walk of his life.

Not that he was complaining. They were lucky enough to end up in a deserted landing bay before anyone realized the bay doors had been opened. The next best thing would have been a nice, fast ship to escape in. No lucky break there. They stood in the middle of an empty bay.

Grey tugged at the back of Cidra's survival suit, releasing the seal so she could remove it. "All we'd need is one of those Saurelian fighters. We could be clear of this bucket and into hyperspace before they knew what happened."

"They're only single man fighters," Cidra reminded him.

From behind her, he slipped Cidra's suit off her shoulders. "Then it should be real cozy. They were designed by...."

"Don't say it," Cidra groaned. She stepped out of the suit.

Grey chuckled. He stopped when she turned around. Perspiration soaked her blue flightsuit in all the right places. It took him a second to recover.

"Your turn," she said softly, her blue eyes hooded. He unleashed a slow, sexy smile and spun around to let her help him.

Without the hindrance of the survival suits, they moved quietly through the landing bay. The silence was unsettling. The only sounds were their footsteps on the hard floor.

When they reached the closed exit door to the corridor, Grey pushed Cidra behind him and lifted the laser rifle. He stepped into the door's activation field, but it didn't open as expected. He frowned and slipped the dead guard's pass into the authorization slot. Nothing.

Cidra asked, "What's wrong?"

"We're locked in."

Suddenly the open landing bay doors began to close, cutting off the glorious view of deep space.

Grey ran a hand through his hair. "And there goes the other option."

"I think we've got bigger problems than that." Cidra's eyes took on the far away look that Grey had seen before.

Then all hell broke loose.

* * * *

"Dropping out of hyperspace now. Outside *Expunger*'s scanner range," Coon announced and spun around in his chair to face Decker. "If you don't stop that pacing, I'm going to have you medicated."

Decker stopped and glowered at him. "Stick it, Coon. I'm in no mood. I want a complete status report on all of our systems. I want all scanners at maximum range and the automatic warning system on. I want every available body working on repairs. And I want them now."

"And I thought Captain was tough," Coon muttered as he spun back around to carry out the orders. "Anything else?" he sing-songed sweetly.

"As a matter of fact, there is one more thing. Your single, most important duty." Decker bent over Coon's shoulder and punched in a command.

A star chart arose from the bridge's holo deck in front of Coon's station. From the center of the display, a healthy beacon signal was transmitting to *Calíbre*.

"What is that?" Coon asked.

Decker smiled smugly. "That, is Captain Stone. More specifically, his personal comm signal."

Coon's mouth dropped. "We're too far away. His personal comm unit isn't that strong."

"It is if it passes through a signal booster. I planted a high-power relay aboard the K12. As long as he's within range of the K12, we can pick him up across the galaxy," Decker said proudly.

Coon shook his head. "Forget it. The d'Hont will find it in a minute."

Decker laughed. "Not this one. It's one of a kind. My own creation. Get to work on those repairs. I want to be ready when they move."

"What happens if the signal suddenly dies." Coon glanced up at him. Without answering, Decker turned and walked off the bridge.

* * * *

Grey's first thought was that someone was poking him full of holes. His second thought was that his brain had become too big for his skull. Consciousness floated back bit by bit. Needle-like pain radiated in all directions inside his head with every heartbeat. He began to dread each steady beat. He was lying down on what felt like a bed. Where? The last thing he remembered was standing in the landing bay with Cidra.

Cidra. He reached around with his hands for her. She wasn't there.

Another hard poke jabbed into his shoulder.

Grey forced himself to open his eyes and was greeted by the business end of a high-caliber laser rifle.

A voice spoke from somewhere behind the guard pointing the rifle in his face. "Welcome aboard *Expunger*, Captain Stone. I am Commander Plass."

Plass. The big gun himself. Well at least the man had manners. He glanced over the barrel of the laser rifle to the guard holding it. This one looked a long way from polite.

"You won't get many visitors if you greet them like this." Grey winced as the sound of his own voice ricocheted through his head. "What did you do to us?"

The guard with the gun moved away and was replaced by the figure of the man impeccably dressed with perfect posture. His black hair was shot with gray and expertly cut. Dark black eyes were bright with intense perception and intelligence. He carried himself with the bearing and character of a man very much in control. Grey knew immediately that this was the man who tracked them down through all the diversions. This was the mind behind their ultimate capture. Although Grey was impressed, it didn't make him feel any better that Commander Plass was a worthy adversary.

With a heavy groan, Grey rolled to a sitting position on the edge of the large bed and shook off the stabbing pain that shot between his ears. He cradled his head between his hands, resting his elbows on his knees. With a laser rifle trained on him, he felt completely vulnerable. There was no way he could even defend himself in this condition. And where was Cidra?

"You were incapacitated with auditory stun bursts. It will take some time until the residual pain diminishes, but there will be no permanent damage," Plass explained with little sympathy.

Grey grunted. It sure felt permanent. He raised his eyes to Plass. Although he should have been, Grey didn't feel threatened by him. It took his foggy mind a few tries to figure out why. Commander Plass didn't have the eyes of a killer. They were too clear. Grey should have been comforted by that revelation, but it only meant the man probably would order someone else to do his killing for him.

Plass widened his stance and locked his hands behind his back. "You left quite a mess in the landing bay."

Grey forced a wide smile. "I guess they just don't make landing bay doors like they used to."

"And caused the deaths of thirteen good men," Plass continued, ignoring the sarcasm.

Grey narrowed his eyes. "Thirteen stupid men. I gave them time to get out." He shrugged. "It's not my fault they didn't use that time wisely."

Plass stared at him for a few long moments. "Cidra Faulkner is your companion."

"She works for me," Grey sidestepped. "Where is she?"

Commander Plass knew better than to believe the Captain's cool, detached concern. She was more than another crew member. When the guards found them unconscious on the floor in the bay, the Captain's body was wrapped around hers like a shield. Plass knew exactly how to get his answers.

"In a separate detention room. She has yet to regain consciousness. I decided to begin with you."

That phrase earned Grey's full attention. He watched with growing dismay as the Commander began to pace the small room, his hands still locked behind his back deep in thought. It dawned on Grey that the Commander was stalling. Why? Then Plass pulled out his laser pistol. Grey froze.

Then Plass dismissed the single guard, leaving them alone in the room. Grey wondered how fast he could reach Plass before he could pull the trigger. His head protested immediately. He needed more time to recover and he doubted he was going to get it.

Plass stood in the center of the room with the weapon pointed at Grey. "I have come a long way to capture the daughter of Jarid Faulkner. My men are very anxious to kill the last Faulkner."

Grey didn't say anything. The blood was pounding through his veins, clearing his head with amazing speed. He didn't like the direction of the conversation.

"Unfortunately, she is not our real enemy." Plass stepped toward Grey. "Is she?"

Stunned, Grey stared Plass down for a few long moments. Then it hit him. He knew the reason why they were still alive. Equal parts of relief and anger rolled over him. Grey spat out through clenched teeth, "You know."

Plass said nothing, revealed nothing.

Grey stood to his full height, ignoring the pain it brought, ignoring the laser pistol pointed at him. He turned his back to Plass, trying to bring himself under control.

"You know about Tausek. You know about the shipment he sabotaged." Grey swung around to face him, rage surfacing. "How long have you known?"

Plass remained calm. "I *know* nothing. I have suspicions. I am optimistic that you can supply me with additional information."

Grey narrowed his eyes at the man with combination of disgust and disbelief. "Let me get this straight. You want us to tell you what we know? Then what? Then you kill us? Then you destroy all the evidence we have and forget it once and for all? That bastard killed millions of people. Millions. He should rot for that."

Plass' voice was quiet in contrast to Grey's angry words. "I agree."

It took Grey several heartbeats to recover. "You agree?" he hissed softly. "What kind of game are you playing?"

"No game," Plass explained. "You are correct. If Tausek did destroy that shipment, I want him dead."

Grey laughed cynically and shook his head. "Forgive me if I don't believe you. I know how you d'Hont stick together."

"Yes. Especially when we've been betrayed."

Grey regarded his adversary warily. The eyes that met his never wavered, never flinched. "What about your crew? Don't they know the truth? Why do they still want Cidra dead?"

Plass sighed deeply. "They are a different matter. Tausek has hard core loyalty from the d'Hont, due mostly to the incident ten years ago. I need irrefutable evidence. And even then, it will be difficult to persuade them to turn against their leader." Plass met Grey's eyes. "But I give you my word that I will do everything to bring Tausek to justice. It is not only your lives at stake here."

Grey absorbed the final statement. For the first time he realized

Plass' predicament. He was turning against his ruler--alone. He may be a d'Hont, but he had integrity and guts. A guarded respect surfaced as Grey struggled with the changing dynamics of the situation. His choices were severely limited.

"I want Cidra. In here. With me," Grey demanded firmly. "Then I'll give you all the evidence you'll ever need."

Plass studied him for a few long moments and nodded once. "Acceptable." He turned sharply toward the door.

* * * *

Ten minutes later one burly guard carried an unconscious Cidra into Grey's detention room, followed by Plass. After the guard deposited her on the bed and left the room, Grey gave her a cursory exam. To his immense relief, she appeared unharmed. Her breathing was deep and even.

"Why hasn't she regained consciousness yet?" Grey grilled Plass.

"She should be coming around shortly. Better to let her rest. She will awaken in less discomfort."

Grey stared at the Commander, not believing his ears. "Why do you care what happens to her?"

Plass met his eyes. "Because if Tausek is guilty, she is innocent."

"Her father was innocent, too."

"You said you have evidence," Plass replied. "We don't have much time."

Grey nodded and looked down at Cidra. "I hope the K12 is intact."

"It is."

Grey gave Plass a hard sidelong glance. "Will she be safe here alone?"

"For now." Plass waved his laser pistol toward the door. "After you."

* * * *

By the time Grey returned to his detention room, Cidra had begun to stir.

Alone at last, he slid onto the bed and gathered her into his arms. She sighed and burrowed her head into his shoulder, still firmly entrenched in her peaceful dream-like world.

Grey lay there wide-awake, stroking her hair. The trip back to the K12 had energized him. The little craft was in perfect condition, but the bay was indeed a mess. It gave him enormous satisfaction to watch the faces of the guards performing the repairs and clean up. Somehow he got the feeling they had learned a valuable lesson.

He chuckled softly recalling the amazement on Plass' face when he had simply entered the K12 and yanked out the transport's active memory core. Plass' guards had checked every square inch of the ship looking for evidence. They had recovered the vaccine shipment, but had missed the memory core. It never occurred to them that the K12's original core had been substituted by that of the downed transport on Courf.

Unfortunately, Grey never had a chance to view the contents of that memory core. He could only hope it contained the original file transfer of the Galena ambush. If the recording wasn't in the core, there was no hope for them. Even if his instincts held true and the recording existed, there was no guarantee that he or Cidra would live to see another day. All he had was Plass' word. And a ship full of d'Hont who wanted Cidra dead.

He had given Plass the core and outlined the entire story from beginning to end. It was a desperate gamble, but Commander Plass was now their only shot at survival. All they could do was wait. It seemed ludicrous that their enemy should become their savior. Grey breathed in deeply and closed his eyes, trying to have faith in the Commander's conviction and his powers of persuasion.

Cidra shifted. Grey dropped soft kisses on her upturned face and down her throat. He slipped his fingers through her thick hair, inhaling the sweet scent of it. He would never get enough of her. Never. Just the thought of holding her for the rest of his life sent passion raging through him. Heat only Cidra could bring forth.

She stirred against him, the length of her body melting into his. With deep kisses, he drew her back to consciousness. She blossomed under his hands, waking fully aroused and ready.

Cidra moaned softly against his mouth and murmured, "Where?"

Grey smiled. Her complete trust amazed and humbled him. She didn't ask about her safety, didn't worry about her situation, didn't even open her eyes. He didn't want to yank her out of her sensual awakening by telling her how dire the situation really was. "Safe."

She slid her arms around his neck, searching and finding his mouth with her own. Grey shifted on top of her, parting her legs with his thighs and settling himself there. He loved the way she felt under him, the way her form fit perfectly to his, the way the fire built between them. His kisses were soft and gentle, lingering and long. With a single movement she arched against him and shot his slow, easy pace all to hell.

Grey thought about the guards standing outside, about Plass' imminent meeting and a very possible interruption of their lovemaking. Then he shook it off and ground his hips into her. He couldn't think of any other place he'd rather be.

* * * *

The situation was critical. His life was in the balance. The future of the d'Hont was in jeopardy. He was about to change history forever. Plass couldn't be happier.

His executive quarters brimmed with *Expunger*'s highest-ranking personnel. Majors Holtz and Berman were seated on either side of him at the large holo deck table along with Lieutenant Fiske who was operating the holo deck controls on the opposite side. In a semi-circle behind them, stood eight junior officers in charge of *Expunger*'s various systems. They had all been briefed on Plass' suspicions of Tausek and the amazing scenario of events that began with the Avion shipment and ended with the recovery of the memory core and missing vaccine.

Plass knew that not a single crew member in this room believed the account. What he proposed would shake the fundamental goals and foundation of the d'Hont. A foundation built on hate and revenge, on the resolution to never again be vulnerable. The wreckage of the past united the d'Hont into the force they were today. Changing that past meant changing the present and the future.

Even now, Plass felt the skeptical and caustic looks aimed his way. The transition would be painful for them, he mused, but he would thoroughly enjoy watching them convert one at a time.

He had already viewed the holo recording several times with Lieutenant Fiske. It was more than he had expected, more than he could possibly have hoped for. Any doubts were crushed. The truth screamed out with a vengeance.

The room lights darkened for the holo deck presentation. The holo grid in the center of the table shed a ghostly light on the men seated nearby. Major Berman's big arms were folded across his chest, his expression belligerent. Major Holtz sat ramrod straight, his hands folded neatly on the table. He watched Lieutenant Fiske intently.

"We are ready, sir," Lieutenant Fiske reported.

Plass leaned back leisurely in his chair. "Run it, Lieutenant." He smiled in the darkness.

The holo grid sprang to life and began revealing the demise of the Galena. All eyes were instantly glued to the action, transfixed in surprise and confusion. Lieutenant Fiske stated the star date and star map coordinates as the Saurelian fighters faithfully performed their death dance. Each officer watched in rapt fascination, grappling with the truth of his or her own eyes.

Plass could almost hear every breath taken. He let the action run for some time and casually turned to Major Berman seated to his right. "Look familiar, Major?"

Major Berman leaned forward and frowned. "That's us. And that's the refugee ship we destroyed ten years ago."

Lieutenant Fiske shook his head. "Not according to the holo recording stats. That's the Galena loaded with vaccine bound for Dakru."

All eyes turned to Major Berman. He stared at the holo image, looking for support of his innocence. Another Kin-sha escort blew up. The holo recording didn't oblige. Plass watched the heat of anger rise in the Major's face, burning and boiling below the surface.

"No!" Berman snapped. "It's a fake. It has to be."

Lieutenant Fiske replied calmly, "Not possible. The ship signature matches the Universal Craft Identification database. This is the Galena."

The battle unfolded, taking its fateful place in history. Plass gazed around the room at the faces. They were drawn out, shocked, and speechless. Just the way he wanted them. He turned back to the action with mundane interest. "Your forces were certainly efficient, Major Berman."

Plass watched Berman's expression as the Major relived the event that sealed the fate of millions of Dakruians. His forehead glistened with sweat, his breathing increased. He was the only one in the room who knew the ending to this incident. As it drew nearer, the pain in his face grew.

Lieutenant Fiske continued his commentary of the action, blow by blow to its inevitable conclusion. He had enhanced the transport escape path for easy viewing. There was a collective gasp as the transport hit hyperspace a split-second before the holo image died away.

The room was heavy with silence. All eyes remained on the

holo deck as if hoping, praying for a different ending. The lights came up. Plass stood slowly and walked to the viewport, fully aware that all attention automatically turned to him.

"You have the entire truth," Plass said as he stared into the star-studded universe. "Questions."

Major Berman was the first to break the silence. His voice was raw with emotion. "Can you prove that was the original shipment?"

"The date matches the approximate delivery window for the vaccine order," Plass replied calmly. "The exact ship date was purged from our information systems by Tausek to cover up the incident. Captain Stone has offered to verify the dates by infiltrating the Avion archives and securing the contractual agreement. I'm certain the delivery schedule will concur. The serial numbers on the vials of vaccine that Captain Stone retrieved from the transport on Courf match the Galena's manifest. Next question."

"How did the Stone find the missing transport after all this time?" Major Holtz asked.

"Apparently, Captain Stone has many talents besides evading capture. Next question."

"Why now? Why did it take so long for this to come out?" the officer in charge of the medical facilities asked.

Commander Plass replied, "For ten years Cidra Faulkner lived with Syrus Almazan, a friend of Jarid Faulkner's. Almazan kept the holo recording and the information hidden. Shortly after his death, Captain Stone took Cidra Faulkner and the evidence off Avion. I don't know why Almazan didn't pursue it sooner. Next question."

Plass answered every question patiently, cutting away the resistance and chipping away the doubt until the truth stood alone. Eventually the questions ceased, replaced by acceptance and anger.

Major Berman buried his head in his hands. "This is ludicrous. I can't believe Tausek would betray us. I can't believe he would kill millions simply to become the ruler of Dakru."

"Believe it, Major," Plass replied matter-of-factly. "We have been lied to and used. Our lives manipulated. Our families sacrificed. Our world devastated. Can you think of anyone else who had the power and motive to do this?"

There was an agreeable silence. Then the murmurs began, getting louder as the officers began to turn against Tausek one by one.

Plass waited until the increasing anger was palpable. Now he could harness that rage and use it against the traitor. He turned around to face the group. "We have a decision to make. I will not make it for you."

Major Holtz said it first. "Tausek must pay."

The agreement was unanimous and enthusiastic. Even Major Berman conceded. Plass surmised the burly Major would be his strongest supporter.

"How are we going to apprehend him?" asked Major Holtz.

"I would recommend a decisive and lethal assault on his main tower chambers," the female Chief Battle Station officer voiced bitterly.

Plass shook his head. "It won't be that easy. My sources on Dakru tell me that Tausek has already convicted me and all of you by association. He has rebuilt his personal protection structure around himself with new bodies. Stoll has succeeded me. We have all been replaced by Tausek's own private force. No more d'Hont." Plass swung around the face the group. "From this point onward, the d'Hont will be nothing more than his personal weapon."

The officers stared back at him, stunned. Plass continued, his voice low. "We alone know the truth. And we are on our own."

"Then how do we get to him?" Major Berman demanded.

"I have a plan." Plass smiled. "Cidra Faulkner will be our bait."

CHAPTER SIXTEEN

"That's your plan?"

Cidra jumped at the anger in Grey's voice as he shot out of his chair and practically leapt over Plass' desk. She clenched her hands together in the chair next to his, still stunned at the scheme Plass had just outlined. A scheme that would bring down Tausek. A scheme that could cost her and Grey their lives.

The young blond Lieutenant standing behind them pressed a hand to Grey's shoulder to pacify him. Grey swatted the hand off like an insect and glared at Plass. Fury radiated from every muscle in his body.

"What kind of plan is that?" he raged at Plass. "Haven't we

given you enough already? We practically put Tausek in your lap. Do we have to pull the trigger, too?"

Unruffled, Plass steepled his fingers in front of his face. "Tausek is well insulated. A direct assault on him will not work. Besides, we want him alive. In his case, instant death is not punishment enough. I won't force you to help. I can only ask."

Grey lip curled into a snarl. "Well, that's good because the answer is *no*."

"It is a sound plan." Plass regarded Grey with a cool, placid expression. "And the only way to get a confession from Tausek."

"I wouldn't call leaving us unarmed with that madman a sound plan," Grey snapped. "We won't be your bait."

Plass shook his head slowly. "I know Tausek. He will not turn down the opportunity to gloat about his successful deception. Especially if he believes the confession will die with you. It is the perfect trap."

"You can't guarantee our safety," Grey charged. "You can barely keep Cidra safe from your own men."

"My crew and I will do everything within our power to protect you," Plass offered.

Grey's eyes narrowed. "Tell me. Does Tausek know you're on to him?"

The only answer from Plass was the steady drumming of his fingers together.

Grey nodded. "That's what I thought. You can't even protect yourself." Grey reached over and tried to pull Cidra out of her chair. "Forget it."

"No." Cidra pushed his hand aside. Grey stared at her in confusion.

She raised her gaze to Plass. "I'll do it."

She felt the temperature in the room dropped several degrees before Grey responded, "No, you won't."

Cidra refused Grey's hand again, keeping her gaze on Plass. "Commander Plass is right. It's the only way."

"We are not going to do this, Cidra. We've done more than enough already," Grey said.

She could feel the burning heat of his eyes on her, but she pressed on. "This is the one peaceful option. Broadcasting the confession is the perfect way to communicate the truth to all the people and the d'Hont at the same time. Otherwise, sides will be taken, blood will be spilled."

Grey's fury bore down on her. He spun her chair around to face him and planted his hands on the chair arms. His face lowered to inches from hers, his voice hissed low and deliberate. "I don't care how many people die on Dakru. Let them deal with their own problems. *Our* mission is complete, Cidra."

"And what happens when Tausek's forces crush the truth. No one, on or off Dakru, will defy him. Certainly not Avion. He will never be stopped or punished."

Grey shot Plass a murderous look. Then he turned his sights back to Cidra. "It's suicide and you know it." He pointed to Plass. "He knows it."

She realized it at that moment. A line had been drawn. The sudden insight choked her even though she'd always known that at some point this would happen. He was going to make her choose between him and her mission. Make her choose between righting the wrongs of the past and her future with him. He didn't understand that they were one and the same. She couldn't have a future without rectifying the past. What kind of future would they have if Tausek continued to rule? The answer was easy. The choice was not.

Cidra reached out and stroked his cheek with her fingertips and uttered the words that would cost her the most important thing in her life. "I'd rather die this way than be hunted down again. The rest of my days won't be spent on the run." Then she drew a breath, dropped her hand and released him. "You needn't worry. I won't drag you into it. I am perfectly capable of taking care of myself."

Cidra saw the flash of fire in his eyes before they turned cold as ice. She had done something that could never be undone. He might never forgive her for this.

Grey spoke in a quiet voice. "Then I won't stand in your way." He straightened and walked out.

Plass nodded at Fiske to follow Grey.

Cidra didn't dare move for fear her tenuous grip on control would break. She had never seen that much anger in him, deep anger. Hurt and betrayal. Not even a glimmer of mercy. He didn't understand her decision, didn't realize it was a need as great as her need for him. The way he saw it, she had chosen the mission over him. She had betrayed his trust. A crush of pain and emptiness filled her.

In silence, Plass regarded her. The daughter of Jarid Faulkner continued to impress him. Under all that classic beauty was the heart of a saint and the courage of a warrior. Although he wasn't entirely sure of what had just happened, he could tell by the look on her face that she had just made a painful decision. Of all the people involved in this mess, she had sacrificed the most and deserved it the least.

"Everything he said was true. I may not be able to protect you. You owe nothing to Dakru," Plass spoke solemnly.

Cidra met his gaze, her voice hard. "I owe it to the Kin-sha, to my father, and my family. To millions who died for Tausek's power and greed. And myself. That's enough for me."

Plass flicked his eyes to the door. "Will you go alone?"

Cidra paused. "If I have to." Then she raised her chin. "You are."

"Yes, I am," he replied solemnly, but the thought of Cidra alone with Tausek plagued his mind. He didn't doubt she could draw a confession from Tausek, but her safety afterward was a different issue. Plass decided to work on Captain Stone. She didn't have a chance without him. Despite what just happened, he believed Stone was the one man who would protect her to the death.

"Why?"

Her question startled him. "Why am I doing this?" Plass asked. She was assessing his motives and he hadn't given them conscious thought. It took him a minute to analyze all the complex emotions and principles that guided him to this point. Then he spoke reverently, "Tausek took something away from each of us. Some more than others, but we've all suffered. I have committed myself to making sure he pays for that."

Her blue eyes studied him, looking older and wiser than her age. "So have I."

"I think we have much in common," Plass said.

Cidra's expression turned cold. "I doubt it."

Plass remained silent. After what the d'Hont did to her family, he deserved whatever she threw at him.

She didn't give up. "You could escape to another galaxy."

Plass raised an eyebrow. "I could no more do that than you could. We are both victims of Tausek and our own moral standards."

Apparently satisfied, Cidra pursued another question. "You said instant death was too good for Tausek. What do you have in mind?"

Plass smiled crookedly. "I thought he'd enjoy working in the

Thorite mines."

Cidra nodded in approval and rose to leave.

"Will you join me for morning meal tomorrow?" Plass brought his fingers to his lips.

She turned to him. "Do I have a choice?"

"Of course. I am inviting you, not ordering you. I could arrange for a tour of the ship." He knew she'd jump at a diversion from the detention quarters.

She pursed her lips. "Very well."

Cidra headed toward the exit but stopped just before the door with her back to him. Plass watched as she clenched and unclenched her fists. "Were you there that night?"

Plass stilled. He didn't have to ask where she meant. Her home, her family, that night ten years ago. Even though he owed her the truth, he couldn't take the chance that she might back out.

"No."

A deep sigh relaxed the tight muscles in her back and she walked out, leaving him alone with the horror of the past. Plass snarled when he realized Tausek had timed the Faulkner massacre perfectly. The d'Hont were ripe for the kill, their hands still dirty from burying their own loved ones.

When he opened his eyes again, a smoldering amber of hatred remained. How long had Tausek perfected his plan, setting the pawns in place, easing them toward the trap? How cold-hearted could one man be that conscience didn't alter his course? Had he calculated the losses and found them acceptable?

Plass' hate for the man grew by the minute. He vowed to use the hatred fully.

* * * *

If she hadn't had a guard standing next to her, Cidra would have remained frozen in place in front of her and Grey's detention room door indefinitely. She should have asked Plass for another room. Two days in the same room with Grey would destroy what was left of her soul. Reluctantly, she activated the door and stepped onto the battlefield.

The lights were dimmed to near darkness, a sharp contrast to the brightly-lit corridors. When the door closed behind her, she stood in place and waited for her eyes to adjust. She could hear his breathing. There was nowhere to hide in the tiny room as she surveyed the lone chair and the large bed. That's where she saw him, lying on his back across the bed, his hands behind his head. He didn't acknowledge her, but she knew he was still awake.

She stared at him. He was so beautiful, dark and brooding. She loved his seriousness as much as his rare wit. The smile that streaked across his face when he laughed, the tenderness in his eyes when he touched her, the intelligence of his mind when he worked. She loved him down to every fiber of his being. Without a doubt, every one of those fibers hated her right now. No words could cut through that hate tonight. The battle would have to wait another day. The warrior within her was empty.

With a deep sigh, she walked to the opposite side of the bed and laid down next to him, careful not to touch any part of his sprawled body. Her body's automatic reaction to his familiar scent took her by surprise; it was oblivious to the mess her mind had made of their relationship. She turned her back to him, denying herself any further torment.

Defiant silence thundered. In one fell swoop, the weight of the day crushed her. She fought back the tears that burned her eyes, shoved the sob back down her throat. She would live with her decision and the fact that he would never understand or forgive her. But at least he would still be alive.

As sleep drew its heavy blanket over her, she wondered if she would ever forgive herself.

* * * *

Decker paced as a streak of curses came over the bridge comm unit aboard *Calíbre*. Barrios and Coon sat in command chairs while Rourke ranted through the comm unit.

"When I get my hands on that thick-headed bastard, I'm going to kill him," Rourke said. "I can't believe he would get into a mess like this and not tell me. Are you positive they are heading for Dakru?"

"Absolutely," Decker said. "Two days from now. We're following Grey's personal signal, behind them by about thirty minutes."

Rourke mumbled in disgust. "How bad is it?"

Decker sighed. "Bad. I've heard a nasty rumor that Tausek is planning a self-worshipping military celebration with Cidra's dead body as the big entertainment."

Rourke swore. "So tell me if I've got this right. Grey and Cidra were captured by the d'Hont and are now being held in a d'Hont Class One cruiser heading to Dakru. All the d'Hont are going to be there for a military celebration. So basically, we are taking on the entire d'Hont force in their own home."

Decker winced. "Yeah, that's about it."

Rourke launched into a sardonic drawl, "Well, how difficult could it be to rescue them? Dakru only has the best military force in the galaxy with kick-ass weapons and an impenetrable planetary defense. And there's what, three of us? No problem. When do we start?"

Shifting in his chair, Decker piped up. "I didn't say it would be easy. You don't have to help us. We're prepared to handle it ourselves." He ignored the identical horrified expressions on the faces of Barrios and Coon.

Barrios reached out and snagged his arm. He whispered low, "Speak for yourself, Decker. I, for one, want all the help we can get."

Decker waved him off and concentrated on the angry mutterings emanating from the comm. Not that the final outcome was ever really in doubt.

"I'm in," Rourke finally grumbled.

Decker relaxed. "Great. Thanks. Thanks, a lot. Now. All we need is a plan."

"What?" Rourke boomed.

* * * *

Cidra wondered how it had come to pass that she should share a morning meal with her sworn enemy. Her mind was still grappling with the events of the past few days. Emotions warred within her, rising one by one to be addressed by her overwhelmed brain. The stress of tackling it alone was wearing her down.

Melodious, benign music drifted lightly around her and Commander Plass as they ate alone in *Expunger*'s domed executive dining area. The mottled blue-green and gold walls were a welcome departure from the sheer monotony of gray and silver in the rest of the ship. High golden stools ringed an impressive raised center table, topped with a polished black stone slab.

Plass watched her as he ate. She appeared reserved, wary, and tired. No doubt, the conflict with Stone was the reason. She needed to be rested and ready to face Tausek in less than two days. Plass realized he'd have to work fast.

"Is your meal satisfactory?"

Cidra startled but collected herself quickly. "Fine. It's fine."

Plass raised an eyebrow when she laid down her fork and turned to him. "What's going to happen once we get to Dakru?"

Plass reached for his drink. "*Expunger* will remain in orbit around Dakru, directly over the Capital City. You, Lieutenant Fiske and I will take a transport to the surface. Major Berman and his men will land their ships at the city's outer slave bays. Major Holtz and his forces will remain aboard *Expunger*."

"And once we land on Dakru?" Cidra persisted.

"You will be brought to Tausek's chambers located on the top floor of his tower building."

Cidra looked him dead in the eye. "And you? Tausek knows you have turned against him. He will arrest you the minute we land on the planet."

Plass met her gaze. "Correct. This entire plan is contingent on your success. Lieutenant Fiske will see to it that your conversation is broadcast. Once it airs, I should be released." Noting the skepticism in her eyes, he added, "If not, Major Berman's units will protect you."

"You don't believe that any more than I do." She snorted slightly. "I have no delusions, Commander."

Plass waited for her to back down from the plan. She didn't.

The dining quarter doors opened, admitting Grey and Lieutenant Fiske. There was a momentary break in Grey's step when he saw Cidra.

"How was your tour, Captain?" Plass asked.

Grey narrowed his eyes at Plass, knowing he'd been set up. "Most impressive, but I'm sure you already knew that."

Plass looked pleased. "Yes, I did. *Expunger* is the most advanced starship in the fleet. A pleasure to command." He motioned to two stools nearby. "Please join us."

Fiske stepped forward. "Nothing for me, sir. I'll wait outside."

Cidra cleared her throat and addressed Fiske directly, "If you don't mind Lieutenant, I would also like a tour."

Fiske shot Plass a surprised look. Plass gave him a nod.

"Perhaps later today would be better," Fiske began hesitantly.

Cidra slid off her stool. "Actually, now is a perfect time."

She turned to Plass. "I would appreciate it if you could assign me to another detention cell, Commander."

Plass nodded. "Of course."

She turned back to Fiske and flashed him a stellar smile. "Lead the way, Lieutenant." She followed him out the door.

Grey was livid. How dare she act that way toward a d'Hont--cavorting with the enemy? She practically threw herself at the man. She was *his* mate. A rage he couldn't name tightened every muscle in his body.

Plass said nothing as the tension built in silence. A meal was served unnoticed to Grey.

"She is a remarkable woman," Plass said.

Grey raised his eyes slowly to Plass'. "What ... is that supposed to mean?"

Plass continued, "Intelligent, strong, striking. And more courageous than anyone aboard this ship. Wouldn't you agree?" Plass took a bite of food.

"So?" Grey's tone was clipped and barely restrained.

"So much promise. It's a shame to see it destroyed." Plass shook his head. "She will never survive facing Tausek alone. He won't let her leave his quarters alive. She knows it."

Grey snapped, "You bastard. How can you send her?"

"I have no choice. Her sacrifice will save countless lives." Plass shrugged. "Besides, she's sending herself. How can she do otherwise? This is her destiny, her charge."

As Plass spoke, anger swamped Grey. This mission would end up killing her. That was the part that gnawed at him. The part he couldn't accept or condone. She had made the choice knowing it would drive them apart, knowing it would destroy their future. When all she had to do was walk away.

Plass was saying, "After *Expunger* is in orbit over Dakru, you will be allowed to contact your ship. They can pick you up anytime."

"No, they won't," Grey mumbled.

"Did you say something, Captain?"

Grey glared at him. "Cidra's not going to face Tausek alone."

Plass gave him a pointed look. "I don't think she wants your help."

Grey stabbed a piece of food with his fork. "You let me worry about that."

* * * *

"This the stupidest idea I have ever heard," muttered Barrios. "No one is going to believe that we are entertainers, much less musicians."

His round face was propped in his hands as he eyed the comm unit in the center of Grey's office.

"What do you expect on such short notice? You're lucky my people work fast," Rourke's irritated voice came through the unit. "Can you think of another way to get down on that planet in one piece?"

"But why a band?" Barrios questioned in exasperation.

"Every available performing act in the sector is being recruited to play Dakru for this celebration," Rourke answered. "Hangtime is a popular new group from Vaasa. Three male band members. We fit their general descriptions close enough to pass. We can't ask for more than that. It's a perfect cover. It will position us in the middle of the capital city. We can even smuggle our weapons inside the equipment."

Decker tapped on the table in thought. "When was this group scheduled to arrive?"

"Tomorrow afternoon. A day early to setup," Rourke reported.

Decker nodded. "The timing is right. We won't raise suspicions by arriving unexpectedly. When will your ship reach the coordinates we agreed upon?"

"We'll arrive early tomorrow morning," Rourke stated.

Decker said confidently, "*Calibre* will join you mid-morning."

"And the d'Hont cruiser?" Rourke asked.

"Unless they change their minds, tomorrow morning just before us," Decker said. "What are we going to do if the real band shows up? Our cover will be blown."

"Not a problem." Rourke chuckled. "Being creative souls, they don't take orders well, especially from Tausek. They were more than happy to accept my offer to find a replacement for them. I've got the security code they were issued to land on Dakru, boys. We are in."

Decker shook his head. "You do work fast. I appreciate it. We'll be ready to go the minute we drop out of hyperspace over Dakru. See you tomorrow."

Decker cut the communications and leaned far back in his chair.

Barrios pressed his fingers to his eyes. "This is never going to work."

Decker grinned. "Worried about being mobbed by crazed fans?"

"No," Barrios mumbled. "I'm worried someone will ask me to sing."

* * * *

Cidra entered her newly assigned quarters with profound relief. The *Expunger* tour that had taken most of the day was little more than a blur. She had monopolized Lieutenant Fiske for as long as she could, but her mind and soul were still occupied with the most recent confrontation with Grey at breakfast. His furious expression remained etched in her mind.

She surveyed the grand room, slowly registering its contents. It was about as far from a detention room as she could imagine. Official guest quarters would be her guess. Being considered a pampered guest aboard a d'Hont cruiser did nothing for her state of mind.

Subtle lighting splashed over the rich burgundy colored walls, an elegant couch, and several chairs in a deep rose and gold. Plush flooring picked up all the colors in the room. Lavishly ornamented tables and trim work accented the grand quarters. But it was the massive, graceful bed that caught her attention.

Weariness claimed her as she laid down on it, stretched out, and closed her eyes. "Lights ten percent," she ordered the computer. The lights dimmed, plunging the room into near darkness and turning the opulent surroundings to gray and black.

"How was your tour?" a familiar voice asked from the darkness.

Cidra shot up on the bed. "Lights one hundred percent," she gasped.

When the computer obeyed, she found Grey leaned against the lav doorway, his arms crossed, his gray eyes dark and cold.

"What are you doing here?" Cidra snapped as she rolled to the edge of the bed. "These are my quarters."

"I'm your mate, remember? You don't go anywhere without me," Grey reminded her, his hunter's eyes watching her every move.

She stood next to the bed facing him. "As I recall, you gave up that position in Plass' office."

"And it didn't take you long to find a replacement," he countered, his anger flaring. "Did you enjoy yourself with Fiske?" He silently berated himself the minute the words came out. He was making a mess of this.

He had gone slowly mad waiting for her to return with Fiske. The idea that she was spending so much time in the Lieutenant's company had taunted him relentlessly.

By the time she returned, he had worked himself into an explosive emotional state, one he had no idea how to diffuse. The first glimpse of her lying on the bed was enough to make him forget the carefully prepared apology. The desire to possess was overwhelming.

Cidra glared at him and pointed to the door. "Out. Get out."

"Not until I have my answer." He shoved off the doorway and stalked toward her, unhurried and resolute.

"I don't owe you anything," Cidra fired back, not budging from her position even as Grey stopped a mere step away.

He stared at her for a few long moments. "I'm going with you tomorrow."

Cidra replied tightly, "I can handle the mission alone."

"Too bad," Grey said. "I made a promise to Syrus. Part of that promise was to keep you safe."

For a split-second Cidra looked wounded, but then she lifted her chin. "I see. Well, I wouldn't want you to break that promise. Right now, I'm perfectly safe. So if you don't mind, I need some rest. Alone."

Grey's eyes narrowed and he waited. He thought she would say something else, change her mind. Nothing. A chill ran through him as he stared into her defiant eyes. He turned and stalked out.

CHAPTER SEVENTEEN

The Dakru sun was just beginning its slow, grisly descent in the bank of windows that stretched across one end of the room.

"Are the ceremonial preparations underway, Commander?"

From behind Tausek, Commander Stoll answered. "Yes, sir. A planet-wide celebration has been declared in your honor as you requested. The parade will begin with a d'Hont show of force, headed by our ground forces and our most impressive military weapons."

"And Faulkner's body?" Tausek prompted.

"Will be the center attraction in the parade," Stoll boasted. "A victory for you and a warning to our enemies. It will be a celebration like no other. The day will go down in history."

"Excellent." The word rolled off Tausek's tongue. "The celebration must be a success, Commander. I expect no less. Are the plans in place for the arrest of Plass?"

Commander Stoll answered. "Yes, sir. I will be waiting for him when the *Expunger* docks at the orbital station. He will be apprehended as soon as he delivers Faulkner's body. Plass and his crew will be transported here and interrogated. Plass' execution is planned after the celebration."

Tausek suddenly swung around to face Stoll, wiping a smug

smile off the new Commander's face. "He is a traitor to the d'Hont. Undermining the organization and pursuing his own warped interests at the expense of others and in direct conflict with my orders. Make his execution public and painful. And I want the entire *Expunger* crew present."

A droll smirk touched Commander Stoll's face. "Yes, sir."

Tausek spun back around and stated flatly, "You are dismissed."

Commander Stoll exited in silence.

Alone, Tausek smiled openly. He had guaranteed that Plass would go down in history as a traitor by convincing Stoll that Plass had defied several direct orders. The undertaking was so effortless, a lie here, a mistruth there.

For Tausek, it was no less the truth. Plass was a traitor to him and him alone, but no one would ever know that. Even if Plass managed to convince the *Expunger* crew, no man or woman would dare speak after Plass' horrific execution.

The situation had given Tausek another opportunity he had been waiting for: to replace the d'Hont positions vacated by the mutinous *Expunger* crew with his own personal agents. Men and women loyal to Tausek alone. The personnel guaranteed to take him to the next step in his master plan with no petty issues like d'Hont integrity and honor to get in the way.

The path to ultimate control of the sector was clear and stronger than before. The recent events would provide him with renewed backing from the people and reduce the d'Hont to nothing more than an enforcement role. The executions of Faulkner and Plass would provide a brutal demonstration of Tausek's power to the rest of the galaxy. He had already chosen the first planet to invade and add to his kingdom. Avion.

The sunset glowed a ghastly crimson as Tausek basked in his own brilliance.

* * * *

Plass nodded in approval and satisfaction as Grey and Cidra joined him in *Expunger*'s crowded security center. Although they kept their distance from each other when they took their places at the massive holo deck, they were together.

As Plass introduced them to Majors Berman and Holtz, he watched for any sign of belligerence toward the couple. He saw none. If anything, the two Majors greeted them as part of the team. Grey and Cidra seemed wary but steady, with the exception of the searing look Grey gave Lieutenant Fiske. The other senior and junior officers lining the round room eyed them with mixed curiosity and acceptance.

Turning his attention toward the empty holo deck, Plass started the early morning meeting. "Display the layout of the inner city."

The holo deck sprung to life with a flat, two-dimensional map of the Capital City floating about a half meter above the bottom of the deck. All eyes took in the criss-cross of streets and outlines of buildings and landmarks.

"Give me a low-projection, three-dimensional view," Plass ordered. Seconds later, cubes representing buildings and structures rose up from the ground level. A network of tunnels, rooms, and passageways appeared below ground level. A large, circular object in the center of the topographical map projected higher than the rest.

Plass pointed to the tube-like structure. "Tausek's tower. High-level, intensive security system and a guard at every single entry point throughout the building. At twenty stories, it is the tallest structure in the city. Tausek's executive and private quarters occupy the top floor, as well as my office." He corrected, "My former office, now used by Commander Stoll."

Grey inquired, "What are all these passages below the surface?"

"Tausek's secret weapon." Plass smiled sardonically at him. "The underground world below the Capital City. The real heart of his power. Tunnels and passages link all parts of the city's military facilities--detention and interrogation, control centers, communications, planetary defense. The underworld existence is a highly-guarded secret. Troops and units can move freely and discreetly underground. Then suddenly appear on the surface. As you can imagine, that element of surprise works well to keep the natives in line." He pointed out several access areas. "The entrances are placed throughout the city and guarded continually. To the average Dakruian, they look like simple military posts."

Plass indicated the landing point and looked at Grey. "You, Cidra, Lieutenant Fiske, and I will take a transport to this location. I am not planning to conceal our entry. The planetary defenses around Dakru are superior. It would be a futile and fatal effort. Therefore, I expect Commander Stoll will meet us when we arrive."

Grey spoke up. "What then?"

"I will inform Commander Stoll that Tausek expected to see you in person and alive," Plass told him. "Stoll doesn't have the

guts to make his own decisions, so he won't take a chance that
I'm lying. He will bring you to Tausek, probably via
underground. I will also ensure that you are accompanied by
Lieutenant Fiske."

"And you?" Cidra prompted.

Plass turned to look at her. "My sources indicate that I will be
arrested. My execution is already scheduled after the parade."

Cidra paled. "Execution?"

"Public, lengthy, and brutal. Tausek style," Plass replied dryly.
"If he shows up for it, I will know the mission failed."

"It won't fail," Cidra amended, her voice determined.

Plass gave her a small smile. "I hope not. We have come a long
way."

Grey looked around the room. "And the rest of your crew?"

Major Berman stepped forward and spoke in a booming voice.
"Posing as slave transports, my forces will land at three locations
outside the city. We will converge on the tower from all
directions—above and below ground, neutralizing Tausek's
guards as we proceed. Once inside, we will take out the internal
guard units and secure the tower."

Grey narrowed his eyes at the man. He was quite sure that
Major Berman had simplified the whole affair beyond reason.

Plass nodded toward Major Holtz. "The Major will stay aboard
Expunger with a skeleton crew." He swung his gaze toward
Grey and Cidra. "I've ordered *Expunger*'s guns aimed at
Tausek's tower. We will have four hours to accomplish our
mission. If Major Holtz does not receive counter orders from me
before that deadline, he will open fire. I will not take a chance on
losing Tausek. If our plan fails and we can't get a confession
from him, I want him dead at all costs. The battle for power
afterward will be bloody, but unavoidable at that point."

Grey looked at Cidra and muttered, "Whatever you do, Plass,
don't lose your comm unit."

Plass smiled and addressed the holo deck once more. "Zoom in
on Tausek's tower. Scale to size. Full schematic, classified
version."

The holo deck complied, filling the viewing space with
Tausek's towering fortress. Grey studied the impressive, circular
structure. Other than the two entrances on the lower level, there
were no outstanding features. The exterior looked smooth and
unscalable. No other windows or doors were displayed on the
nineteen floors leading to the top. The word 'impenetrable' came

to Grey's mind.

The top floor that housed Tausek spun slowly on the tip of the structure, half of the exterior wall appeared to be windows. A solid, small domed structure topped the entire tower, effectively prohibiting a spacecraft from landing on it. Unlike the rest of the plans, it was not a viewable grid shape.

Grey pointed to it. "What's in here?"

Plass shook his head. "I don't know. Even the most classified schematics didn't have it listed. It was included based on a visual observation."

Fiske took over the plan of attack, addressing Berman's units. "I will cover Tausek's upper level. Major Berman will be in charge of the tower assault. There are only two entrances on the lower level--a formal front entrance and a large rear entrance. Both are heavily guarded, both equally difficult to breach. I would suggest we concentrate on a discreet attack on the underground access level instead."

"Once inside, we are faced with another problem." He pointed out a highlighted tube running from the lower level to the top through the center of the tower. "This is the only lift in the structure. It will be automatically locked out the minute our assault begins on the tower. However, there are access points throughout the building." He ordered the access tubes and stairs lit up on the schematic and turned to the group. "Unfortunately, each access shaft is located at a different point on each level. They don't line up from floor to floor."

Grey noted with dismay that the units would have to scale to one level, then locate the next access point and scale that one and so on. Without the lift, getting from the lower level to the upper level would be a slow and exhausting effort, not to mention nearly impossible without a map.

Fiske added, "You will all be issued micropads containing the tower's structure and access points. I suggest you memorize the points in case the micropads are lost or confiscated."

He returned to the attack plan. "We have no choice but to charge the access shafts one at a time and overwhelm any guard units by sheer numbers alone. I estimate the total elapsed time to reach Tausek's chambers under optimal conditions via this method will be twenty-five minutes."

Grey and Cidra's eyes met. *Twenty-five minutes alone and unarmed with Tausek.*

Fiske continued unaffected. "If our attack is discreet, we may be able to access the lift. However, you must take a tower guard with you or the lift system will not operate. It is programmed for their embedded ID units. Via the lift, arrival time is thirty seconds."

Plass spoke up. "Once you reach the top, your first priority is to rescue Grey and Cidra. Your second mission is to capture Tausek any way you can, preferably alive."

All heads nodded in understanding.

Lieutenant Fiske began handing out the miniature micropads. "These micropads contain all the information you should need. We will drop out of hyperspace over Dakru in one hour. Be ready to deploy seconds after that."

"Any questions?" Plass asked the group.

When no one spoke up, Plass dismissed them. He turned to Grey and Cidra. "Join me in my executive quarters. I want to explain the communications plan."

* * * *

Plass smiled at the chaos surrounding his transport jet docked in the main landing bay located on Dakru's Principal Transportation Center. With its contemporary architecture and gleaming interior, the preeminent transportation center showcased the very best of Dakru for all the delegates and foreigners who visited the planet. It was a far cry from the slave bays on the outer edges of the city.

As he had hoped, the confusion caused by their unexpected arrival at the Transportation Center instead of the orbital station worsened an already frenzied situation. Traffic in and out of Dakru before the biggest celebration of the decade had pushed the city's transportation centers to the limit. This terminal was no exception. The atmosphere bordered on riotous as people moved in waves and currents throughout the terminal. Muffled announcements blared overhead. Arguments arose over the precious few public ground shuttles.

Plass stood outside their transport flanked by Fiske and their prisoners, Grey and Cidra. Although Plass and Fiske had not been placed in restraints, they had been disarmed. Four security guards surrounded them, weapons ready, unsure what to do with the unanticipated group. An endless stream of people milled around them, eyeing the proceedings with curiosity.

The Commander glanced at Grey and Cidra. Side by side, they appeared calm even with their hands locked behind them. Plass had not told the guards who his prisoners were. He couldn't risk a glory-hungry guard with a quick draw. He prayed no one would recognize them until Stoll arrived.

Finally, the Head Security guard appeared. He looked haggard and frustrated as he wordlessly motioned for the entire group to follow him. The churning crowd gave the armed escort a wide berth as they approached the bank of lifts. The Head guard activated one of the lifts.

After the doors slid shut, Grey felt the brief sensation of falling. They were going underground just as Plass had predicted. It wasn't good, but at least it was expected. He tested the strength of the restraints. *They* were not part of the plan.

He slid Cidra a cautious glance. She was taking in all the details, checking the guard's weapons, watching for weaknesses. He suppressed a smile. No other person in this room knew what she was capable of.

The lift halted almost immediately. The door opened into a wide, deep tunnel lined with endless doors and rooms. The stone walls were dark with black dirt, smudged and smeared by people and vehicles that rubbed against them. Harsh overhead lights ran down the center of the corridor ceiling casting a sickly green glow over everything. The air hung thick and foul. An insidious low hum seemed to vibrate from the walls themselves.

At gunpoint, Grey, Cidra, Plass, and Fiske were ushered down the corridor and into a small, dingy room. Grey studied the strange marks on the walls and floor. It took him a moment to recognize the substance that created the stains as blood. This was an interrogation room. He tugged on the wrist restraints instinctively. Then he caught Cidra's eye and gave her a reassuring smile, hoping to keep her distracted from the room's horrible distinction.

Grey and Cidra were halted in the center of the room behind Plass and Fiske as a door in front of them opened admitting a tall man followed by two guards. Grey eyed the lead man, no doubt Plass' replacement. The new Commander was a big bastard. Tall and broad with an arrogant saunter that made Grey dislike him on sight. Chin-length, jet-black hair was combed straight back from his forehead. His upper lip was curled in a permanent sneer. His eyes conveyed power and hate. Grey's dislike turned to concern.

Plass regarded Commander Stoll with amused contempt. He knew Stoll as a man who backed a guaranteed winner. It didn't matter whether the cause was just or whether the fight was fair as long as victory was assured.

But there was another factor that made Stoll dangerous. He had tried and failed the discipline and rigors of d'Hont training. It was a failure that fueled his ruthless disdain for them. Tausek had picked the perfect man to harness and shackle the d'Hont.

Stoll stopped directly in front of Plass, using his size to intimidate the smaller man. His smile was superior and arrogant. "Welcome home, Ex-Commander."

"Stoll." Plass ignored the Commander's position.

The new Commander's face turned cruel. A slow smile returned as he looked at Lieutenant Fiske and nodded. "Welcome back, Lieutenant. I see our plan worked perfectly. You have served me well."

Plass turned to Fiske, his eyes narrowing.

Lieutenant Fiske saluted and stepped forward to address Stoll. "Yes, sir. I apologize for the loss of communication for a short time. It was beyond my control. However, the mission was a success regardless. The Ex-Commander is all yours."

Cidra rocked on her feet. One look at Plass' pale face told her that this was not part of the plan. Fiske had betrayed them.

Stoll grinned like a lunatic at Plass. "You failed. You should have checked out your crew more thoroughly. Lieutenant Fiske works for me."

Plass continued to stare tight-lipped at Fiske. "You've seen the evidence yourself. How can you deny the facts?"

The young Lieutenant snorted. "I don't know how you live with those high moral standards you have. Did it ever occur to you that I don't care how Tausek came to power? I have my own position to think about."

"You bastard," Grey snarled. He dove forward and head-butted Fiske in the stomach. They both hit the wall with a resounding thud.

"Grey, stop it," Cidra shouted. Fiske gripped Grey by the shirt and pinned him back against the wall.

Drawn by her outburst, Stoll turned his full attention to Cidra as he took a slow walk around her. The hair stood up on the back of her neck.

"A live Faulkner. Tausek will be most pleased to see you." He stopped in front of her, his gaze drifting down her body.

Cidra felt the chill descend over her. Although he was inches from her, she couldn't feel any warmth emanating from him. The cold blue eyes that met hers had no depth.

"Most pleased," he repeated slowly. Cidra froze under his lurid gaze.

He spun around and motioned to two of the guards. "Take Plass to the detention center. The prisoners will accompany me to Tausek's tower."

Fiske stood at attention next to Stoll. "Request permission to join you, sir. I would like very much to see this mission through to the end."

Stoll nodded and walked out of the room.

* * * *

"It's showtime, gents. Mind your manners now," Rourke said as he released the hatch door of the transport. He took one step out of the craft onto the landing bay platform on Dakru and came face to face with the spitting end of a laser rifle.

"Howdy, boys." He grinned wide at two stone-faced entry guards. Decker and Barrios exited behind him.

The transportation center they had been directed to on their entry into the Capital City bustled with activity. An astonishing assortment of species and races crammed the landing bay, most looking destitute. The smells of food cooking close-by wafted above the stench of body odor. The landing bay must have been impressive once, but signs of decay appeared everywhere: cracked and broken windows, the floor indistinguishable under the layers of dirt, the walls lined with beggars and thieves.

From amid the madness, the Head security officer appeared and demanded to see their IDs. As he verified them in the security system, another guard began a man-to-man body search.

"You boys don't talk much, do you?" Rourke persisted as the guard roughly frisked him.

The Head security guard glared at him. "Quiet. Your identification checks out." He motioned to a pair of armed guards. "These are your escorts for the duration of your stay on Dakru."

He addressed the guards. "Shuttle them to the stage area and their quarters." Handing the ID's back, he said matter-of-factly. "You will be shot if you are caught without escorts."

"Their welcome committee could use some work," Barrios muttered to Rourke as the Head security guard disappeared into the crowd without another word.

They boarded the small, fully enclosed shuttle with the guards taking positions in the front. Rourke and Decker sat behind them, with Barrios in the rear just in front of the band's equipment and luggage.

The shuttle leapt forward and exited the landing bay structure. Dakru spread out before them. The dismal view didn't get any better. Even at this time of the morning, it was a dark, solemn city. Rundown one- and two-story buildings crowded the litter-lined streets. The inhabitants looked like walking dead, their faces and eyes sunken as they moved along in slow motion.

Barrios grimaced. "What a pit."

Decker whispered back to him. "Imagine what it looked like before they cleaned it up for the big celebration."

Pointing to pictures of Tausek plastered on every structure, Barrios said, "At least we know what the arrogant bastard looks like."

Rourke caught Decker's eye and discreetly slipped the concealed Flint laser pistol from his jacket. He had lifted it when they transferred the equipment. Decker smiled back and slipped his own out.

Rourke leaned over and whispered, "At the next stop, you take the one on the right. I'll take the one on the left."

The shuttle had barely halted at an intersection when Decker and Rourke leapt forward, each getting a headlock on a guard and pressing the Flint pistols to their heads. The stunned, wide-eyed guards were then yanked up and out of their seats, restrained and gagged in a matter of minutes.

Rourke jumped into the front seat and took control of the transport leaving Decker to quiet the guards.

Barrios whistled. "Nice work, boys. Now what?"

Decker reached around and dug the tracker unit out of the band equipment behind him. "Now we find them." He activated the unit once he located it and jumped into the front seat beside Rourke. He began a sweep of the city as the shuttle lurched forward with Rourke at the controls.

"According to this, they are moving due south. You need to take the next right, Rourke," Decker told him.

"Got it." Rourke whipped the shuttle crisply around the next corner.

Decker concentrated on the tracker unit and frowned. "This can't be right. According to this, they are underneath us."

Barrios piped up, "What did you do, Rourke? Run them over?"

"Back seat navigator," Rourke muttered.

"I'm serious. They are right below us," Decker insisted. Then he jumped up. "They turned off, due south."

"What? Where?" Rourke slammed a fist on the console. "What is going on?"

Rourke suddenly pulled the transport over and turned it off.

Decker looked at him in disbelief. "What are you doing? They're getting away."

Rourke ignored him and pointed at small, guarded building on the corner of the next intersection. "What do you make of that? There was a similar one a few blocks back."

"Too small to be of any practical use," Decker thought aloud. "Maybe a control center or part of a security grid." He glanced around and frowned. "It might be used to access something underground."

"With an armed guard standing watch?" Rourke asked. "Must be some real special infrastructure down there. Wouldn't you say?"

Rourke and Decker looked at each other and grinned.

* * * *

Cidra tried to take in as much of the underground layout as possible while the shuttle whisked silently down one side of the wide tunnel toward Tausek's tower. She spotted Stoll riding in the shuttle in front of them and shuddered involuntarily at the thought of such a cruel man wielding so much power.

Wedged between Grey and Lieutenant Fiske in the center seats of the shuttle, she could only glimpse an occasional intersecting passageway in the endless and monotonous underground world. She wondered where in this maze Plass was. Despite his role in her past, he had earned her respect and her concern. His fate was now as grim as their own.

Cidra tried to push the desperation of their situation to the back of her mind. It proved a futile effort. Without Fiske, the entire plan was ruined. They had trusted him implicitly with the communications, making him a critical link in the plan to broadcast Tausek's confession. She couldn't believe she had been so completely deceived. But the moment he had taken his position next to Stoll, she had watched the youthful, innocent face turn hard and cold. His whole body had matured in a flash. Only now could she see the years in his eyes.

Maybe Grey was right. Trust was an illusion.

Next to her, Lieutenant Fiske abruptly fumbled with the micropad he was reviewing and it fell to the shuttle floor beside her foot. He bent low over her knee to pick it up. She froze as his hand slid under her pants and slipped something cool and flat inside her boot. He retrieved the micropad and straightened in his seat, turning his attention once again to the unit as if nothing had happened.

Cidra stared straight ahead in stunned disbelief and fought the overwhelming urge to look at him. Instead, she wiggled her foot slightly to verify her suspicions. It felt like the tiny comm unit that Plass had showed them on *Expunger*. The unit that Major Fiske was supposed to give her before their meeting with Tausek. Could it be that he had not betrayed them after all?

Another thought crushed her elation. It could also be a simple explosive device. Maybe Fiske planned to blow them all up and blame Tausek's death on her in some sinister plan to make Stoll the next ruler of Dakru.

Out of the corner of her eye, she slid him a cautious glance, but his demeanor was detached and stoic.

A sliver of hope glowed. It was all she had to cling to.

CHAPTER EIGHTEEN

Decker stood watch in the underground tunnel as Barrios leaned against the wall behind him and wheezed. "Who thought this was a good idea? In case you hadn't noticed, my running days are over."

"Keep it down. We don't need any company right now," Decker whispered over his shoulder. "I can't see a thing, and there's no cover in this corridor. When Rourke comes back from reconnaissance with a clear sign, we're off again."

Suddenly, a laser blast and a small explosion filled the corridor. Barrios jumped. "What was that?"

Decker swore, lowering his pistol. Smoke drifted from the scattered pieces of the Servo-unit he'd just shot. The smell of burnt wiring filled the air.

"It came up behind me so fast, I thought it was a guard," he explained, holding his hands up helplessly.

Barrios gaped at him. "A half-meter tall guard? And since when have guards whizzed along sucking dirt off the floor?"

Decker shot him a scathing look. "Hey, be grateful I was covering your big butt."

Then he froze as footsteps approached. He turned back around, leveled his weapon and waited.

Rourke emerged from the darkness almost on top of them. He raised his eyebrows at the laser pistol aimed at his midsection. Breathlessly he held up a hand. "Easy, Decker. Don't get tight on me now."

Decker lowered the weapon and frowned. "Sorry. This place is getting too busy. Next time, whistle first."

Rourke looked down at the charred remains of a Servo-unit and turned to them with a look of disbelief. "I leave you boys alone for a minute and you start terrorizing small, defenseless cleaning equipment. New rule. No shooting unless the enemy comes up to your knees."

Decker hung his head. "This is going to be all over the galaxy, isn't it?"

Rourke smiled wide. "You got that right. I haven't had a good story for the saloons in a long time."

"Do you think they'll miss this one?" Decker looked down at the smoldering metal.

Rourke snorted. "I doubt it. There's about a million of those things down here."

Decker's expression brightened. "So what did you find?"

Rourke leaned back against the wall. "This corridor empties into a larger one about thirty meters down. Looks like pedestrian traffic only, lots of doors running along it. Can't tell the direction, but I'd guess it's east/west. No activity that I could see, so I checked out what would be the west branch. It intersects with a main artery--double lanes of motorized traffic. It was pretty busy, but I'd say that's our only option at this point unless you want to spend a lifetime down here trying to find another way. Sooner or later, that artery is going to hit something big."

"Just how extensive are these tunnels?" Decker gasped.

Rourke wiped sweat off his forehead. "Very. I'd say they run under the entire city."

"That would explain why none of the buildings are over a few levels tall. This underground infrastructure could never support them," Decker surmised. "I'll bet the natives don't have a clue what's down here."

"That means that everyone we meet is going to be armed and dangerous," muttered Barrios.

"Exactly right," Rourke agreed. "Sounds like we have a borderline plan. Let's go."

Barrios asked, "Speaking of plans, what's the escape route for getting out of here once we find them?"

Decker looked at Rourke. "Well?"

Rourke put his hands on his hips. "Hey, I got us down here. I thought you were going to come up with getting us out."

Decker raised the tracker unit in self-defense. "Don't look at me. I'm in charge of navigation."

Barrios shook his head and lumbered down the corridor in disgust. "Forget it, just forget it. What was I thinking?"

They covered the first leg of their journey unspotted. A primary artery appeared exactly as Rourke had described. Rourke brought them to a halt behind a doorway as an occasional shuttle whizzed by. Traffic was light with a slow stream of shuttles and supply vehicles.

Rourke studied the traffic. "Looks like most of the shuttles run on timed intervals. They probably have pre-programmed destinations as well. Unless we want to walk all the way to the tower, we're going to have to steal a shuttle. One that's not on autopilot."

Decker groaned. "That means a driver. A driver means a weapon."

"Generally, yes," Rourke said, his attention locked on a lone shuttle some distance away closing on them rapidly. "That's the one. Two guards in the front."

He nodded to Decker. "If you see a firearm, shoot. These guys are too good to mess around with. Here we go."

Barrios demanded, "How are you going to stop an armed shuttle?"

Without answering, the two men stepped out from the cover of the doorway together. Immediately, the shuttle driver raised a weapon. Rourke and Decker fired their laser pistols simultaneously. Rourke's blast struck the shuttle driver in the head. Decker's took out the guard on the passenger side. Without a driver, the small shuttle slowed to a stop almost at their feet. Only then did they notice another man in the semi-enclosed passenger section.

"Nice going." Barrios grinned as he emerged from the doorway.

"Hold on," Rourke warned, holding a hand up to stop him. "There's another one in the back."

He approached the man with his weapon raised. He could see through the open sides that the man wore wrist restraints.

"This is your stop," Rourke told him.

Decker came around the side, took one look at the man he'd seen during his recent research into Dakru's files and leveled his weapon at the man's head.

"Plass," Decker snarled.

Stunned, Rourke glanced at Decker. "Isn't this the man who captured them?"

"Yes," Decker hissed. "At least I'll make sure he dies for that."

Before Decker could fire, Rourke put his hand on the end of the weapon and pointed it to the floor. Decker turned on him. "What are you doing?"

"Let's think about this first." Rourke addressed Plass. "Why the restraints?"

"I am now an enemy of Tausek's. If you would give me a few minutes, I can explain the entire situation."

Rourke's head shot up, his eyes searching for what his ears could hear. "Incoming traffic. Get in. We need to move."

The men scrambled into the shuttle with Rourke at the controls and Barrios riding next to him in the cockpit section. Decker sat in the back with Plass. They accelerated quickly, putting distance between themselves and the shuttle behind them.

Decker checked his tracker unit. "The signal's not so good down here, but I think they are south of us. We need to take the right branch."

Then he turned to Plass. "You better have one good story or I'm going to feed what's left of you to the Servo-units."

* * * *

"How much further to the tower?" Rourke called back to Decker.

Decker checked their coordinates on his tracker unit and replied, "About a kilometer to go."

Barrios looked at Rourke. "Problem?"

Rourke shook his head and checked behind them for traffic. "The closer we get to that tower, the nastier it's going to become. Do you have any idea what our chances are of finding them? Stone must be crazy. No woman is worth this kind of trouble."

Barrios grinned. "Jealous?"

Rourke snorted. "No. In fact--"

"Look out!" Barrios shouted, pointing to the left.

A bulky ground shuttle shot out of a side tunnel beside them, veering into their lane. Rourke jerked the controls hard to the right, but it was too late. The other vehicle caught their back end and knocked them into the side wall. The impact spun them around until they were facing the massive shuttle head-on. Braking thrusters roared as the big shuttle slid to a halt before them--nose to nose. Both sets of occupants were too surprised to do anything but stare.

Then Rourke bellowed, "What's the matter with you?" He pointed at the spot where Berman's shuttle had entered the main tunnel. "Can't you read the signs?"

Barrios nudged him hard. "Rourke, shut up. I don't think it's a good idea to piss them off."

Rourke rounded on him. "Why not? Those idiots could have killed us."

"That's why." Barrios grimaced and nodded toward the other shuttle. No less than ten weapons were pointed at them as d'Hont poured from the rear entrance of the shuttle.

Breath hissed through Rourke's teeth. "Good point."

A clearly annoyed, very large man barked, "Kill them all and leave their bodies inside. Quickly and quietly."

Barrios muttered to Rourke, "Now would be a good time for a brilliant idea."

"Major Berman, that won't be necessary." A voice came from behind him. Plass stepped out of the passenger section. The restraints were gone.

Berman blinked in surprise and smiled broadly. "Commander. Good to see you alive."

Plass grinned back. "It's been an interesting journey. The details can wait. We need to get moving before another shuttle comes along."

"What about them?" Berman pointed to Rourke, Decker, and Barrios who were exiting their disabled shuttle at gunpoint.

"Lower your weapons," Plass ordered the d'Hont team surrounding them. He turned to Berman. "They will be joining the rescue. I have briefed them. They have agreed to the plan." Plass nodded toward Berman's shuttle. "I can fill you in along the way."

Grey's rescue team and their weapons were loaded aboard the back of the slave shuttle Berman's unit had seized, crowding an already packed rear storage section. Plass and Berman took a position in the rear section as well, directly behind the small hatch door to the cockpit section. Although they were blind to the outside, a communications link to the cockpit would let them know what was happening.

"I assume your units had no problems, Major," Plass began as the shuttle accelerated.

Berman snorted. "The plan worked perfectly. We flew in as slave freighters and secured our target landing bay in under ten minutes. All the other units are in position around the city and moving toward the tower now. We will be in position at the designated time."

"The plan has been altered," Plass said coolly. His eyes met Berman's. "Lieutenant Fiske has betrayed us. He reports to Stoll."

Berman's nostrils flared with anger. "That bastard. He had us all fooled."

Plass continued. "And don't expect to see many d'Hont. Stoll is fully in charge. The majority of their positions have been replaced by regular military faithful to Tausek alone."

"Then where are the d'Hont?" Berman asked in disbelief.

"Parade duty," Plass muttered.

A nasty snarl formed on Berman's face. "Just as well. At least we won't be killing our own. So now what?"

Plass looked at Decker. "Are you still getting Stone's signal?"

Decker checked his tracker unit. "Yes, they just arrived at the tower."

"First, we rescue Stone and Cidra." Plass turned to Berman. "Then we kill Tausek and Fiske."

"That's too good for either of them," Berman growled.

Plass nodded. "Agreed, but our choices are limited now. I won't let Tausek live even if we do start a civil war by killing him." He glanced at the time. "We only have two hours before Major Holtz decimates the tower." He looked back at Berman. "And us along with it."

"Checkpoint Beta coming up, sir," the pilot interrupted over the communications link above their heads.

The d'Hont unit automatically came to attention while the vehicle rolled to a stop. No one moved or spoke in the rear section as they listened to the conversation between the pilot and the checkpoint guard. A few words were exchanged before a thud was audible over the comm.

A few moments later, the driver reported the status. "Checkpoint Beta is now closed for the day. Arriving at Checkpoint Alpha in three minutes."

As the shuttle surged forward, Berman addressed his team. "Checkpoint Alpha will be heavily guarded. As soon as the shuttle slows down, you are to exit via the rear hatch. Follow the shuttle closely, using it as cover. We will take the checkpoint by force. After that, we are on foot."

* * * *

Grey glanced around the wide concourse their shuttle had been sitting in for ten minutes. It surrounded a round, central structure containing several doors. He guessed the inner circular room to be the underground portion of Tausek's tower. He wondered which one of the doors would lead to the tower's single lift.

The curved wall behind them was lined completely with guards at regular intervals in typical Tausek style: overkill.

He was trying to come up with an escape plan when he caught Cidra watching him, her eyes clear and calm. Lord, he loved her. He wanted to touch her, wanted to hold to her. What a fool he'd been. He may have blown his chance to tell her he loved her but he'd make sure she got out of here alive. With or without him. Now was their last chance to escape.

Slowly, she shook her head at him. He blinked at her. Did she know what he was thinking? She glanced at the contingency of guards, back at him and mouthed the word 'no'.

Grey stared back. She didn't want to escape? When she gave him a small smile, he realized she must know something he didn't. His natural instinct to escape warred with her eyes pleaded silently at him: *trust me.*

Grey closed his eyes. *Trust me.* Once they were in the tower with Tausek, there would be no chance for escape. *Trust me.* Tausek would kill them. The mission would be lost. *Trust me.* Do nothing. Trust her. Could it be that simple? Did he love her that much?

He let out a long breath, relaxed, and put his life in her hands. When he opened his eyes, a single tear was trickling down her cheek and a sweet smile played on her lips.

Finally, Fiske approached the shuttle and assisted Cidra out. Grey was handled roughly by a guard on his side. They were led briskly to one of the doors in the tower. Grey bared his teeth when he spotted Stoll watching Cidra with blatant interest. Grey shuddered to think what would have happened to her by now if he hadn't agreed to accompany her.

The door to the lift opened before them. Stoll ordered all his men but Fiske to remain in the concourse circling the tower. Then he took Cidra's arm and led her into the lift with Fiske and Grey following. Stoll's hand was on Cidra's arm, stroking it lightly. Her expression remained stoic but Grey could see the effort it took. He, on the other hand, was itching to kill someone and made no effort to hide it. Stoll eyed him knowingly and smirked.

The tower lift opened less than a minute later on the top level of the tower. When the door opened, they walked around the corridor that circled the lift. Additional hallways veered off the circular corridor like spokes. They took one such hallway and halted in front of an intricately decorated door.

Stoll turned to Fiske. "I will deliver them to Tausek myself."

The Lieutenant hesitated slightly. "Of course, sir. I will stand guard."

* * * *

The attack on Checkpoint Alpha succeeded with a barrage of gunfire and a pile of dead bodies.

The sealed tower entrance now loomed before them, unguarded but impenetrable. Plass and Berman were joined by Rourke and Decker outside the entrance near the security panel.

"Now what?" Rourke asked.

Berman frowned at him. "Our security clearances aren't registering. Entrance can only be granted from the inside without proper clearance. We'll have to blast the door."

Plass shook his head. "It won't work." He turned to Decker and Rourke to explain. "The base of the tower is surrounded by a full circular concourse. About fifty guards are on duty at all times. Any one of them can activate an alarm that will drop shield doors across all the entrances. Nothing can penetrate those. We won't get two meters inside before we are cut off and killed. We'll have to call our ground teams to attack the above ground entrances and hope the distraction draws some of the guards away."

Rourke watched a Servo-unit buzz happily by. "I don't think that will be necessary," he muttered. He snatched up with the little unit just before it dove into a tiny hatchway. The men looked at him in surprise.

He lifted the cleaning unit up to them. "Now where do you think this little guy is heading?"

Plass eyed him carefully. "Probably into the tower concourse. They cover all parts of the underground."

Rourke smiled. "That's what I thought. How tightly sealed is that concourse?"

"Completely," Plass answered as he watched Rourke peel a concussion charge off his weapons belt and attach it to the

Servo-unit. Understanding dawning, he asked, "You have a remote. Right?"

Rourke looked up from his task indignantly. "Of course. This concourse is wide open, three-hundred sixty degrees around. Right?"

A smile tugged at Plass' lips. "Of course."

Berman's eyes widened. "That concussion charge is going to ricochet all around the concourse." He shook his head in disbelief and understanding. "You're going to knock out fifty men with one air burst and leave the room untouched."

"I think we need to reevaluate our security, Major Berman," Plass summarized.

Rourke placed the little unit back on the floor. It continued on its merry way as if nothing had hindered its duty, disappearing immediately into the hatchway.

"Get your teams ready to blast the entrance doors, Berman," Rourke called out as he headed for cover.

Everyone cleared the entrance doors. Rourke pressed the detonation device. A muffled sound emanated from the other side of the entrance.

"Fire!" Berman yelled. Laser cannons tore gaping holes through the center of the door. Immediately, Berman's team rushed through the jagged opening, guns firing.

Rourke and Decker followed Berman. The concourse was filled with smoke and smelled of melted metal, but otherwise still and silent. Unconscious bodies littered the floors with the Servo-unit wandering innocently among them.

"I want them all in restraints before they recover," Berman ordered.

Plass walked directly to the tower lift. It was still operational and the door opened at his command. The alarm hadn't been sounded, but he remained cautious. He would feel better when all the guards in the concourse were accounted for.

He turned to speak to Berman.

Suddenly, the silence was replaced by the tower alarm. The shield doors immediately dropped, sealing them in the concourse. Plass spun around in time to see the lift doors close on a stunned Barrios. As the lift doors sealed shut, Plass swore. The old man must have walked right into the lift and set off the alarm. So much for the element of surprise and the use of the lift. They would be using the access shafts--all twenty floors of them.

* * * *

Cidra swallowed hard just as Stoll was about to activate the door to Tausek's chambers. His comm unit beeped.

"What's the problem?" Stoll barked to his chief security officer.

A deep voice replied, "Unknown at this time, sir. An unauthorized user has accessed the lift. It sealed and deactivated automatically. We have no other security issues at the moment. Perhaps it is a malfunction."

Stoll pinned Grey with a savage glare. "Somehow I doubt that. I will be in my office. Report there as soon as you isolate the problem."

He turned to Fiske. "Hand them over to Tausek. Then remain on guard outside the door. I won't take any chances." He warned the young Lieutenant. "There is no need for Tausek to be aware of the security issue. I will deal with it myself."

Fiske answered, "I understand."

The moment Stoll rounded the corner out of sight, Fiske stepped behind Cidra. He released the restraint mechanism, but didn't remove them. She looked at him as if afraid to believe. "What are you doing?"

He smiled slightly. "Giving you a fighting chance. The restraints are released. One good tug will free them completely."

She gazed at his face in amazement. It appeared to soften and grow younger before her very eyes. "The comm unit...." she began.

"Is in your boot," he finished, looking up at her through long lashes. "Don't do any dancing or the transmission will suffer."

Grey asked, "Whose side are you on, Fiske?"

Fiske turned to face him. "I am a d'Hont guardian. My loyalty begins and ends with them. Not Stoll, not Tausek, not even Plass. I am part of a secret order dedicated to the preservation of the d'Hont."

He looked at Cidra, his voice sympathetic. "We saw what happened to the Kin-sha--destroyed by one incident. My order was formed shortly after that for the sole purpose of preventing a similar incident from decimating us. Our preservation effort extends beyond the political realm, beyond the power of any ruler. Even Stoll is unaware of it. I've been watching him for some time, earning his trust, and keeping close. The time has come to eliminate him as a threat to us."

As he spoke, Fiske stepped behind Grey and released his restraints. In one swift move, Grey pinned Fiske to the wall behind him, crushing his throat with his hand.

Grey hissed. "Give me one good reason why I should believe *anything* you say."

Cidra answered, "We need him to establish the communications link, Grey. We have no choice. We have to trust him."

He turned to look at her and she saw the shadows in his eyes lift. He released Fiske and stepped back.

Fiske massaged his throat and looked at her. "Thank you. I was having some difficulty vocalizing." Then he narrowed his eyes at Grey. "You're faster than you look."

Grey's mouth kicked up. "You should see her."

Fiske gave Cidra a nod. "It is time to face Tausek. Are you ready?"

"I'm ready."

"I'm not." Grey pulled her into his arms, restraints and all. He kissed her hard, desperation turning to passion to tenderness. Cidra leaned into him, welcoming the heat and harbor he offered. A soft moan slipped through her throat. He did this so well. And she needed him so much.

Grey broke off the kiss and spoke in her ear. "Cidra, I love you."

She smiled. She had known he loved her when he trusted her in the shuttle. "It's about time. I love you, too."

Grey smiled back. "I'm a slow learner. Lucky for you, I don't give up easily."

Fiske fixed Grey's restraints. They turned to face the door to Tausek's chambers.

Cidra eyes met Grey's for a long moment in a silent declaration of a deathless bond. Fiske activated the door, and they stepped into Tausek's chambers together.

CHAPTER NINETEEN

Rourke felt the heat from another laser blast zing past his head and yelled, "You have *got* to be kidding. There must be another way to the top."

Behind him Berman bellowed, "Shut up and shoot or get out of the way."

Rourke gritted his teeth and concentrated on the gun battle. They were advancing up the tower at a crawl. This was the third such battle since the lift had been sealed and they had been forced to scale the tower level by level. Each battle grew hotter as more guards from the upper levels descended to protect their ground.

Laser blasts ricocheted off the corridor walls and floors at dizzying speed. The haze of burned materials and flesh hung in the air. Berman had already lost several men and they still had a long way to go yet.

As usual, when the last tower guard went down, they all scrambled to reach the next access shaft.

Decker ran up the corridor behind Rourke. "This is taking forever. There's no way they will still be alive by the time we reach the top. Plass tells me we have another seventeen levels to go."

Berman turned on them in fury and yelled, "You have a better idea? Let's hear it."

At the entrance of the next access shaft, Rourke stopped and relieved a micropad from one of Berman's team. He studied the floor plan, level by level. He gazed up and down the hall and finally straight up at the ceiling.

Rourke turned and stood toe to toe with Berman. "Do you have a laser cannon with you?"

Berman's eyebrows furrowed. "Of course, we do. Why?"

"How long are your rappelling cables?"

Stunned, Berman answered, "Long enough to scale the outside of this tower if there was any way to get back into it."

Rourke nodded and said, "Bring the cannon here. I want the longest, heaviest cable you've got and your best marksmen."

* * * *

Blood. It was the first word that came to Cidra's mind. Crimson red flooded Tausek's chambers and its sparse contents. Cidra scanned the big room quickly. There was one other door besides the one they had entered through. The most spectacular and savage red sunset she'd ever seen burst through a long, unbroken window.

They halted behind the silhouette of a man, his back to them as if commanding the sun, feeding off its power. The sight robbed her of coherent thought. Instincts, swift and powerful, subverted her control.

When he turned slowly to face them, her breath froze in her

lungs at the black, menacing figure before her. His face was pure white, sinister and angular. His eyes were even more disturbing, black, dark and inhuman. Bathed in red, he looked like a demonic sentinel standing at the very gates of a fiery abyss. Cidra fought the urge to turn and run.

Tausek nodded once to Fiske, who saluted and left quickly.

A terrifying silence followed. Fine clicking drew her eyes down to the two furred creatures at Tausek's feet. Corvits. Plass hadn't mention corvits. She had heard of them--beastly creatures capable of ripping a man to pieces in minutes. Somewhere in the insanity of the moment, she wondered if two of them could do it twice as fast.

Fear clawed at her throat, threatening to suffocate her. She closed her eyes tightly, refusing to let it undermine her task. From within her rage grew, slowly at first, fed by the anger at her own fear. Thoughts shifted from herself to her family, Syrus, and her father. Then the voices arose--pleas and cries for justice and vengeance. The silent faith of a million souls killed by Tausek drove her on. The strength grew and built, crowding out the fear and anger, replacing them with determination, honor and reverence.

Cidra opened her eyes and faced her demon.

"Cidra Faulkner," Tausek began. "I've been waiting for you."

* * * *

Seated at Plass' desk, Stoll glanced up at Fiske in surprise and irritation. "I told you to stand guard outside Tausek's chambers."

Fiske stood motionless just inside the doorway and said nothing.

Stoll's face reddened. He pushed himself to a standing position. "Did you hear me?"

"I heard you. The d'Hont no longer take orders from you." Fiske raised his laser rifle to Stoll's chest.

The Commander's eyes narrowed with hate and anger and a low growl rumbled through him. He lunged around his desk at Fiske. The laser blast caught Stoll squarely in the chest. His face contorted in pain as he collapsed on the floor.

Fiske stepped over the body and went to work at the communications center.

* * * *

"Ready?" Rourke asked.

Berman nodded and hefted the laser cannon over his shoulder into an awkward position, lining the sights up at the ceiling over his head. An instant later, the machine bore a perfect two-meter hole through the ceiling, followed by the ceiling of the level above, and the next.

"Nice and steady. If you hit anything structural outside the corridors, we're going to be digging out from under this building for a long time," Rourke muttered over Berman's shoulder. "And remember only fifteen levels. We don't want to spook Tausek."

Berman grunted, sweat beginning to spread across his brow as the laser ate a perfectly round, two-meter wide tunnel through the tower levels.

Rourke turned to Decker who was fitting Plass with his rappelling harness. The three of them wore harnesses with clips in the back, ready to take the harrowing ride up through Berman's new tunnel. The marksman stood by with the harpoon gun and cable.

"Looks like we're taking the express route." Rourke grinned.

Decker stood next to him and watched Berman's progress skeptically. "Are you sure this is going to work?"

Rourke balked. "Hey, it was my idea. What do you think?"

Decker shook his head. "You don't want to know what I think. Is Barrios alright trapped in that lift?"

"Alright?" Rourke snorted. "He's safer than we are. Plass said it would become operational once they shut off the alarms."

Finished, Berman cut the laser cannon fire and dropped back. "Harpoon gun."

A split second later, the marksman was targeting the ceiling of Level Eighteen and pulling the trigger. The cable attached to the harpoon zinged upward and snapped taut.

The marksman reached over and clipped the three-man rigging unit to the gun barrel and hoist. He then clipped each man's harness to the rigging, facing outward. As soon as he stepped clear, Berman addressed them. "All yours. Good luck. We'll be backing you up."

Rourke nodded and activated the hoist control behind his head. The initial jerk nearly ripped them out of their harnesses. Higher and faster they ascended through the narrow tunnel.

"Keep still, boys." Rourke looked up, gauging their velocity. "Banging into a floor section at this speed is going to hurt like hell. And whatever you do, don't look down."

Above them, a laser blast shot perilously close to the thin cable they now owed their lives to.

"That didn't take long. Next level. Your side, Decker," Rourke ordered.

"Got it." Decker slowly raised his laser pistol and began firing continuously as the level approached. He pumped artillery into the waiting guards.

The ascent seemed eternal and before they reached the end of the line, all three men were returning fire on every level they encountered.

The ride ended abruptly with the trio hanging fifteen levels up, staring at two surprised tower guards on the eighteenth level. Outnumbered and stunned, the guards were quickly eliminated.

Rourke unclipped his harness and shoved off the other two men, clearing the gap to the floor. He reached out and hauled Decker and Plass to the safety of solid ground.

Decker exhaled a long sigh of relief.

Rourke grinned at him. "Feel better?"

"I'm taking the lift *down*," Decker muttered.

As they removed their harnesses, Plass looked around at the empty corridor. "Where are the rest of the guards?"

"Probably heading for the lower levels," Rourke answered. "Fine with me. Let Berman handle them." He looked up from the micro micropad to the corridor ahead of them. "Access shaft that way."

* * * *

"I expected you to be bigger." Cidra squared up her shoulders. She could feel Grey's quiet strength next to her, giving her the lead.

Tausek's expression didn't change. "I expected you to be dead."

"And miss the honor of meeting my family's murderer? Never."

"Your father killed millions of my people by denying us the vaccine. He deserved to die," Tausek uttered in supreme domination.

Cidra's eyes narrowed. "The real beauty of history is how easily it can be rewritten as new facts emerge."

Tausek's mouth twitched. Their eyes locked.

"We know what you did," she continued fearlessly. "We know how you did it and we know why."

Tausek's eyebrows raised a millimeter and settled back down. "Well done. I underestimated you. No doubt the reason why you've proven so difficult to kill."

"I had help."

Tausek looked at Grey. "Grey Stone. You are unexpected and unwelcome."

Grey smiled broadly. "I'm only here to watch you squirm."

Tausek's eyes narrowed minutely. "It is you who will squirm."

"You betrayed your own people and used the d'Hont," Cidra prodded.

Tausek turned back to her. "The d'Hont are no more than a weapon at my disposal. They served me well and will continue do my bidding."

Cidra persisted. "The millions died because of you."

"It was a small price to pay for my rightful place," Tausek concurred.

Victory flooded Cidra in a rush. She could only hope the confession made it beyond these walls.

Grey stepped forward. "Lucky for you, the plague came to Dakru when it did."

Tausek gave a short snort. "Luck," he gloated, "had nothing to do with it."

The words hung between them as the revelation turned to horror. Cidra's resolve faltered. She choked out, "You brought it here? You infected your own people?"

Tausek cast her a pitying look. "Of course. It was the opportunity I'd been seeking."

Grey cut in. "Why didn't the d'Hont die as well?"

"I needed them. The vaccine was given to them as part of their regular inoculations," Tausek answered him smugly. "I planned for everything."

"But their families?" Cidra stammered.

Tausek leveled his eyes at hers coolly. "It's amazing how the death of a loved one or two can guarantee more loyalty to the cause than mere credits can buy."

Air rushed out of her lungs in shock. Her voice shook. "Why?"

Tausek's mouth slid into a demonic curve. "How else would the son of a female slave hand become the most powerful man on the planet? I was the product of a d'Hont rape. It is only fitting that they made me what I am today."

Suddenly, the communication's device in her boot emitted a short squeal of feedback. Cidra's breath caught as Tausek stared at her boot and slowly raised his gaze to hers. Then he hissed low. The corvits came to life, advancing slowly on her.

She heard Grey's low curse next to her just before he stepped between her and the corvits.

Tendrils of primal fear coiled within her. Tausek casually turned and walked to the second door, leaving the corvits guarding his prisoners. The door opened and Tausek stepped inside. He turned to face them.

"Cidra, come to me," Tausek ordered. His arrogant voice cut through her.

Grey cast her a hard look.

Tausek kept his eyes on Cidra. "I will order the corvits to kill Stone if you refuse."

Cidra's heart thumped wildly in her chest. A vision of Grey being viciously ripped apart flashed by.

"No, Cidra," Grey whispered over his shoulder.

She looked from his broad, vulnerable back to the terrifying creatures of muscle and claws. Tausek wanted her, not Grey. If she left now, he could escape or be rescued. He had a better chance without her.

Cidra turned and followed Tausek, testing her wrist restraints gently. She stepped through the doorway and looked back at Grey.

His eyes were fierce, his body taut and poised. She could see the transformation. The hunter had come alive. And he was not happy.

Tausek moved behind her. Cidra watched in stunned disbelief as Tausek slowly raised his arm and pointed a finger at Grey. "Target!"

Her scream of "No!" rang out and was abruptly cut off by Tausek's steely arm around her throat. The other arm wrapped around her waist and jerked her tight against his body. The door closed as Tausek dragged her into his private chamber.

* * * *

"Hurry up," Rourke yelled. "We're almost there."

Running backwards, Rourke fired behind Decker and Plass, covering them as they sprinted by. More guards pursued them, rushing up from the lower levels. The final two floors had been a virtual gauntlet of gunfire.

Plass ran to the final access shaft leading to the top level and began entering his access code. Tausek and Cidra's voices could be heard clearly over the tower's communication system. He didn't know how or why, just that Fiske was the only person who could have established the link. The fact that his access codes were once again working only deepened the mystery.

As the access door slid open, they all dove for the cover the access shaft offered. Laser blasts criss-crossed down the corridor behind them. Rourke and Decker alternately returned fire.

Plass said, "You are going to have to stay here and hold them back. I'll take care of Tausek."

Rourke snapped, "Forget Tausek. You take care of Grey and Cidra. Or we'll stop shooting at them and start shooting at you."

He turned to fire at the newest wave of guards to attack their position. "You'd think these guys would give up after Tausek's confession."

"They aren't d'Hont. They work for Tausek," Plass snarled as he headed up the shaft.

As Plass breached the top level landing, he froze as Tausek's 'target' and Cidra's scream riveted him in place. Heart pounding, he began racing down the corridor towards Tausek's chambers. Just as Plass rounded the corner, he caught the sight of Fiske running flat-out from the other direction. The Lieutenant waved his laser pistol and yelled to him, "Kill the corvits!"

They reached the door at almost the same time, triggering the activation field. Stepping inside, they took in the gruesome sight. Grey was alone, flinging one corvit off his bloody right arm and sending it careening into the wall. The other corvit was ripping into his neck and back as he tried to pull it off with his other hand.

Plass aimed and picked the corvit off Grey's back. It shrieked as it flew across the room. Fiske shot the other corvit just as it leapt. It joined its lifeless mate on the floor. The only sound that remained was Grey's labored breathing. He slumped to the floor on all fours, his teeth bared in pain.

Plass ran to him. Blood was running down his arms, pooling around his hands. His back and neck were shredded, but it didn't appear that any major arteries were severed. He would live if he got medical care soon.

"Cidra," Grey grimaced. He tried to stand, slipping in his own blood. Plass helped him to his feet. Grey pointed to the second door. "He took her in there."

Fiske rushed to the door but it didn't open when he breached the activation field. "It's secured," he told Plass helplessly. "I don't know the access code."

"I do," Plass said.

* * * *

Rage and fear guided her as Cidra shook off the restraints.

Tausek gave her no leverage to reach his body and he was much bigger and stronger than she anticipated. He had one heavily muscled arm around her neck and one wrapped around her left arm and waist. She fought the instinct to grab the arm that was choking her and instead reached with her free hand for Tausek's eyes. His head jerked back. He roared as she clawed at his face. She was rewarded with a tightening of his death grip on her throat, cutting off her air supply.

She reached down and behind her, intent on inflicting serious groin damage before she passed out. With her first dig, he jerked his body away from her and flung her across room. The side of her head hit the wall with a violent thud. Her vision clouded with silvery stars.

Cidra dropped to the floor, rolled onto her back, and groaned. She shook her head to clear the dark edges that threatened to close in on her. With tremendous effort, she focused on Tausek standing two meters from her, his features contorted. She could see the damage she'd inflicted on his face. The scratches were bright red against his white skin. He wiped a hand across his face and glanced at his bloody fingers. Then he gave her a cold, cold look.

"I shall enjoy killing you with my bare hands."

As he started toward her, a ragged voice cut through the air. "Get away from her. *Now.*"

Cidra's eyes widened. *Grey. Alive.* She grinned victoriously into Tausek's face as it twisted from savagery into rage.

"Now or die," Grey said from behind them.

Tausek slowly backed away from Cidra and turned to the three men at his chamber door. His lips curled as he looked at Plass and Fiske. Then he eyed Grey's bloody clothes.

"You're going to have to find yourself some new pets," Grey said. Then he spied Cidra struggling to stand. His gray eyes burned into Tausek. "First, you will pay for that."

"I don't think so," Tausek smirked. Suddenly the chamber went black.

Plass shot once where Tausek had been standing, but the light from the laser blast showed no target.

When Fiske finally located the lights, they looked around in disbelief. Tausek was gone.

Plass turned to Fiske. "He must have gotten by us. Notify Berman that Tausek has escaped. He's probably heading for a transport on the lower level."

Fiske gaped at him and countered, "How would he get out of the tower?"

"Try the lift. See if its functional again." Then Plass asked Grey. "Is she alright?"

Cidra was already in his arms when he answered, "Yes. She needs a medic."

Plass nodded. "So do you. Find one. We're going after Tausek."

As their footsteps retreated out of the chambers, Grey held her. Then his mouth captured hers in a desperate kiss, slanting over her lips again and again in an effort to convince his mind that she was safe. He couldn't hold her close enough, couldn't kiss her deep enough.

Cidra slid her arms around his waist. He flinched. Quickly, she stepped back and looked at her hands covered in blood. Frantically, she began checking the wounds on his back, neck, and arms.

"I'll live." He smiled grimly. "Once Tausek is caught, we'll both live."

She stopped. "I don't think they'll catch him." Then she said quietly, "I could swear I smelled fresh air when he escaped."

Grey squinted at her. "Fresh air? This tower is sealed up tight. The closest outside exit is twenty levels down."

Cidra looked into his eyes. "Maybe he didn't go down. Maybe he went up."

Her insight jolted him. He quickly scanned the room. Other than the one door, there was no visible exit. That left only one option.

"An escape passage," he muttered, disgusted at himself for not seeing it sooner.

"If you could smell it, the doorway had to be close to you." Grey walked to the wall behind her and began pressing along it.

Cidra grimaced at the trail of blood he left across the room and smeared along the wall. To her surprise, an entire section of wall slid silently out of the way, revealing a passageway.

Grey disappeared into it and Cidra followed him when she realized that he was going to investigate. "You need a medic, Grey. We should go back. Let Plass take over."

He was already heading up. They had reached the roof before Grey cast her a tight smile over his shoulder. "Tausek's long gone by now. We'll leave it up to Plass to track him down. At least we know how he escaped."

He stepped onto the roof and stopped dead. "Cidra. Take a look at this. It's a landing bay." He started walking around, reciting the inventory. "Small transport jets. Weapons. Ammunition. Survival gear. Food stores. All the necessities of life. Unbelievable."

"Grey," Cidra said, looking up at the high domed roof curiously. "How would he get a transport out of here?"

"There must be a retractable opening," he answered absently, his full attention on the warehouse of weapons and supplies before him. "You know, a man could hide up here for months and no one would know it."

Cidra scanned the roof for an opening and frowned. "I don't see one. I think he would have to break through that barrier to take off. Don't you--"

Suddenly a laser blast shot by her head and caught Grey low in the shoulder. He dropped to the floor with a deep groan and went perfectly still.

Cidra spun around behind her to find Tausek standing there, the laser pistol now pointed at her. He stood between them and the only exit. She took a quick glance at Grey behind her. He hadn't moved.

She slowly lifted her eyes to Tausek, a deadly calm stealing over her. Reality became an illusion, insignificant and expendable. "You killed him."

A low growl rumbled through Tausek. "And you are next. You have ruined everything. My plan, my place, my *right*."

"You had no right," she screamed at him, her rage making her invincible. "The judgment to live or die is *not* yours to command. It never was."

Tausek's face twisted, his voice escalating with every sentence. "I built Dakru. I made it what it is today. I can do the same throughout the galaxy. I am Tausek!"

Cidra stilled. The galaxy. He wanted the whole galaxy. She already knew he'd do anything to get it. And she knew something else. He was completely insane. Uncontrollable, unpredictable, and deadly. Past reason, past logic. No matter the cost, she couldn't allow him to escape.

She had one last weapon against him--her body and her life. There was five meters separating them. A few steps. She could make it. "I will never let you out of here alive."

A hideous kind of laugh rumbled through Tausek. "You can't destroy me with your inferior Kin-sha skill." He lifted the laser pistol and pointed it at her head. "Good-bye, Cidra Faulkner."

Cidra ran straight at him and leapt forward, hoping to inflict some damage before she died. She heard the blast, saw the flash of light. Ignoring the shot, she slammed into his mid-section, hurled him backwards and landed on top of him.

A second later, she was staring into his open mouth, his unseeing eyes. The smell of burnt flesh choked her. Tausek was dead. *What happened?*

She raised her eyes slowly to the feet planted several meters away at the entrance to the roof. She knew those feet.

Cidra looked up to find Barrios smiling at her, his laser pistol firmly in hand. "That was for you, love."

EPILOGUE

Cidra sat alone in the moonlight on a planet she both loved and hated. The grass in Syrus' clearing felt cool and thick beneath her. Avion's giant moon hung possessively in the night sky, casting its brilliance across the Lake of Ares. A hush of light wind whispered through the trees in a sweet, voiceless song.

The breeze caressed Cidra's face like a loving hand. She gave a contented sigh. *She was free.* The very thought brought bittersweet tears to her eyes. She would enjoy the future that her family had been denied.

Avion's elaborate burial ceremony would have to be enough to heal her wounds. There were no apologies, no thank yous from the Central Consortium. Her father's honor had been restored and her family celebrated. It wouldn't bring them back, but it was more than she could have hoped for. She wiped away the tears and accepted what was.

Cidra turned her head and glanced over at the spot where Syrus was buried. Sometime in the past few days she realized that he knew exactly what he was doing when he set this mission in motion. He even picked the right man for the job and for her.

Cidra froze. She spoke aloud, "Trying to sneak up on me?"

She heard the low, rumbling laugh moments before Grey dropped to the grass behind her and pulled her back between his legs and against his chest. "That sixth sense of yours is going to be a problem."

Cidra laughed. "Not for me. Something tells me I'm going to need all the advance warning I can get."

Grey slid his hands around her waist and listened to her laugh. It was a sound he wanted to hear every day for the rest of his life.

He looked over her shoulder at the lake. "Decker contacted me again today. I think he's anxious to get back to work. He mentioned the Lost Mask four times." He paused. "I was thinking of letting him take *Calíbre* and get it himself."

Cidra stiffened in his arms. "Why would you do that?"

Grey shrugged. "Thought we could use some time alone here at Syrus' cottage."

"Is that what you really want?"

Grey kissed the top of her head. "I could handle it for a while."

Cidra leaned back into his chest, sliding her hands over his. "That would be nice. It'll give you a chance to teach me everything you know about treasure hunting."

"That's a deal, partner." Grey grinned. He'd teach her more than just treasure hunting, starting right now.

Cidra let her head roll back, careful to avoid his healing shoulder. "Have you heard anything from Dakru?"

He swept her hair to one side and contemplated the slender, exposed neck beneath. "I talked to Rourke over subspace a few minutes ago. Plass was sworn in as ruler yesterday. He's already appointed Fiske as his Commander."

Grey shook his head. "They have a lot of work ahead of them. The environment on the planet is a mess. He's initiating some steps to create more humane working conditions in the mines. It's going to take some time to undo the damage Tausek did to Dakru and the d'Hont."

"Not to mention the Kin-sha," Cidra said. "Ten years of hatred and persecution won't disappear overnight."

Grey nibbled along her neck and shoulder while his hands started a slow exploration of the fasteners of her shirt.

"So what is Rourke up to now?" Cidra asked distractedly as the first fastener released.

Grey chuckled softly. "Last I knew, he was making the saloon rounds, dazzling the ladies with some strange story about Decker and a Servo-unit."

Cidra melted against him as he slid his hands inside her shirt, cupping each breast. His breath came in fast and hard.

"Grey." It was a sigh and a question in one.

"No one knows we're down here," he murmured in her ear. He

tugged her arms out of the sleeves and peered over her shoulder at the sight of moonlit breasts.

"Barrios does," she whispered.

Grey's hands caressed the curves of her body. "He can get his own woman."

Cidra laughed. "He already has. He can't wait to get back to Vaasa. I want to thank you for offering your house as his new Kin-sha facility."

"Our house," Grey corrected. "I can't blame him for not wanting the Kin-sha on Avion. Besides, Rosa loves the idea of playing hostess to a bunch of young students. The biggest battle will be over who's going to do the cooking."

His fingers slipped inside the front of her pants.

"Oh no, you don't." Cidra twisted around and pushed him gently but firmly onto his back in the grass. He looked up at her in surprise. Her expression was mischievous as she straddled him and began unfastening his shirt.

Cidra pulled his shirt back, exposing his broad chest.

For a few moments, she just stared at him.

"You like this position?" He grinned at her.

She gazed into the quick silver eyes of the man who had given her flight and freedom, the man she'd spend the rest of her life loving.

"Of course," she said in a husky drawl and a wicked smile. "It was invented by a woman."

THE END

Printed in the United States
52349LVS00001B/217-243

9 781586 086831